Bearskin

JAMIE ROBYN WOOD

Bearskin

SWEETWATER
BOOKS

an imprint of Cedar Fort, Inc.
Springville, Utah

This is a work of fiction. The characters, names, incidents, places, and dialogue are products of the author's imagination, and are not to be construed as real.

The views expressed within this work are the sole responsibility of the author and do not necessarily reflect the position of Cedar Fort, Inc., or any other entity.

ISBN 13: 978-1-4621-1716-1

Published by Sweetwater Books, an imprint of Cedar Fort, Inc.
2373 W. 700 S., Springville, UT 84663
Distributed by Cedar Fort, Inc., www.cedarfort.com

LIBRARY OF CONGRESS CATALOGING-IN-PUBLICATION DATA

Wood, Jamie Robyn, 1982- author.
Bearskin / Jamie Robyn Wood.
     pages cm
Heppson's enchantress mother commands him to kill his step-brother Conrad, but he escapes to the desert, setting off an adventure in which he, Conrad, his stepsister Moiria, and forest sisters Heart and Lark must learn the truth behind the enchantress's actions or suffer from the witch's magic.
ISBN 978-1-4621-1716-1 (perfect : alk. paper)
1. Fantasy fiction. [1. Fantasy.] I. Title.
PZ7.1.W65Be 2015
[Fic]--dc23

                              2015008585

Cover design by Rebecca J. Greenwood
Cover design © 2015 by Lyle Mortimer
Edited and typeset by Justin Greer

Printed in the United States of America

10 9 8 7 6 5 4 3 2 1

Printed on acid-free paper

to Elena,
for talking me off the cliff, time after time

to Justin,
for telling me who should wear the Bearskin,
and changing the whole story

and to my children,
for being awesome nappers,
and loving me when they woke up

BEGINNING

Heart

The night Heart's faint and mewling cries first broke the still of darkness, her mother died. The arms that took her in their tender, trembling grasp were small and slight. Her sister's hair, a falling shade of darkness, lent protection to Heart's barely pulsing frame and fuzzy, fire-hued brow.

Lark, a sister turned to guardian in an instant, worriedly smiled at the babe. Amidst the wails and darkened candles of the room, she stretched her love out wide, determined not to let this tiny life blink out before her eyes.

With fumbling hands, she tightened a blanket around Heart's body and tucked the fabric's warmth around the fresh and chalky infant skin. Pulling her newborn sister deep within the curve of her strong arms, Lark dredged what joy she could from the bottom of her freshly shattered soul to whisper hope. In doing so, she determinedly kept Death back from his second prize that night.

And even as a babe, Heart felt her do it.

PART I

Moiria

Moiria knew Heppson had no real choice. Not once the Queen spoke and directed her implacable will toward his.

"Kill him," their mother said in her low-timbered voice, unruffled as always.

As she spoke, the Queen handed Moiria's half brother the knife she'd asked Moiria to retrieve from their old forest cottage earlier that morning. It had been a tricky retrieval and had required a transportation spell; the very first Moiria had operated on her own. Because of this, Moiria had known all along it was not the meaningless errand her mother insisted, though she never guessed the day had actually arrived for Prince Conrad's death. Could it have come so soon? With both she and the crown prince barely reaching their seniority in the coming fall? Could Moiria be so ill-prepared?

The Queen pivoted away from Heppson to straighten a book on a nearby table, her insistence on order and perfection attending even in this highly-charged moment. "Kill him," she said again, the book now unerringly square with the table's edge, "and when you're finished, you'll have the throne of Alastair yourself—when your father's gone to Death. A simple matter that, once this task is complete."

Moiria watched, as she often watched such things, from the obscurity of her mother's walls – hidden behind one of the massive tapestries hanging about the Queen's darkened chamber. Hers was not a difficult form to hide, even had the tapestries been absent, for despite her nineteen years, Moiria was small in stature and easily mislaid. Currently, her long black hair draped down and wrapped about her, a natural cloak of protection, which she cowered inside.

"*Darkest starlight hair,*" Heppson had once called her locks.

And truly, its color was reminiscent of lake water in deepest night, its surface reflecting slivers of light.

Moiria marked the change in Heppson's face as his hand twisted the knife given him. She saw the pain that crossed his eyes as the initial command was uttered, as well as the pretended veil of indifference that dropped about him when he knew the action had been irrevocably decreed.

Of course, Moiria knew her mother had allowed her to hide among the room's hangings; the Queen most certainly realized her eldest child stayed near enough to observe. The Queen would force this murder upon Heppson and make the act a mark of her son's submission; a submission meant for both him and his sister to remember in the years ahead. The years when they must continue to serve as vessels of her far-reaching desires—or risk the consequences. Nothing Moiria's mother did was ever left to chance; not even a daughter overhearing a private interview.

And yet, even if her mother did know that she watched, Moiria could not help but slink beneath the sweet-smelling fibers of the tapestries, as though the pretending made her presence unreal, imaginary. As though by hiding, she might dismiss her own unnecessary presence and make the truth of what would happen when her brother left this room disappear.

But truth was a difficult thing to deny. Even the cloying odor of the fabric surrounding Moiria reminded her of her mother's intricate spells and all they represented of that woman's ill-gotten power. These were spells Moiria had known since a time when she did not live in the castle—when Heppson had not yet wailed his first pathetic cry. These were spells meant to harm and take away.

With her magic, Moiria's mother had managed to accomplish the impossible. She had dethroned the previous queen and set herself, a common villager, in the dead woman's place. She had duped the king and the entire kingdom of Alastair into bowing down before her and her will. She had birthed a son that she meant to take the throne outwardly, leaving her free to act behind the scenes in whichever way she chose. And now she would use that son to murder the prince who stood between her and complete success.

Oh yes, the witch was everywhere and in everything: in the smells of Moiria's childhood, in the inanimate trappings of this room, in the futures she prescribed for all her children and herself. The Queen's power was complete. And each of the three inside the chamber knew it.

Even though the Queen had allowed Moiria to remain and witness this event, Moiria had made sure her presence was not so obvious to Heppson. Where she stood, she was almost completely blocked from his sight—though not quite, if he had cared to search. She had meant it to be so. She had meant to be there, but also not there. Moiria always operated this way. Present, but not present. Helpful, but offering no real help.

Now she glared at Heppson, her hands grasping her skirts in carefully smothered apprehension. If only he would look her way. If only he would ask for the assistance she did not dare to offer on her own.

Deep inside, she knew he would not look. He never had. He never did. This would not change today. Moiria felt sure that Heppson's mind had moved forward already. Forward from their witch of a mother and forward to the task at hand. Forward to the one person he assumed would make it all right and prevent the murder the witch had dictated. To the one person Moiria knew he trusted above all others in this darkened kingdom. Forward to Prince Conrad.

The two stepsiblings, charming Conrad and shadowed Moiria, had been born three years before the witch wrenched Alastair's future to her bosom, and four years before Heppson's birth. As such, Conrad's rights of heredity were unquestionably clear and unassailable. That is, as long as he managed to breathe his days both in and out.

Conrad was the crown prince, beloved by all who knew

him, and fated to die from the moment Moiria's mother took the throne. Fated to die, and now doomed to do so at his half brother's hands. The two boys may have been tied together by the commonality of the father who sired them, as well as by the friendship they'd built since they were children, but the Queen would make certain they became each other's worst enemies, even if it took every power she had.

Moiria knew where her brother looked for deliverance today. She knew where Heppson headed in this moment of desperation. But she could not fool herself enough to think the two of them might succeed. She could not fool herself enough to forget the curse her mother had just uttered, or the strength that waited, crouched behind it.

Heppson

Ignoring his surroundings, Heppson angled himself downward and out of his father's crumbling castle. He left the looming masses of the walls behind; their black-lined stones a subtle reminder of the newly dropped weight upon his soul. He trained his feet toward what remained of the castle's once-impressive gardens, hoping he would find his brother there. After all, the gardens' derelict vestiges were the last evidence of happier times long past.

When Heppson finally spied the crown prince, he found his half brother lounging across a dirty and neglected bench among the garden's weeds, the rocks and mortar of its long-past creation tumbled about him in the mud of spring. Three puppies wrestled near the prince, their long lolling tongues of crimson the only color Heppson could see beside his half brother's vibrant sun-hued curls.

Everything else around them, including the wrinkled clothes both brothers wore, carried the dampened shades of gray and brown that made up their father's castle and the immediate grounds surrounding it. It was as though the castle could barely manage to survive beneath its new Queen, as though any flavor or color had long since been sucked dry, leaving behind a reality of rainbow-less sludge.

Heppson noted that Conrad did not turn at his approach. Instead, the prince kept his gaze upon his dogs' spirited antics, their playful and oblivious scrapping an incongruous sight in the dreary world occupied by the two princes. Of course, the crunching of Heppson's feet against the scattered stones of the garden walkway had most certainly announced his arrival. A fact made obvious when the crown prince spoke to Heppson, though his face remained directed toward the puppies' rollicking efforts.

"You've found me," he said, his voice pleasant and smooth.

"Why, it's only noon, dear brother. You mustn't be so needy of my company!"

Heppson did not reply. The cheerful banter they normally tossed about had no place in his mouth today.

In response to his brother's irregular silence, Conrad straightened and turned, the puppies dismissed and forgotten in the oddity of Heppson's lack of biting response. Conrad's eyes went quickly to Heppson's hand. "What is that you carry?" he asked.

"You know what it is, and you know for what purpose it is sent," said Heppson coldly. "After all, we both knew it would come, in time."

Conrad stood. His frame righted itself more easily than any stranger watching from afar might have supposed, based both on the extent of his previous lounging and the length of his legs and upper frame. This size and build came to him from his father, a historically able warrior in his own right. Heppson held a similar advantage of strength and massiveness, as he had recently edged his way inside the borders of manhood. At that similarity, however, the two half brothers departed in every particular.

One was light: hair gold, eyes blue. The other was dark: black pigment dominant in his dusk-etched eyes. One carried himself loosely, sure the world should rightly have been made for him. The other kept his movements tight and under watchful guard. In this way, each of their mothers' influence held sway within them; a genetic and nurtured beginning neither could overcome. Brothers, but not through and through—a fact which no one would deny.

"And what will you do with that knife, now that she's handed it to you?" asked Conrad.

Heppson grimaced, and cast his gaze toward the garden's furthest wall, almost ten feet beyond them, and another ten feet in height. Beyond it lay a prolonged courtyard of emptiness, and beyond that a much more formidable wall built by the Queen— this one to separate the vanquished villagers' domain from that of the castle residents.

Even so, the garden's sturdy vines worked to pull the stones they clung to into manageable pieces—pieces they could easily consign to destruction in their silent, imperceptible way. Wishing he could oppose his mother's purposes as easily as those vines, Heppson began to flip his mother's knife from hilt to blade and back again, its edge a strange flash in the sickly light of evening that fell around them.

"You ask me that?" he said finally.

"That woman is both your mother and a witch," said Conrad, his voice more serious than Heppson had ever heard it sound before, "and she sent you here to thrust that blade into my heart. So yes, I ask you what you plan to do with it. It seems a natural question."

Heppson's eyes centered on Conrad. He watched his brother reach to the narrow rope, which lay about his neck. He watched him twist the golden ring, which hung from its lengths, between his thumb and forefinger. Heppson knew it was the only tangible reminder of the mother who once held Conrad in her arms, before the new queen came to take her place. His half brother wore it always, and often tugged at it when his mind became troubled.

Heppson took a breath. "I will not lie to you. We both know her power will force me to do the deed in the end," he said. "The same way it brought your own mother to Death, so that my mother might become queen."

Conrad nodded. "An undeniable truth," he said.

Heppson blinked, surprisingly unhinged by his brother's placid agreement. "And will you kill me first then? It is a serviceable option. That small blade kept within your boot would do the job. It could be finished here, and her plan would be thwarted."

Conrad laughed harshly, kicking at the dirt beneath him. "No. I will not kill you."

"Are you sure?" said Heppson. "I am an assassin now, you know. You are duty-bound to defend yourself, if only for the sake of this kingdom. It is your right to rule when our father, the king, should drop his addled head and die."

"Oh, stop this nonsense," said Conrad, a wave of his hand pushing aside Heppson's words. "If you'd wished, you might have stabbed me in the back five minutes before this ridiculous conversation began. You needed only quiet your steps when you entered the garden, and the task would've been complete. Neither of us is going to stab the other in the heart today. So tell me, do you have a plan? Or have you come here to demand one of me?"

Heppson sighed. "Well, you are the eldest, by at least three full years. Shouldn't any plan be yours? What do I have to offer against this witch?"

"For one thing, you are the man with the knife."

As he grimaced, a flash caught Heppson's side vision; he sensed a presence against the closest wall to his left. Heppson knew Moiria had stolen into the garden and hidden beneath the vine's wild growth to his side. He also knew she would be fully aware of what might happen this day—of the order of death their mother had given. She had watched in his mother's tower, a fact he felt certain of, even if he had never seen her. She always watched. She always knew.

But why would she come here, in this moment of madness, to view a battle in which she played no part? Did she come as a spy for their mother? Did she come to report on his actions? Heppson could never tell how willingly his older sister took part in the witch's requirements. He could never tell how deep their mother's darkness reached into her soul. His sister was unfathomable.

Regardless, Heppson blinked and forced himself to dismiss Moiria from his thoughts and plans. Time was an overwhelming consideration when dealing with the Queen and her edicts. Time was the only thing standing between him and the murder of his brother. He did not have any leftover moments to work out the puzzles surrounding Moiria. In fact, he did not have time for much at all.

"I may have the knife," he said to Conrad, concentrating on the crown prince once again, "but I must admit I have no plan to avoid it."

"I wish I could say I had more, brother. Unfortunately, I have nothing to offer that might solve the problem at hand. We knew that the order was coming, but we are both of us unprepared to bring its defeat."

Heppson's eyes flashed, and his heart tripped inside him. "You must have a plan! I counted on you to make it right. You've always known the way ahead before I've found the path."

Conrad's voice hardened, an unusual occurrence for him. "And why should I have a plan? Because I've lived a measly three years longer than you? Because I'm meant to rule a kingdom which is currently under the control of our puppet father and a witch? A kingdom whose economy is falling to pieces, what with the horrible crops we've managed to harvest of late? What would give me all this wisdom you've come here expecting? Why would I magically have a plan to circumvent the Queen? You ask too much of me. You expect too much."

Heppson's shoulders fell with his brother's words. "We cannot let her do it."

"And yet we have no real choice. A fact you've been well aware of since the moment she handed you that blade."

"I will not use the knife," insisted Heppson, his voice hard. "I will do anything to leave this task undone."

"And I agree that I will not use mine either. But you know she will win, somehow. The same as she did with my mother. The same as she has with our father. Neither of us has the power to stand up to her. You obviously didn't have the will or the courage to tell her 'no' when she asked. And there will come a time when you will not have the power to hold back when it comes to the actual deed. You must know that I will not blame you for it."

Heppson's eyes locked on his brother's. Conrad's words were a slap in the face, but like all the words his brother offered, they were true. He should have said 'no' from the beginning. He should have refused to take the knife. He should have forced her to kill him rather than give in to her plans. But he had been weak. He had done as she said rather than oppose her. He had slunk from her sight in meek submission. And he would do so again, and again, always acting as she wished. Unless . . .

"Then I will leave," said Heppson, his eyes now firm on Conrad's. "It is the only way."

Conrad dropped his hand from the golden ring, surprised at Heppson's response. "But she will hunt you down. She will wreak havoc on anyone standing between her and yourself until she finds you hiding in their midst. The blood of your protectors, should you find any, will run the streets. And if she finds you, she will only force more pain between us. She will only require more evil at your hands."

"You speak truth. And perhaps if I tried to make it to the wilderness beyond the village—perhaps then she might attack the people along my way. But not if I escape in another direction. Not if I escape to the desert. There is no one there for her to punish. There is no one there I might betray. Even she cannot pass into its depths without fear. She is human like the rest of us, in that, at least."

Conrad stepped forward and pointed roughly at Heppson. "That's because no one lives inside that place," he hissed. "No one. I might as well take you with my own knife, if that is the conclusion you seek."

"But you won't end it that way. You've already said as much. Neither one of us will consent to kill the other. Neither one of us will employ the knife. Which means my going is the only answer. You know this to be true. It will be better than taking what she's offered. It will be better than taking part in her darkness. Besides, you never know, I might find a way to live."

Conrad let out a disbelieving laugh. "And if you did? If you bested a desert which even that witch avoids? Would it achieve your purpose? Tell me, what will keep her from killing me herself, once you are gone? How will your sacrifice be of any use, if she still achieves her purpose?"

Heppson's mind raced to understand his own plan, a plan

which bloomed like a wild weed that none had planted and none could understand. He caught upon a subtle realization that had come to him long ago. A truth he'd guessed at in the past, but had never spoken aloud. A truth which told him years ago of the price his mother would eventually demand at his hands, long before she spoke the fatal words.

"Tell me, Conrad," he said. "What has held her back all these years? Why would she wait for you to grow in strength and apparent wisdom before bringing you to your knees? I do not know for certain, but there is something that requires that I do the deed. There is a reason she has waited for me to be of age to take the task. I feel this must be so. And if I am far from you, you can only be safer as a result."

"You think that you can kill me when she can't? An interesting theory. With no foundation. No proof."

"All I know is that I call you brother, even when the blood between us is not complete. Whatever it is that protects you from her wrath, perhaps it is this fact of brotherhood that might let me circumvent it and take your life."

"This, inexplicably, you believe?"

"Yes, I do," said Heppson. "I think I've always known it, from when we were quite small. She's always meant to use me for this task, because she must. Because mine would be the only hands that could spill your blood. Otherwise I do not think she would have ever allowed our friendship. Not unless she meant to use the friendship as a tool of her own darkness."

"And so you'll go. And you'll assume I've lived through the aftermath." Conrad once again kicked the dirt beneath his feet, upturning dust and stones onto his boots.

"It is the only way," said Heppson.

Conrad sighed and looked to the side. "Oddly enough, I am bound to believe you. At least it offers us a chance, assuming you survive that desert. I would not consider it if there were any other hope. The truth is, it is your decision to make. I would not have you die wrapped tight in heat, but I do not wish a murder on you either."

Heppson nodded.

"Tell me, when will you go?"

Heppson flipped the blade once more within his trembling hand, the hot handle slick with his own sweat. He voiced in a whisper: "I must go before the knife can meet its mark. I do not trust myself to stay one evening. Her power already pushes at my will."

The flash of movement came in his sight once more, and this time, now that his decision had been made, Heppson allowed himself to look toward his sister. His eyes found hers, glinting in the shadows of the vines. Their darkness matched, the two born of the witch.

As children, they had built a sort of friendship of their own, similar to the friendship between Conrad and Heppson. But time, and Moiria's eventual assistance with their mother's spells, had separated them. Now a barrier stood between them. A barrier as wide as Heppson's lack of understanding regarding Moiria's role in all his mother did.

Would she take this tale to the witch? Would she turn him in for his inaction and watch the punishment that came? Did he and Conrad have only a moment before she left to make their rebellion known to the one who would bring their defeat? Heppson could not say. He could only hope.

He turned to Conrad. "To tell the truth, I do not completely trust the walls which watch us speak. I must go before the Queen makes this path impossible also. I must leave immediately."

Conrad nodded, his fists clenching and unclenching at his sides. "You will take the knife at least," he said. "You'll certainly need it."

Shaking his head, Heppson threw his mother's blade upward. It caught light again, its flowing arc of movement twisting 'round and 'round into the sky, and then downward again, until it came to rest in the ground between them, its pointed tip submerged in earth.

"I will take nothing," Heppson said. "I will take nothing at all."

Moiria

Her brothers never thought of Moiria. She never crossed their minds. At least not anymore.

Perhaps when they were children, the three of them trapped by their stumpy legs inside the moldering castle walls her mother so fiercely controlled. But not when they grew a few inches more, and her brothers ran off to live the smallest of adventures away from their mother's prying eyes. And especially not in the past year or so, when each of them clung to every sane thought in their minds, in hopes of escaping the Queen's demands of death and division. Not when they started to view Moiria as part of the Queen.

No, Moiria's brothers never thought of her. Of what she might offer. She was not a part of them, or so they had decided. That much was obvious from their conversation in the garden. Moiria knew she could have helped them, if they'd thought to ask. And in the only way she knew, she had given them the opportunity to request her assistance. She had followed Heppson, on the off chance that he might ask for her involvement. It had been her one last attempt to be part of what they planned.

But Heppson turned away. He left Moiria forgotten, a relic of his abandoned life, an unnecessary sister, hidden from his sight and memory by a convenient garden wall. Heppson fled to protect a half brother with whom he shared no more blood than he did with her, yet he did not even say good-bye. It was that, she thought, which brought the coldness in her middle, the coldness that dared her to act, no matter the consequences.

Well. Moiria would show the both of them that she knew how to say good-bye. Even if they did not.

It's true that she'd been forced to watch her mother during all those years of mixing potions, and that she'd assisted with the spells a time or two. Along the way, she'd learned that saying good-bye properly depended on knowing what another person desired, in the deepest depths of his soul. She learned this from her mother, the type of witch who never wasted energy or effort in her many machinations. The type of witch that did not rely on the crutches and trappings of the outside world to make her magic happen. The type of witch that used a man's own heart to dig his grave.

For instance, it had been simple for her mother to enslave the King's will and take his power for her own. She had only to remove the one he loved most dearly, Conrad's mother, and then force her way inside the aching gap left by the prior queen's death. The King had wanted love and devotion and he would give anything to regain it. In the end, he gave everything he had.

Now the King wandered the castle as a shadow of himself, a figurehead to charm the villagers. The same villagers who were forced to grovel beneath the Queen and her supporting cronies, offering their pitiful tributes of crops and slaughtered beasts. Useless in any attempts to shake the darkness her mother had brought, the King's will was captured by his enemy with the simplicity of a proffered kiss. His kingdom was lost too.

Moiria watched the way her mother worked her magic as the witch moved through Alastair. She watched hearts broken into, secrets stolen, and people's own love used against them. If Heppson and Conrad had thought to ask, she would have shown them the possibilities of what she'd learned. She would have shown them the path to defeating the woman they so feared. Because Moiria knew what it was her mother wanted. She knew the desire of that wicked woman's soul.

This meant she also knew her mother's undoing, as clearly as though it had been written in the stars.

It was obvious, really. The Queen wanted only that her own blood-borne son sit upon the throne as king, with her acting as master manipulator behind. Then she would be the true ruler of the kingdom, and her own grandchildren its future heirs. Once

Heppson had taken a life he loved with his own hands, his blood tie would make him easier to manipulate than his father. Heppson would be more a pawn within her grip than the current king. This ambition drove the witch's every action and deed, making it apparent how deeply the desire was rooted in her heart. Her child. On the throne. Her son. The king.

Moiria knew the way to conquer the Queen. Though what good it would do to either Conrad or Heppson would go unmeasured. They'd never thought to ask. They'd never thought to learn about good-byes.

Which meant that rather than joining together to defeat the witch, Moiria watched Heppson run from the castle's domains, his steps solitary as they disappeared from sight. Her puzzled thoughts circled inside her as she saw him go. She saw him climb the garden wall, knowing there was so much that must follow, like the hurried passage through the courtyard and the sneaky darting through the outer gates. Moiria could see none of this, and she would never know if he managed to take actual refuge in his escape.

All she saw was that he was gone from her life as she knew it. All she knew was that he would likely die, a martyr to the desert, and their mother. This then, as far as she was concerned, must be the end of her brother. An empty darkness spread inside her at the thought, blocking the deepest of her breaths; though nothing could be done to change the truth of it.

After he'd left, Moiria watched Conrad gather his hounds and turn toward the kennels. When he abandoned the gardens for the castle, the foolish prince left the witch's knife where Heppson dropped it without a glance in its direction. Moiria did not think he'd want to touch the blade meant to slit his throat.

Perhaps Moiria had counted on him leaving it behind, once she began to formulate her plans, once it became clear Heppson would leave her behind. Neither of them thought of the sister they once had, the sister that should be part of their revolt. Well, she would have no brothers either. She could manage that good-bye, and her own rebellion, all by herself.

Moiria gathered her dark cloak around her, the chill of evening lifting goose bumps along her flesh. She crept from the garden wall, where she had hidden, and toward the rocky path. Her feet were silent, though no one listened for her steps. Soon enough her mother's knife rested in her hand. It was not heavy. A small knife for such a large purpose. And yet, despite its lack in size or weight, Moiria's hand shook. She trembled from head to toe at what she'd chosen to take in her grasp. The knife seemed near alive.

Catching herself and forcing her limbs to still, Moiria took a deep breath and repeated the arguments of her plan inside her mind: What did her mother want? And what would Moiria do to give it to her? The answers were simple, and their words calmed the shaking. Certain again of her decision, Moiria wrapped the knife in her handkerchief and slid its bulk inside a small bag attached to her billowing skirts. She wrapped her cloak across her middle and moved toward the chambers of her runaway brother.

Heppson had left quickly, and so far no alarm had been raised at his departure. He had jumped from the garden wall and slunk into the night, a few cascading rocks the only evidence of his passage. He'd carried off this trick many times before, in a bid for any slice of freedom from the oppression of their mother. Moiria knew the servants and guards would not think to note his disappearance. And she knew Conrad would not mention their brother's departure, in an effort to aid him in his flight. Which meant Heppson's room would remain unguarded for a bit longer. The Queen would not know of his subterfuge or betrayal immediately.

Moiria slipped through the castle's hallways, skirting those paths most traveled by her mother's people. The Queen had replaced all servants in the castle with the most dependable of her conquests. Anyone who saw Moiria would be more than willing to report her odd behavior. Still, moving swiftly, Moiria reached Heppson's chamber without crossing another soul's path. After all, she had not lived her entire life in shadows without gaining certain skills.

Swallowing another breath, Moiria lifted the latch to her brother's door and slipped inside his room's darkened depths. Once her eyes adjusted to the meager light afforded by the narrow and half-blocked windows of Heppson's room, they took in the complete disorder that made up his chamber.

Stray tunics and cloaks were thrown wildly about the cold and drafty room, the few pieces of furniture in the room covered almost completely with Heppson's dirtied things. Half-chewed crusts of bread littered the floor, while platters and cups were shoved on any spare surface left uncovered by her brother's discarded clothes. Moiria wrinkled her nose in distaste, the odor of her brother's sweat filling her nostrils.

Of course, she understood why her brother locked out any servants that might have cleaned the mess and established order. She knew why he kept the hands his mother controlled far away from his private life. Moiria had done the same in careful self-preservation. But Heppson could have done better than live in this mess. He could have cleaned after himself, instead of living in filth.

Moiria lifted her feet to step through the clutter and detritus. As she moved, she gathered the clothing she'd need. She and her brother were dark children, both of them recipients of their mother's physical characteristics. No one could deny the relationship between them. True, Moiria had none of Heppson's height or weight, his form having recently filled out as he'd passed his fifteenth year, but her mother's desires to see her plan fulfilled would complete the deception. After all, the Queen wanted to see Heppson before her. Heppson, conqueror of Conrad. Heppson, bearer of a triumphant knife, and newly minted heir to the throne.

Once she'd gathered the items she needed, Moiria settled her own cloak and bag onto her brother's rumpled bed. She shrugged out of her long dust-colored gown, and allowed the dingy gray skirts and underskirts to drop to the floor. There, they disappeared silently into the other leavings that speckled the fur-draped stones of her brother's chamber.

Rushed along by the room's chill, Moiria pulled her brother's trousers onto her legs. She folded the ample material about her waist, and constrained it with a bit of ribbon yanked from the lacing of her now discarded gown. She pulled one of Heppson's shirts over her head, tucked it inside the pants, and hid the entire mess beneath one of his cloaks instead of hers. Lastly, she bundled up her long dark hair, weaving it together and twisting it beneath one of her brother's hunting caps. True, he normally wore these caps only when he left the castle walls, but she doubted her mother would think to question the alteration in behavior today.

Fully clothed, and feeling odd in the massive bulk of her brother's things, Moiria retrieved her bag from where she'd dropped it on the bed. One last task remained to complete this delicate ruse, which stood as the foundation of her plans.

Hands shaking, Moiria opened her bag and pulled out her mother's knife. The blade shone weakly in the dying light of evening. Moiria turned the knife in her hands. She knew if the spell were to work, this knife would be the key. After all, to achieve her goals, she must make it appear that she could offer what her mother wished most to receive.

A knife tinged with life. A knife marked by blood.

Moiria took another steadying breath. She gritted her teeth and closed her eyes to halt the sudden fizzing that ran up and down along her spine and behind her eyes. She must do it, to make the charade believable. Her mother never balked at any method required in her spells, and Moiria must not allow herself to turn away from the required methods either.

She opened her eyes and gripped the knife, lifting it to where she could easily make out the strange etchings pressed into the metal of the blade. It was not an ordinary knife, and Moiria had already wondered why her mother required it for Heppson's task. Why had she been sent to retrieve this specific blade from the old cottage, which belonged to their life before? A cottage the witch never visited. A cottage Moiria could not help but think of with the only real affection of her childhood?

Because this knife had been present in the last of her earliest memories—part of the first spells her mother had done, those many years before. In this way, the knife was part of the change that marked Moiria's life before her mother's twist into evil and after.

But her mother had not brought the blade, with her other things, when she moved into the castle walls. She had left it behind, hidden beneath the bricks of their old hearth. Apparently, the Queen had not wanted it, or the power it apparently held, close—at least not until now. So strange, when the knife's appearance in their life had marked the beginning of all the darkness of her mother's wants.

To tell the truth of it, Moiria only remembered bits of that 'before' part of her life: the parts that happened prior to her mother becoming the witch, and prior to their descent upon the throne. She knew Conrad and Heppson had none of those half-colored memories, and that they could not guess what her mother had once been, in the time of the cottage, in the time before the knife. They would not guess how the Queen had once rocked Moiria in the crook of her arm as a forest mother, the same as any other common woman in the land. They would not guess how she had cradled Moiria's baby cheek inside her hand, rubbing a finger gently across her nose. They would not know what to make of these memories of Moiria's, these shadows of the mother she'd once had. Just as Moiria didn't know what to make of them, or how to let them go.

For this reason, Moiria didn't know what to make of the knife either. Puzzled, Moiria spun the hilt of the knife in her fingers, her eyes on the blinking of its metal blade. Carefully touching the curls and tufts of the knife's patterns in deliberate inspection, she realized she felt a pulsing, almost as though the knife itself beat with the passage of another heart's blood. The longer her finger stayed upon the etchings, the more solidly the pulsing bore into her skin. The feeling disturbed her and for a moment, her fingers loosened, as though to drop the knife and let it fall to the ground below. But how could she succeed in her plans without the blade? The actions she'd set out to complete must be finished, no matter how her fear threatened to choke away her breath.

Decided, and before she could think any further of her past, or of this weapon's part in its darkness, Moiria pushed her brother's loose sleeve up her arm. Quickly, she moved the knife sideways against her skin and sliced the blade cleanly across the soft flesh of her upper arm. Blood surged from the wound, not needing any more encouragement than the slight pressure Moiria had dared offer. Its thick and vibrant hue stained the metal of her mother's knife, blood seeping into the metal's grooves as the crown prince's blood had been meant to do.

Moiria hissed as her body reported the pain of her action. She dropped the knife, surprised at the hurt such a small cut could bring. The knife spun to the floor clumsily, her smeared blood staining the rug. She grabbed at another shirt of Heppson's and pressed roughly at the new ache in her arm. She forced herself to take air in and out. The blood was necessary. She knew this. Her mother would look for it, and she certainly didn't feel up to killing Conrad to get it out of him. But she had not known it would feel like this. She had not expected all this dizzy swirling in her mind.

Twisting her brother's shirt with one hand, Moiria wrapped the fabric firmly about her arm. She shut her eyes against the pain and against the sudden awareness she had of her own heart's beat. It was almost as though she could feel her veins emptying themselves into the rag she held against her skin. Almost as if she had felt the knife suck at her blood when it cut into her flesh.

She should have torn strips before she made the cut, she should have been prepared to make the red and sticky sweetness of her bleeding disappear. It would have been easier. She could have dismissed the pounding rising in her ears, if she had made a more deliberate plan. But this discarded cloth would do as well. The cut had not been deep, and the flow of blood would end soon enough. Then she would forget the sight of her blood. She would forget how it had illuminated the etchings of that horrible knife, as though it had somehow momentarily brought them to life.

Minutes later, having finally settled her wound and staunched the flow of red, Moiria bent down and picked up the knife from where it had fallen. How odd to leave the blade unclean. How odd to see her own blood drying on its surface, not quite so stark-looking as before. Of course, it looked real enough. It was real, after all. Which meant she must now find her mother, and convince her of what had not truly been done.

Moiria turned around in her brother's chamber, wishing Heppson would emerge from some corner and join her. Wishing he would tell her that what she'd done was right, and that all that pulsing dizziness which had come before meant nothing more than a weak stomach of some sort. But when the room remained empty, Moiria squared her shoulders and headed to the door.

He would not come here again. He had left forever. And so must she.

Moiria

Standing outside her mother's chamber, Moiria dug deep inside her heart to draw up one last image of her brother. This was the image she must carry into her mother's presence, the image that must partner with her brother's clothing, and the blood-stained knife she carried, to tell the tale of victory that the witch so desired to hear. The image came easily to Moiria, a simple manipulation of light, which took no effort at all, considering how hard it had been to swipe a simple knife, only moments before. But Moiria had taken on the images of others often enough, at her mother's request, so this part of her plan felt familiar and simplistic.

Speaking words of power she had dealt with for years, Moiria stretched her brother's image out to reach the width of his shoulders and the crown of his head. She filled his loose clothes with the breadth of his appearance and covered her face with his. Lastly, she filled the air around her with his scent and the heat of his body. Satisfied that she looked and smelled the part, Moiria clasped the knife more tightly in her hand, ready to begin the final stage in her plans.

Wouldn't the Queen marvel at what Moiria did today? The planning and the cunning in her attempted revolt. All this time Moiria had slunk away in the curtains of her mother's life, but now she'd finally stepped out into the light. Her mother had never looked at her to see her, not since that woman had come to this place and taken up the throne. She had only assumed Moiria followed in her wake. But if she had known what Moiria did now, perhaps the Queen would have seen her the way she had so many years before, when it had been the two of them alone inside the cottage.

Of course, the witch would never know what Moiria had learned. She would never know what Moiria could do. Not if things went as simply and quietly as Moiria had planned. A shame, really, when no one else seemed to care about it either. But it was an unfortunate side effect of Moiria's chosen methods. For all rested on the Queen's not guessing she faced battle when Moiria entered her rooms. All rested on her not employing her own well-developed powers against the fledgling magic that Moiria hoped to use. It must be a surprise attack, when brought to its most basic level. Always take the easiest course to power. She had learned that from her mother.

Feeling her brother's gauzy form fall in place about her, Moiria breathed in deeply and once again convinced herself the path she took would find success. She absentmindedly rubbed the bandage on her arm, feeling the sting of her recent wound. As she did so, she felt that distant ache she'd felt before, when she touched the knife's blade in her brother's room, but this time she no longer feared what it might mean. Instead, she took a strange courage in its constant beat. What she had begun must be finished. She would do what no other dared to do. She reached her hand to the door and knocked.

"Enter," came the witch's voice, its echo reaching out into the corridor like a snaking hand.

Moiria took two longish strides inside, awkwardly attempting to mimic her brother's gait.

"Have you done my bidding?" said the witch, her back facing Moiria. "Is he dead?"

Moiria dared not speak, fearing her speech might stretch this charade far beyond her present ability, especially considering the fear that hammered inside her chest, just below the beating drums of her wound's blood. Instead she waited, and soon enough, drawn by curiosity, the witch turned.

She had been bent over one of her many tables of books, her fingers tracing the knowledge and legends that strengthened the magic she used. Now her eyes narrowed on the figure where her daughter waited in disguise.

For a moment, Moiria doubted her own ability, and her

insides urged escape. How could this powerful woman fail to see past the faulty offerings of her own first attempt at independent sorcery? How could she fail to mark the quivering of her limbs, or the girlish frame hiding behind her brother's image? And yet, from the look of her continued gaze, from the lack of anger raging in her eyes, she seemed to see what Moiria offered. She seemed to see Heppson instead of her eldest child. It was what she wanted to see.

You've brought the knife?" said the witch. "Give it to me so I might taste Conrad's blood and know that he is dead with certainty."

The darkness of her mother's intent did not surprise Moiria, so she stepped again toward her mother. She held the knife close, knowing she must come within the circle of her mother's trust if she meant to cloud the witch's judgment as she planned. The spell she'd prepared to trap the witch was a simple one—a sort of veil made of another's dreams. She'd watched her mother mumble similar words before, when she'd dropped spells such as this upon others, people the witch meant to keep alive, in some deluded fashion. Moiria felt sure she understood the words and their proper usage correctly.

To complete the spell's placement, all Moiria needed was to step forward, as her brother, into her mother's inner circle of being. She would lift the veil she'd created with her words upward, the spider web of magic she'd prepared growing as it fed on the Queen's desires. When it had stretched high enough, she would drop it about her mother as a blanket of dreams that could not be lifted.

Once in place, the spell would tell a pleasing story to the witch: the story of a dead crown prince and her own son on the throne. The witch would watch the tale Moiria had built, frozen in space and time as she forever considered the dream that she had most wished to make reality. And with her fervent appetite for the dream to be the truth, she would swallow Moiria's lies and let them eat away at her will and strength until nothing reminiscent of her old self remained. She would be trapped by her own heart's tale, reduced to a weak and doddering invalid.

Moiria needed only a few more steps to make it so.

"I knew you would see it my way," said her mother. "I knew you would join my cause eventually. And now that Conrad is gone, Alastair's throne belongs to us. Everything I've desired has come to pass. What a small sacrifice to make on your part for a triumph such as this. Besides, I am sure you no longer regret your actions, not now that you've used that knife to take your dear one's life. You will see the rightness in our path now."

Moiria took another step, her mind barely catching the witch's words. But suddenly, she knew she was close enough, and all she could do was consider the task at hand. If she reached her hand just one length forward, she would touch her mother's robes. The time had come to act. In her mind, Moiria began to lift the veil. She stretched it up about her mother. Behind the image of her brother, Moiria's mouth began the incantation to complete the trap.

As she began, the witch's eyes narrowed, her gaze reaching from the soft soles of Moiria's feet to the top of where Moiria's head should be, if Heppson's image had faltered in any way. And from that barely perceptible movement, Moiria knew her mother knew. With this knowledge, time seemed almost to stop, wrapping around Moiria and splicing itself into infinity. As time slowed, its length increased immeasurably. The conclusion of all Moiria had done appeared startlingly certain. With the knowledge of Moiria's actions, her mother could not be stopped. The fight was finished, unless Moiria was willing to do much more.

It is true that Moiria had thought, when she cowered against the garden wall and made her decision to act, that it might go in one direction. That she might veil her mother's mind in the same way she veiled her body to appear as that of her departed brother. She had thought she could leave the witch alive, but misdirected to such a degree that she would be rendered impotent. The witch would be caught by the belief that her schemes had met success, and Moiria would not need to take further action of her own. She would have won the battle with nothing more than a harmless trick.

She had hoped her mother would not see through all she'd prepared. That the threat of the witch's own attack would not require more than she actually wished to give. But looking back, she realized that deep inside she had guessed that coming here would result in this instead. Wasn't that the reason she had trembled to take a knife intended to bring Death? Wasn't that why she had forced herself to swipe it once before, to draw blood in practice for a final confrontation? Hadn't she needed to make certain she could do it again? And hadn't she almost felt the blade speaking to her of what must surely come?

Now, there was not time to think. There was only time to feel the force that drove her forward and to her necessary task. In a moment, her mother's power and anger would lash outward with a strength buoyed up by years of evil deeds. She would sacrifice Moiria to the failure of her bid for Heppson's will. She would punish her daughter for daring to think she might act against a witch as powerful as herself. She would kill Moiria in a second, not sorrowful at losing a child so intent on rebellion and rejection. Moiria knew it; she knew it in her soul. She had ceased to be any more than a pawn to her mother years ago. Pawns were meant to be thrown aside in battle.

And so, Moiria gripped the knife tightly and with moving purpose, doing her best to forget it was her own flesh and blood beyond the blade. She slashed it upward into the waiting cloth of her mother's robes, past the material and into the flesh beneath it. She pushed the knife with the ache and fear of all she'd felt during her years inside this castle. She pushed it further and further into her mother's belly with the knowledge that if she failed and left her mother able to launch a reciprocal attack, her own heart would cease to beat with only a miniscule flick of her mother's fingers. She pushed it, feeling the pull of the knife to complete its task.

Then, with one last thrust, Moiria twisted and released the knife. She stepped back, her eyes captured by the witch's glassy gaze, her careful charade of Heppson's image falling to the stones below—now that the lie no longer mattered. The witch dropped downward to her knees and the floor, her legs collapsing beneath the blade's invasion. Blood spilled outward from her belly.

Behind them, the witch's chamber door flew open, the solid wood crashing itself against the wall. Startled, Moiria broke her gaze away from that of her dying mother's and turned, amazed to find Conrad standing in the room. Why had he come here? How could he possibly have known all that she'd planned? What would he think?

"You've killed her," he said, his voice a whisper full of fear and awe. "You've actually killed her."

Moiria fought away the glazed feeling which suddenly threatened to overwhelm her. She had left the knife inside her mother's body, and as she'd released it, all her original trepidation had returned, surging its way upward through chaotic thoughts of what she'd done. Besides, she had seen in her mother's eyes a threat that Conrad could not even begin to comprehend from where he stood.

"Not quite," she said, speaking what she knew to be the truth, speaking what she'd seen in her mother's eyes before Conrad's unexpected entrance, speaking of the danger that still remained.

For, behind Moiria, with what must be the last effort of her angry life, the witch lifted her hand toward her daughter, just as Moiria had known she would. In fact, Moiria felt certain a new desire ruled the Queen, a new insistence of the heart. She would do one thing more, before Death came to claim her. She would take revenge on her meddling daughter, the daughter who had brought the knife and ended her reign.

"No, not quite," said Moiria again, her voice low and lost in a realization of her absolute failure.

For, after everything, after taking what could only be considered the worst of options, her efforts had still not been enough, and now it was too late. She had thought she could succeed, but she was mistaken. Conrad and Heppson had been right not to ask her for help. They had been right to consider her worthless and of no use.

To her side, the witch's mouth began to move, her words blurred by pain, but uttered all the same. Moiria marked the mumblings and waited for the final blow to fall. In seconds, the witch's words were finished. Shakily, she lifted up her hand and directed her gruesome hatred toward her daughter.

Moiria pulled herself inward and prepared herself for the blow. She closed her eyes. She would forget the woman who did this, deny that the one who brought her death was her own mother. Instead she would consider her memories from long ago. Her memories from the cottage, and from the woman no one here had ever known.

And then, in that moment of her own disappearance, Moiria felt herself shoved aside, her shoulders pushed roughly out of the witch's line of fire and down to the ground. Moiria gasped inward as she fell against the stones of the chamber floor, but her eyes rushed open, eager to see what had been done. As she fell, swept aside by Conrad's hands, it occurred to her that her stepbrother would die in her place, of all the unreasonable turn of events, considering what it was she had meant to do. But then she remembered: her mother could not kill Conrad, not with her own two hands.

"We all must act, it seems," said Conrad, from where he stood between the fallen Moiria and her mother. His mouth had set grimly, as though to take a blow.

When the flailing curse struck her stepbrother, a blinding flash of light overtook the room. Moiria blinked away the pain of its brightness. She must keep her eyes open. She must see the curse's impact. What would happen now, when the curse meant for Moiria struck at Conrad so wildly?

In moments, the curse's light broke into pieces where it should have touched the prince, reflecting backward from the rope strung around Conrad's neck. Moiria realized that the Queen had never managed to remove the simple protection left behind by the old queen inside her marriage ring. That ring had been welded by love. It was meant to keep both that love and its fruits protected and whole.

Heppson might have ended Conrad's life *because* he loved his half brother with the same tenderness of the departed Queen. The ring would not have viewed him as a threat to fight against. That's what her mother had counted on when she left Heppson and Conrad's brotherhood whole and then handed Heppson the knife.

The witch had likely tried to kill Conrad, time and time again as he grew to manhood, though she had failed miserably with each attempt. Moiria's mother had never done well confronting natural magic. Natural magic did not negotiate with her kind of manipulation.

Moiria had watched the incantation build as her mother mouthed the words. She had read her mother's lips and viewed her fate. Because of this, she knew her mother meant to draw out her daughter's life force and take it for her own, even before the curse went shooting through the air. Moiria had tried to kill her mother, and her mother meant merely to reverse the action, trying to take Moiria's life as fuel for her own continued breaths.

Now, the Queen's curse, fueled by the lifeblood that puddled around her, fought to take Conrad's life force. In this way, the Queen's last curse most definitely held more power than her magic had before. It would fight a bitter fight against Conrad's ring. It would not win the battle completely, but it would take what triumph it could.

Moiria watched the spell coil its tendrils around her stepbrother as tight as his mother's ring would allow. It snaked its way about the prince, reaching inward to where her stepbrother waited within the protective ring of his mother's love. Moiria saw it suck at the power of Conrad's soul, grasping for any morsel it might wrap inside itself and take away.

As it caught at bits and pieces of the prince, yanking them from him in desperation, Moiria's mouth opened in disbelieving horror. Caught between two powerful forces, Conrad fell to his knees within the lights and shadows, his eyes blinking rapidly, his entire body twitching.

Still, despite the pain on the prince's face, despite the stench of burning flesh that filled her mother's chamber, Moiria could do nothing more than watch the struggle continue. Her last two efforts at stopping the witch had already failed, reducing her to the role of bystander in this particular battle. She pulled her knees to her chest and wrapped her cloak about her legs. She began to inch backward, away from the spectacle of the fallen witch and the trembling prince.

Then, abruptly, the curse's power met its limit. It had obviously taken all it could from Conrad's innards, as its shadowed darkness ricocheted back from the light of the old queen's ring and fell to pieces on the ground. Its evil quickly skittered away into non-existence, its purpose and strength completely spent. It might have yanked and pulled at Conrad with all its might, but it could not offer up any gift of prolonged life to the witch.

As the curse fell, Moiria heard the Queen exhale, her arm continuing to reach toward where Moiria last stood—where Conrad hunched forward now—as though she could not comprehend that her daughter had escaped and lay beside her, instead of beneath the shards of her broken spell. A few more evil words slipped across the ground with her dying efforts, words meant for Moiria as much as the others had been. Moiria was not surprised. After all, she always expected something more when it came to her mother, a woman who would never accept a complete defeat.

Across the room, frozen where the curse and ring had fought, Conrad remained crouched in place, unaware of this last attack.

True, he continued to breathe—alive as a result of the ring's powerful intervention and battle—but he did not move or defend himself in any way. Moiria listened as his lungs greedily gulped at the lightning-filled air that dissipated about the room, making it sound as though he had never breathed before. His arms hung lank and heavy across his bent-up legs, his frame apparently exhausted with the struggle he'd just faced. Why would he think to defend himself against the Queen's last words?

And so, the words fell. They settled on Conrad's shoulders and sent him into a fit of convulsions until, despite his weakness, he stood. What had Conrad lost from the first spell? His will, his memories, his sense of self? It had not been able to take his beating heart, so did it take what stood behind it instead? And what did he feel now, with this new and latest power pitched against him. What brought his body to stand and turn toward the door? Moiria clenched her fists together, hypnotized by the scene.

"Leave," hissed the witch, her mouth gurgling with the effort of the words. "Leave this place forever. Go to the forest and never return."

Moiria's eyes jumped from Conrad to her mother, understanding flooding her mind. If the witch could not kill the object of her anger, she would send it away. She would force the victim of her curse to disappear forever from the kingdom's civilized boundaries. To lose everything, as she had done.

With these last words spoken, her mother's head tipped downward, a darkness overtaking her eyes. Her hands fell to the ground, the fingers soaked in her own blood. One last breath coughed its way out and the Queen was finally dead. She would not move again.

She's dead, thought Moiria, blankly. *She's dead, and I'm alive. It actually happened.*

Amazement surged from Moiria's stomach, cancelling out all the terror she'd felt only moments before. She turned toward Conrad, the only other who might appreciate what had been done.

The Queen was dead. The witch was no more. She could help Conrad overcome whatever it was that had happened to him, and together she and her stepbrother could call Heppson back, they could make things right inside the kingdom.

But where Conrad had stood before, there only a wretched empty room. Conrad was gone. Gone.

Leave, the witch had said. And he had gone, just as she ordered. He had left Moiria all alone.

Heppson

The desert existed before memory. Once simply the eastern border of the land, the witch had transformed it into a graveyard of hopes, dreams, and downtrodden souls.

At its edge, the desert choked off every outstretched weed that worked to tumble its way inside its bounds. The weeds struggled against the sand, as all weeds must, fighting for any moisture the earth might retain, but a few yards into the desert's clutches, their efforts failed and ceased. All that remained were countless granules of sand. Sand, sand, sand. Coarse sand. Its yellow color reflected the heat above.

Due to the lack of vegetation, and with enough walking, those traveling in the desert's depths completely lost sight of the line that separated ground and heaven. Their eyes burned to see all around them as golden.

Nothing lived inside the desert. It was home to no one. As such, Heppson knew the witch would not follow him into the desert's boundaries. His mother had long avoided the dominance of nature, an obvious and insurmountable dominance in the desert's world of rushing grit and wind. Its sparseness and its endless hills of ever-moving, mound-shaped billows held nothing for the witch's hungry hands to absorb or shape into her darkness.

In this way, it was the last escape for all who would not bend beneath her evil. Even though that escape necessarily dictated the arrival of dreaded Death. Heppson had truly done what he must to evade his mother when he stepped onto the desert's lifeless soil. The desert served faultlessly as an escape for the witch's fleeing son.

Did he think that he would die when he fell forward into the dust, committed to avoiding the assassination the witch required? In actuality, he knew it. It was only a matter of how and when the end would come that remained to be seen.

With halting steps, in thickly layered sand, Heppson continued to walk. Three days passed in quick succession. By the time the last day dawned, he could barely recall the first, or how it had felt to leave his life and its promise of a future behind.

Over those days, when the sun rose high, heat scorched Heppson, blisters bursting outward all about his body. Each erupted sore allowed more raging sunlight and windswept sand to grate against his damaged skin, the pain like scraping fingernails against his tissue. When the sun went down and coldness clasped about his body, Heppson's limbs trembled against an earth that would not fold itself around him to offer any warmth.

Meanwhile, hunger grew inside him like an elephant knocking its way against his belly and his ribs, although this ravenous desire for food shook itself away as the endless ache of thirst rose above it.

Thirst: a thought that never disappeared in cold or heat. His swollen throat and sun-cracked lips dreamt all on their own of water and the liquid relief its memory promised. Though memory was the only part of this particular dream that remained. True to his word, Heppson had taken nothing when he entered the desert—not even a half-filled skin of moisture to placate his bloated tongue.

At the close of the third day, Heppson knew Death must approach before night arrived. His body manifested this truth to him with every step he took. In fact, he was surprised that he had lived so long.

Shallowly, his mind measured the length to which he could drive his failing frame. He walked onward, all other pathways now closed. At least his own will had chosen this direction for his end. At least he had not sunk his mother's knife into Conrad's belly. He had not felt his half brother breathe a last breath beneath his own two hands. He would die young, but he would die his own master.

And as for what he'd left behind—father, brother, sister,

kingdom, and any possibility of future happiness—what did that matter? Deep within him, Heppson knew that if he could not overcome his mother or her arrangements of evil, the only choice was to leave and not become a part of them. And now he would die, his decision heaving its unavoidable consequences directly onto his defeated shoulders.

All of these thoughts circled around Heppson's water-starved mind over and over again, time both moving forward and keeping itself at a standstill while he waited for the end. So when the unexpected happened, when a strange figure appeared before him in the sand—most obviously not Death, for it rode no horse of fire as Heppson had always been taught—his mind stumbled at any attempt to understand what it might portend. He had seen nothing and no one for so long that his eyes refused to acknowledge the reality of the figure's appearance.

Still, as Heppson's stilting, dragging crawl carried him close enough to the specter for his eyes to adjust, he found himself hungrily evaluating the person who waited before him. Here stood a sight besides sand, when Heppson thought sand was all he would ever see again.

The man, for it most certainly was a man, when viewed at this close proximity, was green. Not green in skin or face or hair, but dressed in green. Dressed enough to seem quite overwhelmingly green to Heppson's troubled and moisture-empty eyes. The man's ends all came to points. Long, slender limbs with sharp-tipped endings. A cone-shaped hat. Of all the strange and wondrous things about the figure, it seemed most odd to see it wear a hat like that.

The green man sat upon a rock, his eyes fixed on Heppson's floundering progress. Though where he'd found a rock to hold him up in this world of sand, Heppson could not begin to guess.

Despite these strange details, Heppson found himself unable to halt his progress forward and investigate further. He was unable to do any more than lean and drag his legs beneath him before he fell. In this way, Heppson found he had almost moved past the startling, green-hued apparition that was his only fleeting interest in this desert. Anyhow, what energy did he have for speaking with a dream? What energy did he have for a conversation with a stranger, when he drew so close to his own demise?

Death must come and Heppson had prepared to meet him. He could not keep himself from this last encounter for a hiccup of the mind that dressed itself in green. But then, just as Heppson would have completely passed the green man by and carried himself forward to his final end, the green man spoke to him and jarred him from his quest.

"Down in luck," the green man said. It was not a question, but a statement of truth. "Ready to throw it in and end the bitter fight?"

At these words and the conversation they somewhat magically began, Heppson somehow forced himself to lean against the drive that moved him forward. Surprisingly, he came to a firm stop and did not fall to his knees as he'd thought he might. Instead, he halted beneath the green man's gaze, his shoulders weaving back and forth with his sudden change in motion.

"In search of a solution?" the green man asked, with his eyebrows raised. "Or are you past that now?"

Heppson did not answer, for what might he say to questions such as these?

"Listen here," the cone-topped man began, as though Heppson's silence bothered him not at all. "If you like, I'll make you a deal."

The green man stood then and walked toward the place where Heppson trembled. Beyond the green-hued figure, Heppson watched as the rock the figure had sat upon wavered in the heated air snaking between it and its recent resident. It looked as though the rock might disappear if given the chance, and Heppson could not help but wonder if it were even a real rock at all.

"Listen!" said the man in green, forcing Heppson's wandering eyes back to his with a quick little clap. "If you make this deal with me, I'll give you your life back. What do you say to that?"

Silence hung again between Heppson and the apparition, the dizzying implication of his words too much for a three-day-dead boy to evaluate so quickly.

"Of course, there must be an appropriate exchange, when life is in the mix," the green man said. "You would agree with that, I think, even in your present state. For my part, I'll help you survive this heat-drenched wasteland you're currently drowning in, but in return, you must take another gift from me: a gift you may not desire to make yours."

At this, the green man pulled from behind him a massive length of hide and shag and dirt. Where the hide had been a moment before remained unclear to Heppson, his mind struggling to keep up. Still, the man lifted its brown-shadowed blackness to his side, as though any examination Heppson might make from this vantage point would tell him what the hide could be.

"I'll give it to you," he said. "After all, I must give it to someone. And if you take it, you will have eternal life as its almost-constant companion. Your present grapple with Death will come to an end, and you will come off conqueror."

Heppson blinked at the absurd statements thrown at his head by this strange and angled figure. *Life*, he had said. *Life. Life. Life.* The green man's words, though downright incomprehensible, and just as unbelievable, did more to animate Heppson's will than he'd ever thought a promise could do. After all, he might have done great things, if his mother had only disappeared and let him. The desert had worn away much of his past, and the desires that went with it, but he could almost remember having dreams of his own.

He had known he would die in the desert from the moment his plan of escape had formed inside his mind. He had worked to accept it over three never-ending, heat-entrenched days. He had accepted his closed future as a fact that could not be erased. He had imagined the appearance of Death and how the stripping away of his soul might feel when it came. And now, these words of life? Of living again? Could the desire that welled inside him be so real and yet so strong? Could a nonsensical proposition such as this so quickly start his heart to rapid beating again?

This apparition of a green man offered life, an offer Heppson did not think he'd ever have again. And now that he had heard it, the green man's flippant offer of a future immediately awoke a grasping need to live. An irrational tremor in his hand sought to yank the dirty hide and its attachment of life into his grip. Even when it made no sense. Even when it seemed a puzzle.

Curling his cracked and swollen hands tightly into fists, Heppson held himself back. The control he'd practiced under the constant watch of his evil mother aided him in his efforts at forbearance. Rather than yank at the cloak, as his pleading heart begged him to do, Heppson instead struggled to make his mouth spit words. He struggled to voice a truth that a life lived beneath his mother's constant jurisdiction had proved as an unassailable reality.

For nothing could be as simple as what this man had said. Nothing could be so simple as a stranger offering life without real cost. Another boy his age might think this could be so, but not him.

As Heppson worked to speak, the green man waited, apparently unworried by the effort or time it took for the prince to complete his deliberations. In fact, it looked as if he knew the prize he offered must necessarily overwhelm the possible downsides of the transaction. And so, the green man stood. Calm and unhurried. He held the hide carelessly, mocking Heppson's desire to hold it—and the promise of life wrapped around it—in his own two hands.

With effort, Heppson's words began to scratch out from his lungs. It had been so long since he'd made the effort to speak, but he forced the breath past his teeth, insistent on voicing his confusion and concern. "And does that hide have strings?" his mouth barked. His words were dry, hoarse, and painful to more than his ears. In fact, his throat felt as though sand had scraped the surface layer from every inch inside, and he clasped his hand to his neck as though to press against the pain.

Apparently unimpressed by Heppson's speech, the green man laughed. He laughed as though at a joke, as though Heppson's words could not possibly be important enough to be offered in so desperate a manner.

"Strings!" said the green man. "Why, I'd say it has some ropes. But that is not exactly the point, now is it? You see, the fact is, you either live or die today. And this hide is your only option for making it out of this desert in one piece. That is the most important matter to be spoken of between us, not a question of ropes or strings."

Heppson's head spun with both misery and lack of under-standing. His body responded slowly to his efforts at comprehension, and he struggled with the arguments of this green man's words. If only his dried-out mind would follow what the green man said more clearly. But it had been too long since drink or food had passed his lips, and the sun had burnt too deeply beneath his skin. He could not play this game of wits with any skill. He could not engage in this type of loaded exchange.

Instead, without meaning to and without any way of know-ing why it mattered, he thought of the last time he had seen his brother in the castle gardens. He thought of his mother's knife spinning 'round and 'round in the sky before it fell to the ground, its mission denied. He thought of the choice he had made before, and what he had given up to avoid his mother's paths. He thought of the reality he had embraced for three days now.

"Death would be better than a deal which carries the unknown," he mumbled.

"Ah. And that bit of cowardly bravado is your answer? A sure and speedy conclusion sought, instead of an attempt to arrange things in your favor." The green man leaned in closer. "You are telling me that you can look Death in the eye and take his gift without a squirm or shiver in your spine? You are prepared to accept your final end so soon? Well, you'll find Death much more frightening than me, or my ropes. You'll find your evaluation of this situation to be slightly off in its conclusion, I think."

"But he is expecting me," croaked Heppson. "I feel it. Who am I to force a different outcome?"

"Of course he expects you. Look at the state you are in! And, if you wish to know your fate with any accuracy, he waits just beyond that next-most pile of sand. Death is ready to make you his, and your halting feet will take you no further than that. Are you ready to meet him, then? Are you ready to meet my brother? If that is the choice you have made, you might as well get on with it. I can find another to offer my prize. I do not have to help you live."

Heppson's shoulders shook, as they had before at the green man's offer of extended life. His mind grappled with the man's unanticipated words, with his callous tossing away of the remaining moments of Heppson's too-short life. Then, in his mind's slow tumbling through the green man's strange argument of words, he caught upon a stranger puzzle; a puzzle which his former, water-fed mind would have felt important to a deal such as this.

"Your brother?" he asked, his dark eyebrows drawn together in confusion.

The green man's voice went quiet. "Yes, you heard me right, my attentive little friend. It's true I spoke of my brother just before. But my brother is not a mystery to you. In fact, you know him well. He's dressed in black. He rides a horse with a mane of fiery flames—or some other such frightening nonsense told around a late night's embers. I'm sure you'll recognize him when your eyes take stock of all he is. Especially with such a matter-of-fact expectation as you currently carry."

"What brother does Death have?" said Heppson, his mind

grappling outward from the pit of golden sand which held him captive in his head. "Are you here to do his work for him? Is this all a sly charade?"

The man before him brushed sand from his green-clad legs, then twisted his head to look Heppson in the eye. "Death might wish to deny our brotherhood. He does not enlist me in his efforts. But brothers we are." He straightened his spine to grow an inch or two, an effort which showed perhaps how it felt to live with Death as sibling. "You see, I am Trickster. And, as such, I have my own important tasks and purposes which bring me to your side."

"Trickster?" said Heppson, shaking his head. "I've never heard of such a being."

The green man scowled and straightened his hat on what looked to be a head very empty of hair. "I'm often forgotten, it's true, though never quite dismissed by those who know their proper history. You see, I am he who causes trouble in this wide expanse of life. Then I laugh as you fools try to set things right. It is an amusing pastime, and it keeps me busy enough, even if I have no wandering souls to collect as my better-known brother does."

"So you are a jester of some sort who finds joy in other's pain?"

"A jester!" exclaimed Trickster. "You would find that I do much, much more than jest. And that is all you need know of me for now, I think. For this particular trick has to do with you, not me, you see? This is your question to answer, not mine."

Heppson clamped his mouth together tightly, a sharp wind setting his body swaying once again. His clothes hung ragged on his body, ragged and loose. The limbs that had held such strength just three days previous struggled to keep him upright. His skin was covered with abrasions, which might have oozed if they had any moisture to do so. His mind tumbled inside him, even with the returned strength of the last few moments. So many changes in such a short time. He felt incapable of a decision such as this;

incapable of working out the twists and turns of his possible future. What should he choose?

To his front, Trickster examined the nails of his empty hand. After many moments, and apparently finding them in reasonable repair, he looked to the silent prince. "The time has come, my friend. Tell me, will you make the deal or not?" he said. "You see, I must have your decision now. A simple 'yes' or 'no' will do. If you choose to make the exchange, we two will leave Death waiting for his prize. A small pleasure I might add to my side of the balance."

"And what else do you gain if I take this hide?" said Heppson in a last attempt to ferret out his path. "I must know, before I make you any answer. Do you wish only to cheat your brother, or is there some other purpose to this?"

"Ah," said the Trickster. "You continue to wonder at my reasons, do you? Well, let me tell you this. I cannot truly cheat my brother. He will take you in the end, in some way or another. You must prepare yourself for that, despite our deal. Unfortunately, I have no true power over Death, not in the long run. No one does. But there is another side of this agreement that would benefit me greatly. If you agree to take my gifts, I'll tell you more of it. If not, I'll leave you to the Dark One and his horse."

Heppson shook his head, unsatisfied by the Trickster's explanations. "I ask again, what do you gain from this exchange? What is my life to you?"

"It is a life," Trickster snapped, his calm demeanor lost for one short moment. "And that is all I need right now. Besides, you must stop thinking what it is to me, and think instead what it will mean to you. Or, if that matters not to you, think of your dear brother, left behind to face that horrid mother whom you claim. I have dealt with her before."

Heppson froze, his body stiff with Trickster's words. The mention of his mother and her deeds caught his breath inside him.

"Oh yes, I know about all that," said Trickster. "Tell me, does your death here do anything to help your brother take his throne? You think by running away you've done them all a favor. But are you so sure that's the case? Are you so sure further evil has not struck while you've wasted away in this large expanse of sand?"

The sharpness of this thought struck Heppson, its verity quickly outdistancing the strangeness of the Trickster's knowledge of his past. True, he had not thought the witch could kill Conrad herself. But was his belief in such a theory really strong enough to make it so? When all he could do was run and die to keep his brother safe, that truth had been enough to make escape the correct choice. His efforts at protection had outweighed his cowardly behavior. But if he could live without his mother's knife within his grip, must he not expect himself to do more—to try again?

Heppson took a shaky step toward the Trickster, his mind now suddenly made up, a bit of his former self straightening upward with his spine. "Give me the hide," he said. "I will make your exchange."

And Trickster smiled, the deal completed as he wished.

Heppson

Once he'd agreed to the deal, the Trickster had gone silent regarding any further details of what lay ahead. Heppson should have insisted on more information at that point. But what was done was done. It had been hard enough to make the agreement in the first place.

In order to keep Heppson from Death, the Trickster necessarily quenched his thirst and did a little for his hunger. He did this in a way Heppson could barely understand, placing his hand upon the prince's head and allowing some tendril of his power to sink into Heppson and supply his body's wants.

In his hand Heppson now dragged the Trickster's hide. He felt no closer to understanding its meaning than when he'd first seen it in the Trickster's grasp. Brown. Soft. A fur. How many times could he internally list off these realities without coming any closer to a knowledge of what they foretold? He may have regained the clarity of mind he needed to reconsider the decision he'd made, but what good would such worrying do him now? He could not go backward and make better sense of it now.

As best as Heppson could tell, an hour had passed since he should have died. In that time, the Trickster had laid hands on him yet again, this time bringing to his mind a darkness, which lasted several moments and multiple struggling breaths before it ended. By the time he came to himself, his entire location had shifted. Trickster had somehow left the desert and had crossed into the wilderness Heppson knew was situated far south of Alastair.

Here, towering trees both fat and thin blocked the sun from Heppson's burnt and scabbing skin, their branches heavy with the unfurling leaves of spring. From the very beginning, this forest would have been a much more appropriate place to hide from his mother, if only Heppson could have transported himself in whatever way the Trickster had managed to do, which he could not. With the Trickster's backhanded help, the distance between Heppson and his mother's domain had tripled, though what that would mean for his new future, Heppson could not say.

The dense foliage around them lent a feeling of protection that bordered on claustrophobia to Heppson. He had been so long in the empty air of the desert that the upright closeness of this wilderness felt constricting. The vines, trees, and bugs of the forest pressed about him, their proximity an itch against his ears. Of course, the air felt crisp and light instead of heat-heavy, as it had in the desert. It was a small mercy Heppson appreciated as he walked forward. He had never traveled to this forest and his eyes could not help but consider the scenery that came before them.

With continued travel, and a deeper penetration of the wilderness's lengths, a second hour passed. Heppson dragged his feet with increasingly failing efforts. Vines dotted with blue-petaled blossoms tripped him as he went, their tendrils curling forwards and backwards. The hide grew more and more massive in his grip. His energy was limited, and if the Trickster did not halt their journey soon, Heppson knew he would fall to his knees. Even in the best of health, this would have been a difficult day for him. Considering that he should have died this morning, he was amazed that he still stood. Still, Heppson did not request a halt in their travels. He would not reveal his weakness to this strange green being.

Another half hour passed. The sun moved across the sky in its daily pattern, as though nothing out of the ordinary took place below. Still, they walked. Heppson barely managed to move himself forward, counting tree trunks as they passed his sight. Forty-four. Forty-five. Forty-six. Forty-seven. Forty-eight. And a fallen tree. Should he count that as one? His eyes jumped from trunk to trunk, no longer caring about the beauty he had never seen before. He wondered why the Trickster had not transported them closer to their destination. Why were they forced to labor for these last few miles? But he did not ask.

Then, Trickster spoke suddenly, his voice a surprise after their long travels in silence. "I bet you wonder where we're going," he said.

Numbered trees fled from Heppson's mind, and he lifted his head in response. His feet slowed to a standstill, but he did not make any verbal reply.

"Well, even if you won't ask, I'll supply the answer." Trickster reached his hand up into an expectant flourish of some sort. "Kind of me, don't you think?"

Heppson bowed his head. He did not offer the biting retort of irritation that came to mind; fully aware it would not serve him well. He knew his role must be that of captivated audience, if he meant to learn anything here. He had played this role of feigned humility often for his mother, when she'd had some deed of evil she wished acclaimed. And so, he allowed his ears to listen and his demeanor to appear subdued.

"You see," said the Trickster, as he turned to continue their journey and stooped beneath a slanted limb, "I recently had a run-in with a bear."

"A bear," repeated Heppson, his fingers rubbing the pelt he dragged in his hand, a nugget of necessary information finally falling in place.

"Yes, a bear," said Trickster. And then he shook his head. "Of course, this was not an ordinary bear. Not some ambling beast of the forest, just woken from its winter sleep."

Trickster paused and looked about the wilderness. To Heppson it seemed he looked either to the many trees crowding their path, or to the faraway sky, which broke in sharp shards through the canopy before sliding its way down to the ground. When Trickster spoke, Heppson could tell these particular words were not meant for him.

"But who was I to know the bear was more than mortal?" said Trickster. "The beast looked ordinary enough to me. Several hands high, shaggy, and brown. Down on all fours, and rooting for berries."

Heppson stopped walking and stared at the Trickster, waiting for him to continue. With time, the Trickster's eyes lost the gleam they'd held when he spoke to the wilderness and sky. He shook his head and glanced at Heppson again.

"Who was I to know the bear was a Guardian in these parts?" he said, his voice turned upward in well-practiced consternation. "Who was I to know he was part of the wellspring of strength that this forest is meant to play for your entire land?"

"Guardian?" asked Heppson, his curiosity betraying him.

"Ah, you wonder at that word," he said. "And well you should. Your mother does not speak of them, I think. She does not acknowledge the reasons she stays away from places like your desert exile and this forest. She wouldn't want you or your people to know what makes her hesitate to show her strength in places of the earth, in places where the old patterns of power continue to hold sway. Well, I'll tell you a little of the Guardians, since I am in good humor today."

Heppson did not bristle at the Trickster's condescension. After all, he wished him to speak, no matter how mocking the tone. The idea of some Guardian his mother might actually fear awoke in him a sense of hope that he'd never felt before. Could his agreement with the Trickster make it possible for him to help his brother? Would he now learn of a weakness to his mother's plan? Of some fail-safe defense the earth itself could offer against his evil mother?

True, he had known his mother did not prefer to enter the desert, but he'd always assumed that had been because the desert was so empty and bereft of tools to fuel her power. And true, he knew this disjointed southern wilderness was nothing his mother ever sought to make an official part of her kingdom. But it was so far from the castle and its village settlements. It was the background noise for the reality that always held center stage in his mind.

Besides, in his heart, he'd always thought she only waited to put her son upon the throne before attempting a far-flung venture such as conquering this wilderness and the few free souls who peopled its deep unknown. He had not thought for a moment that she left it alone because of fear.

A fact she must have relied upon.

How had he dared assume he knew his mother's purposes and limitations? How had he dared to leave any rock unturned that might make possible the vanquishing of her madness? And what would Conrad say to this new information of the wilderness's apparent strength? Of the possibility of it serving as some buffer against her evil? What would he say of these unknown Guardians?

Beyond Heppson, the Trickster continued speaking, apparently unaware of his listener's frenzied thoughts. Heppson quieted his mind. There must be more important information in all that Trickster said. If he meant to help his brother and their kingdom and make this new deal worth the price, he would need to hunt the useful morsels of truth out of the rest of the green man's ramblings.

"There are four Guardians of this wilderness," Trickster was saying. He turned and held up four wriggling fingers. "One Guardian prepared for each season." He pressed his fingers down one by one. "Spring. Summer. Autumn. Winter. Four in total, you see. And this bear I happened upon turned out to be the Guardian of Winter, instead of the simple lumbering animal of the forest I assumed. It's an oddity, really, when you think that a normal bear would be sleeping through the winter season. But I suppose a person would find that magic has many strange reasons for such seeming contradictions. I've often noted so, when I find unusual circumstances upon the land."

Heppson raised his eyebrows, and the Trickster shrugged as though admitting his deficiency in understanding.

"Well, it is not winter now, you know. And apparently that made a difference in our little confrontation. Some sort of rule that the Guardian's power is the strongest within season. A silly idea when you come down to it. As though power is useful only in bits and pieces, even the earth-spun, wrap-around power of these Guardians. Of course," said Trickster, and he shrugged his pointy-green shoulders, "out of season, this Guardian could not escape the arrow of one of Death's brothers. It seems we each of us have a measure of our eldest brother's life-ending sting within our hands—a fortunate fact for me. Though not, of course, fortunate for the bear."

His hands on his hips, the Trickster silently stared again at the trees, lost in thought. Heppson waited and tried to understand anything his companion spoke of when it came to these apparent Guardians of the forest. What did this have to do with the hide he held in his hand? What did this have to do with the new future he'd chosen when he made his deal with the man in green? And, most importantly, what did this have to do with his mother's avoidance of this forest, of her possible weakness? Why would these Guardians be so far away, in this forest he'd never stepped one foot inside?

"Well," said the Trickster as he turned back to Heppson, "as things like that are wont to go, the bear demanded an accounting, once the deed was done. And as it lay there, bleeding out its lifeblood into the forest floor, my sharp-tipped arrow buried in its hairy chest, it spoke the sum."

Heppson stared at the green man.

"You see, I had ended this bear before his time, and certain obligations came as a result. The beast wanted my life for his."

"Your life?" said Heppson, surprised at this sudden turn in events.

"Of course, you needn't worry about me, in that regard," said Trickster. "You see, my life is much too difficult for another to steal so easily. I've hidden it far away from the prying eyes of others. After all, what purpose would I have if I had a life to lose so easily? With a brother like mine, I have learned to secrete my soul well."

Trickster brushed at the branches about him, which poked him back sharply in the shoulders. He turned to press forward again. Heppson gripped the hide and followed.

"And so, it fell to me to find another to take my place. Another life to give the Bear in the exchange. It was the agreement we made. Quite luckily, I felt a weakened soul nearby. A soul that would serve the Guardian's purpose and be willing to do my bidding. It was only a short, desert's expanse away. Nothing to my powers of travel."

Heppson felt a shiver run down the length of his spine, a foretelling of the end of this odd tale.

"You see, I needed another's future to give instead of mine. Let me tell you, the bear did not seem too troubled at the little exchange I thought to make. All he cared was that a life was given. He did not quibble over the source of the required price. It was not his nature, I suppose, to consider the individual, when it came to the greater good."

Heppson halted, a loose branch scratching across his face as it returned to its original position. "Then you will sacrifice me to the bear?" he said. Had he only given up one Death for another? Had this possible promise of a tool against his mother come too late?

"Sacrifice you?" the Trickster turned and brushed dirt from his shirtfront. "How little you understand! Perhaps you will consider it a sacrifice, but I don't think it would qualify in any other's mind. Fear not, lost soul. I do not plan to slit your neck on any altar today. You will not be the Bear's dinner tonight."

"Then what do you want with me?" said Heppson. "Why have you brought me here? Tell me the end of your tale!" He had held onto his practiced disinterest long enough, and a sort of self-preservation woke him to the injustice of the Trickster's half-given answers.

"Oh, enough with the questions," said the green man, waving his hand in Heppson's face, unimpressed by his outburst. "You act as though you were in charge of this little production. And

I assure you, you are not. If you'll only take a few steps forward, you'll find we have arrived."

Angrily, Heppson walked through the opening in foliage where Trickster had pointed, knowing he had no other choice. He lived when he should not, and as such, he must do as Trickster said, no matter how he wished to throw the hide in his hand at that green and angular face. He had made the deal.

"I see nothing," said Heppson, his eyes taking in an empty clearing of the forest floor. "I see no bear."

"Of course not," said the Trickster, now beside him. "I killed him. I already told you that. Any sign of our struggle would be long gone by now. It's not as though a carcass of that sort would be left here to rot. But tell me, mortal man, what do you hold in that hand of yours?"

Heppson looked again to the fur grasped in his fist and realization hit him soundly in the chest: a full-blown understanding where only a sliver of truth crouched before. "I see a skin," he said. "I see the fur and hide of the Bear."

"You know," said the Trickster, "you really should thank me for this. While a Guardian is obviously not completely immortal, he does have more claim to life than you would think. This particular bear had been around for many centuries before I ended what he called life."

Heppson pulled the skin upward and let it fall open before him. He let its folds and shags tumble toward the ground.

"And perhaps, if you have any luck, you might find enough power hidden inside that fur to aid you in your own battles, though the constraints of Guardian might trouble you in that regard. Regardless, we have come to the site of Bear's death. It is now time for Bear to take life again."

"Take life again?" Heppson looked from the pelt to Trickster.

"So many questions. Honestly, you could go on and on if I would let you. If I answered all you asked, we'd be here the entire day. Very dull indeed. But, happily for me, this is not about what you want or need to know. I am not here to do your bidding. Instead, you must do what I say. You must do what I want. That was the price for your life. And I tell you now, mortal man, that I want you to don that cloak. I do not wish to do so, and since the bear could not lay hold of my soul, I have been given this other option to complete my task."

The green man looked once more to the trees around them. The branches had left the two of them alone in the clearing, their leaves of green a protective cocoon, which awaited the exchange which must come.

"Here, old forest spirits, you find your prize," said Trickster, raising his arms to the sky. "I have done as was required."

Heppson felt the Trickster's eyes lock onto his.

"Don the cloak," he said. "Do it now."

In the end, Heppson obeyed him. After all, a deal had been struck, and he would not drag it out any further. He was not the sniveling type. Instead, he flipped the fur about his shoulders. He pulled the ragged, hairy sheath across his back.

As soon as he'd begun, the pelt wrapped him in, smothering and swallowing him as a snake takes it prey. It pulled him close, melting his skin, like a fire burning where flesh touched pelt. It yanked at his form, pulling him bit by bit into the shape it demanded and remembered. Heppson arched his back in agony, bent forward again in torment. His mouth opened to scream, but gave no sound.

"Ah," said the Trickster, his voice far away and smothered by the pelt's constriction and change. "I see it now."

And so did Heppson. He was the bear.

Trickster did not stay long to survey the extent of damage done by Heppson's transformation. Of course, being Bear occupied Heppson well enough without that creature of green to smile at his pain. For, to become Bear was overwhelming indeed, even without considering the discomfort it brought with it. Becoming

Bear did not mean an immediate transformation into a bear of the animal kingdom, with only animal thoughts or cares. Instead, Heppson remained a person—with a person's mind—trapped inside Bear's form.

In the beginning, he could even feel his human body. Contained within an alternate form, it was there all the same, trapped beneath the surface of the fur and muscles he'd developed. He could feel it inside the pelt. His own fingers and toes. His own tongue and ears. This feeling of dual existence made him shake from core to skin. How could he comprehend what he'd become?

Crazed and manic at his body's change, Heppson the Bear hysterically ran circles of miles in the wood, crashing against the trees that contained him. What could he do but run from this overwhelming feeling of confusion that settled about him with the pelt of fur? Run, and run, and run. Run as though he could make it disappear. Even had the Trickster stayed, Heppson would have left him far behind in his frenzied attempts at an impossible escape.

But then, as hours passed and as the day advanced, his awareness of self and memory lessened considerably. Like water dripping from an overturned vessel, he lost track of who he'd been before exactly. The alteration was slow, constant, and, in the end, almost exhaustively complete. Only one small vestige of himself remained within his center. A vestige that whispered the name 'Heppson' shallowly yet steadfast all the same. In all other parts, he was Bear. Caged in an animal's pelt, he had lost everything he'd ever had, or even every thought he'd had. Perhaps Death had been the better choice in this strange exchange.

By the end of that first day, when he exhaustedly sank to the forest floor to drown himself in sleep, the only thing Heppson managed to feel with any certainty *was* the fur, the claws, and the weight of muscle and fat around his middle. The only substantial thing he encountered in his alarmed consciousness was Bear,

Guardian of the forest. No, he was not a simple black bear of the woods. Not really. He could tell a part of him was different and more astute than some animal consciousness might have been. But he had lost himself in all the changing. And this meant something, though he could not manage to comprehend the extent of it; at least not until the sun dipped below the line of trees and land, and left the world to night.

Heppson had collapsed beside a large and tilting tree—the kind that looked as though its life were almost over, the kind that might be toppled by any passing burly wind. He hid himself beneath its sweeping, sloping boughs, wishing he could cease existence. He did not care if any human or beast should happen along and seek to take his life. What would that mean to him now? Without true animal instinct to lead him and without the intricate desires of his human soul to urge him onward, what was he to do with this new reality?

But as night grew deeper, even with the fatigue that seeped and settled inside his bones, Heppson found he could not sleep. Coolness had crept beneath his skin, and he shivered relentlessly against the pelt. Though how a bear might shiver at the start of spring went beyond his understanding.

Regardless, he lay inert beneath the tree's wide limbs. He did not want to move anymore. He had run enough. He trembled again with the chill of night and with the realization of the new life overshadowing him. Turning to the side, he curled in upon himself and pulled his knees into his chest to escape the cold. As he moved, he felt the cloak of fur shift and slide over his iced form, its rough underside a reminder of the new prison he faced.

And then his mind startled to complete and human wakefulness. He understood. He was not Bear, not now that the sun had set. Instead, he was man, clothed as he had been before his transformation, left with the now detached fur strewn lifelessly over his body. Night had returned him to his human form and his human thoughts. How could he not have noticed?

Stunned, Heppson climbed shakily to his feet. He was not Bear, and with his human legs he could leave the Trickster's pile of fur, if he wished. He could let that creature sort this mess to right. He could leave the cloak and all that it entailed—all the pain and anguish of losing his consciousness within the pelt—and never return. If Trickster threw him back into the desert as a result, so be it. He would deal with those consequences when they came rather than bear the burden of Bear and the loss of self it meant, day after day.

But then, within a few short steps of his desertion, a growling voice inside threatened wildly to yank Heppson's heart in two. It demanded he remain with the pelt. It said he could not depart, or even think to leave behind his existence as Bear without dreaded result. It whispered threateningly that his life of breath and pumping blood continued only here, beside this hide that served as form during daytime hours. And furthermore, that as Bear's constant companion, he must also remain within the forest now surrounding him. He could never step again beyond its boundaries. The bear may have retreated, but it had not disappeared.

Crumpling to the forest floor, Heppson realized that the damage had been done. He might not always exist as Bear, but he was tied to Bear. Indeed, a piece of that being was burrowed inside his mind. Heppson's hands knotted the pelt tightly in their grasp, considering the hours and decisions scattered behind him in the dust of his past few days. First to give up life, rather than take the life of his Conrad. Then to take life back, in some strange exchange he barely understood. And finally, to live a half-life. Man by night and beast by day, trapped inside this wilderness.

What had he done?

PART II

Heart

Heart's sister, Lark, found her love one golden, light-refracted, summer afternoon.

Truly a fairytale.

Lark had gone outside to hang their wash, to let it dry in the bright sun and take on all the woodsy smells of late summer that drifted about their secluded cottage home. To do her work, she wore no finery but that which she'd been born with: sapphire eyes that brightened at the sound of any whistling bird nearby, lips as soft and pink as a newborn baby's kiss, and skin that glowed like candlelight. Lark's chocolate hair hung to her waist.

Dressed in an old and faded gown—dusty rose and white, smooth and worn in the way old fabric grows—Lark looked as comfortable in those woods as though she'd unfurled from the ground herself. Her apron, crisp and white as a mountain's tip, circled her waist in its narrow grasp. Rolled to her elbows, her sleeves were still moist from the water she and Heart had tumbled the clothes in moments before.

Oh, how Heart loved her perfect sister. Lark had kept her close for so long, after their mother went from life the dark night of Heart's first breath. In all the years between that day and this, Lark had taught her everything she dared to know or cared to wonder about. The two sisters were a set, a bonded pair of spirits, and they held their love wrapped about them like one of Granny's quilts: thick, tight, and draped from head to toe.

Up until then, the sisters had lived a simple life: far from any civilization, and with only aged, decrepit Granny for company. They saw few strangers, they saw few locals—mostly, they saw no one at all. They managed their lives on their own. Capable, confident, and sufficient to their needs. Their world consisted primarily of the cozy glen of green that their cottage rested safely inside, and the mile or so of protective trees that crowded 'round about it. The rest of the forest served only as a further separation from them and the outside world.

And so that day, when the stranger came walking from between those trees and stepped into the clearing where Lark stood, Heart was not surprised to see her sister jump in astonishment. Startled as well, Heart sucked her own breath in and froze. She had been dawdling near the rear of their home in an effort to avoid the remaining tasks of laundry and she was still several feet away from the hanging line, which spanned the front portion of their little glen.

From Heart's vantage point around the cottage wall, the newly-arrived stranger looked how she would imagine a soldier or vagrant to look, his bearing nothing like the woodsmen she'd seen before on the rare occasions when they'd worked nearby her home. He was covered with dirt. The dirt was nothing new, but his clothes looked as though they'd originally been quite fine— before they'd been worn to bits in long traveling. Also, he was quite obviously burdened with Death, an apparent relic from his travels.

Despite the world of joy Lark had held above her head since she was tiny, Heart's life had taught her to see Death's mark as clearly as she noted a person's hair color or height. Born of Death herself, Heart could not help but find his shadowed leavings wrapped around the necks of others. She'd never taken any pleasure from this peculiar talent of hers, nor sought for it to grow. Now she took note of the evidence of Death hanging on the stranger as the stranger took note of Lark.

"Oh, my," said Lark, when her own moment of fear had passed.

As usual, her voice tripped like water running from a spring, its crystalline tones as fitting to her as birds were to the sky. As she spoke, likely not knowing he did it himself, the traveler lifted his shaggy, tired head. Then, he straightened his back, increasing his height by several inches. In front of him, Lark took a deep and freshly laundered breath. She finished hanging the sheet she held and dropped her hands to smooth her skirts.

"I suppose you'll be hungry," she said, as though his strange arrival was nothing odd to her or to him.

Trembling, Heart watched as her sister reached out a hand toward the stranger. Within her stomach, a deep pit opened wide to swallow her whole. Heart wanted to call for her sister to stop, to call for time to hold still. But she didn't speak. She knew from experience that nothing could stop Lark's gentle love when it sought to heal a hurt. Not with plants, not with animals, and not with people. She knew it with every bit of breath she breathed.

This traveler stood no chance against the comfort Lark offered. Her sister would take him in, and Heart could only watch her do it. Even if she wished it were not so, even if she wished her tiny world held not one part of him or his dark lingering past.

"Come," Lark said to the stranger, her hand beckoning him forward to the cottage. "Come with me. We'll go inside and find some food and drink."

And that was that. The deed was done, without one chance for intervention. Heart could only watch her sister lead the visitor inside and hope that night would bring the traveler's swift departure from her home. Perhaps if she had done the laundry herself, and had let Lark move on to other tasks, it would have come out differently. But now she would never know. Lark had made her mark.

By evening, Granny had joined the cause and found several other ways to make the traveler feel comfortable and at ease. After a quick offering of food, Granny's first form of welcoming was to shoo both Heart and Lark away from the sturdy, one-room cottage so that the soldier could clean himself and trim the curly beard that graced his chin.

Before any more could be heard of the stranger, both girls were sent to gather greens in the woods, a task that passed in relative silence as Heart stewed about the evening's supper and the new guest Granny had insisted on inviting to the meal. She could not bring herself to ask Lark's thoughts upon the matter. She did not want to hear them.

When they returned, Heart found their visitor not exactly terrible looking. But that did not mean she wished he would stay. Clean now, he was clothed in old things belonging to her father, the pant cuffs a full three inches from his ankles. He stood taller than any man Heart had seen before, and his hair was a yellow mass of knots that curled in gently on itself. She would never have thought to see so much color beneath all the dirt he'd shown up wearing, but Granny always did say that a washing could do wonders. It had apparently, and unfortunately, done so with him.

In fact, from where he sat waiting at their wide, cracked wood table with his long legs sticking out the other side, one would almost believe he belonged inside their home. With the fire crackling at the rear and the light of candles flickering against the walls, Heart wondered for a moment if this was how her home had looked before she drew in breath: when her father waited at the table for his daily bread.

Did he stoop a little when he stood, as this blond traveler was forced to do? Or was the middling height of their cottage well enough for him? The pants' lengths certainly suggested so. Had her mother bustled about as Lark did now? Moving from fire to table to narrow cupboard in deliberate preparation; her steps quick, but somehow unhurried as she prepared the meager meal?

Dinner would be simple this night, as it would have been and always was in a home as modest as theirs. It could not matter that tonight they had a guest; circumstances would not allow for any extravagance beyond the rudimentary supplies upon their shelves. Atop the table rested Granny's bread, a scrap of meat furnished by Heart's homemade traps, a small amount of cheese, and, of course, the freshly gathered greens, which Lark had managed to make beautiful in an old and chipped blue bowl. Heart supposed it must have been this way, so long before. Yes, it must have been very much like this.

Still, once they'd all sat down and begun the meal, the visitor did not speak beyond the pleasantries any stranger might offer, and since Granny despised any hint of a prying spirit when it came to strangers, the evening passed fairly silently—not the way a family's meal would have gone. When all had finished eating, Lark stood up to clear the table and Heart set to scrubbing at the dishes in the large wood tub that served them for this purpose, just as they would have done on any other night. Evening had descended quickly following the unexpected arrival of the stranger and darkness approached.

With a cough, their visitor stood from his chair at the table. "I thank you kindly for the meal," he said. "I will, of course, be going now. I won't cause you any further bother. You've been most welcoming."

Glancing sideways, Heart noticed the look of worry that Lark wore as the traveler gathered up his things. Meanwhile, Granny clicked her tongue from where she remained seated at the table. Heart most definitely didn't approve of the signs she saw in their demeanors. Even if he did look handsome with a washed and hairless face, Heart did not appreciate the way the traveler's eyes took in her sister. Not that it was a look to bring fear, but it most certainly seemed too fond for her mind's comfort.

And so, throwing her towel down on the dishes, Heart decided to take a hand in things herself. She hoped she might speed up the stranger's departure, for who knew what Granny might do if he stayed here much longer, with that sad and homely look about him.

"Yes," she said, her voice startling and abrupt amidst the gentle flickering in the chamber, "I suppose you must be on your way. After all, we wouldn't want to keep you from your own family. You must wish you were with them now. I'm sure you have children to return to and feed?"

Granny grimaced and glared toward Heart, everything in her eyes ordering her to continue with the dishes. As though a mindless task of work could halt Heart's efforts at dismissing this strange interloper from their cottage.

"My family," replied the traveler, his words offered in a hesitant whisper. And then, more loudly. "Yes, I must move onward. It is the way of wanderers like myself to move forward always. This much I know."

"Wanderer?" said Lark. "But which direction are you headed?" The words were quick, as though she knew Granny's clicks of correction would follow soon after. Which, of course, they did. After all, Heart's Granny was nothing if not set in her ways.

"Lark, dear, you know it isn't our place to pry," said Granny. "Heart has badgered our poor visitor quite enough for one night."

Lark looked down, and Heart bristled at Granny's words. Badgered! Didn't her Granny see the danger here? What could Heart do but act? Especially when everyone else seemed unconcerned by the visitor's presence?

Granny pushed herself slowly to her feet and shuffled her way toward the traveler. "Please forgive us. My grandchildren are not much used to company," she said. "Their mother died years ago when that dear thing came to us," she said, her hand gesturing toward Heart. "And their father, my son, comes rarely to check on their health, as the heartache of that night does eat at him so."

Granny sighed and shook her head in that way Heart recognized as an attempt to dismiss her painful memories of the past. At the sight, Heart fidgeted and picked up both her towel and another dish to dry. She did not like to think of her own part in the dark story of her birth, or of the way she'd caused the departure of both her mother and father on that fateful night. She could not change any of it now, so why let her own heart ache?

Besides, what did any of it have to do with her ability to converse with a stranger, or with her certainty that this particular traveler must leave as soon as possible? Her Granny should not have brought it up at all—should not have used it as an explanation of her outburst. But Granny continued, and neither Lark nor Heart dared to interrupt her or her conversation. Granny might be old and rather crippled, but her mind remained sharp, and her will a rod of iron when it came to any argument.

"We three live alone in this cottage," said Granny to the stranger. "And we do fine with one another for company. I keep a gun, loaded and ready, which we all know well how to use. There are not many that come this way, and we've never had a bit of trouble in watching over ourselves."

"I am glad," said the traveler. "You have a happy home, as I have seen and felt this night."

"So am I," said Granny. "Though, I must admit, it isn't in us to turn a lost soul like you out into the dark and lonely night of this empty wilderness, even if we've met you only today. No, we are not as callous and self-protective as that."

Heart clamped her teeth together, fighting against her wish for contradiction, fighting against her desire to still her Granny's words.

"I understand," said the traveler, "but I wouldn't wish to . . ."

"Oh, that's quite enough of your empty words and pleasantries, my boy. I offer you nothing I do not wish to offer, and if I felt that you were any danger to our home, I would send you quickly on your way. However, you know as well as I that it would be nice to have a place to sleep for a change. The wilderness beyond our walls is very large, and homes like ours come few and far between." Granny took a breath. "You will find we have a small lean-to, not far from the glen where you first saw our Lark hanging clothes when you arrived. You may sleep there tonight, eat a small meal with us in the morn, and be on your way before the sun grows too warm. Or, if you need the work, you are welcome to stay for the week and earn a few supplies for your travels. There are always tasks done easier by a man of your size than by ourselves."

Heart tried desperately to stifle a moan at her Granny's words. One night might be manageable, but a week with him looking at Lark that way? It would never do. Did Granny wish to orphan her completely with her blasted courteousness?

"I appreciate your thoughtfulness," said the traveler, "and I must admit I could do with the work. It has been a long while since I've had the chance to build up any rations."

Of course he could do with the work! What was her Granny thinking? Heart rubbed at the last cup in her heap angrily. She had known it would come to this, from the beginning. She had known he would not be sent on this night. And now another week of his intruding presence stood between her and his removal.

"That'll be fine then. But be warned, my boy," and here Granny stood and shuffled close to her new friend, her finger held up sharply in his face, "if you come near this place during night hours, you take your own life in your hands. There will be no warning. There will be no chance for explanation. I am a quick shot and am strong of hearing. These girls will have no problem burying you, if you come to give us bother."

"Yes, ma'am," the stranger said. With a sharp nod of his head, he apparently took Granny's words in all seriousness, though it was the first time Heart had seen any hint of a smile about him. It lightened his face in a gentle way, the troubles of whatever he'd left behind disappearing beneath its influence. This only discouraged Heart more.

"Good," said Granny, "then that's settled." Stepping back, she turned to Heart. "Heart dear, as you've finished the dishes, you may guide this visitor of ours to that lean-to of your father's. Take a blanket from the loft to keep him comfortable upon the ground."

Heart grimaced. As though she personally wished to help the stranger stay! It did her no good to have him here a moment longer, so why would she want to help? Though deep inside, Heart did not really wish to send their visitor into the blackness of night without a morning meal in sight. Besides, she knew Granny would not be pleased with any argument she might make about the blanket. So, with an irritated shrug to signal her displeasure, she climbed the ladder, which led to the loft where she and Lark normally slept. What could be done now anyway, with all the words that had been said?

By the time she'd returned from the loft—no need to hurry with the task, even if she'd decided to do as she was told—the traveler waited outside, Lark waited by the door, and Granny had drifted to sleep in the rocking chair they kept for her near the fire.

"I'll guide him out, Heart," Lark whispered from the door. "I know you don't want to do it yourself, and I don't mind."

"I'll bet you don't," Heart whispered back, "Besides, Granny asked me to do it."

"Oh, it hardly matters which of us should take him," said Lark. "She only asked you because you were being such a sour-puss and she wanted you to behave. Do as I say. It will be fine, I promise."

Lark took the blanket from Heart's arms, ready to turn and leave the cottage, but Heart remained unsure. Moving to block her sister's exit, she took Lark's arm and pulled her close so she might see into her eyes.

Did her sister really think Heart didn't know the reason why she begged this task? Did she really believe Heart to be so clueless when it came to matters such as this? Heart couldn't help but feel she had something huge to fear about this moment. Though what that might be, she found couldn't say with words, which left her with no real defense against her sister's desires.

"Fine. I'll let you go," she said, releasing Lark's arm and allowing the glance between them to break. "But you have to take the gun."

Lark sighed and hugged the blanket close. "Oh, Heart, you don't seriously distrust our guest, do you? I don't need to take . . ."

"Take the gun, or I'll wake Granny," said Heart. "I mean it."

Lark laughed, and dropped one hand down to her side, the blanket draped heavily across her other arm. "All right, dear Heart, I'll take the gun. Have it your way, then."

Content that she'd made some gains, even if they were likely pointless, Heart watched Lark lift the gun from its place along the stone wall. Then, still unsettled, she continued to watch as her sister slipped out the solid cottage door that protected their tiny home.

Of course, she knew Lark was right. There was no reason to fear their guest. He would not harm Lark. He did not wish to bring any of them pain. But Heart's fear was not of the traveler at all, not when it came right down to it. Her fear stemmed from that hint of something new in Lark. The something new that made Heart wish so deeply that her sister would stay inside, and far away from their visitor.

Granny had always said that there are moments in life when a person turns a corner, and suddenly everything that person knew before never exists again. She said this happened the night Heart's mother died. She said that life changed. It wasn't bad or good, but it was different. No one could bring back the old road the family had traveled on before that night, even if they tried. No one could have known the change was coming. It just came. And that was that.

Granny said this altering of all a person knew happened in life. And Heart wondered, as Lark went out that door: had it happened to her family yet again? Would life ever be the way it was before this traveler stumbled into their secluded glen and changed the light inside her sister's eyes?

Heart's back trembled with a sudden chill, which spoke nothing of the late summer season that should have wrapped about her by the calendar's accounting. Meanwhile, a voice inside her heart echoed a firm reply to the frightening and loaded question whispering through her mind:

No.

Heart

How did it happen so fast? One week, and it was finished. Just as Heart had feared from the beginning.

Of course, it certainly would have begun that first all-important night when her sister and their unexpected visitor walked beneath the trees. With Granny sleeping in her rocker and Heart pacing in the cottage, the lovebirds' initial conversation wouldn't have had any unwanted spectators.

In fact, when Heart imagined it later, wishing with all her might that she could make it all un-happen, she decided the traveler would have taken the blanket from Lark that night to lighten her sister's load. All chivalry and kindness: that would have been his way from the beginning. Lark would have carried the gun haphazardly in the crook of her arm, its purpose entirely forgotten in the time they had together. If Heart remembered it correctly, the air that night had been smooth and temperate—clearly ripe for late-night conversations. Conversations that Heart could also imagine, for she knew her dear Lark, oh so well.

"Your sister is careful of you," the traveler might have said, his voice filled with the glowing approval he had directed toward Lark throughout the entire maddening week he stayed.

"We've always cared for each other," Lark would have answered. "We are all each other has."

"But you have your grandmother?"

"Yes, we have Granny too, though that is very different."

At that point, in the beginning, what Heart and Lark had built together had been the special and distinct relationship of both of their lives. Before he came. Before he changed it all, and left their sisterhood wilted, and in second place.

Lark would have led him that night toward the dried-up, old lean-to of a shack her family claimed, where roots and wood awaited their needs, where Heart stored pelts for trade, where the traveler would sleep that night and each of the six nights following. Perhaps a breath of the night's wind wrapped about the two as they stepped along the ground's soft paths. Perhaps they slowed their steps as they grew closer to their destination, purposefully stretching the moments between them.

The traveler would have spoken again, of course, wanting to draw out the conversation, wanting to hear Lark's calming voice again. "Your names—your sister's and yours—they are different than any I've heard before."

Lark would have nodded her head; it was a common observation among the few the sisters met. "I'm not surprised," she would have said. "Certainly we are not the usual Gertrude or Marianne."

"And where did the names come from?" the traveler might have asked.

Lark would have smiled, glad to tell such a well-loved, time-honored tale. "Our mother named each of us herself. She had no plan before her, and no interference from our father in the task. By her desire, we were each named the night we were born. She was led by the thoughts that most took her soul at the time." Lark would have paused at that point, remembering, as she always did, the mother who had loved them so, remembering the woman who had given them each life.

"My mother named me for a bird that sang in her window as I came into this life," Lark would have said. "She named Heart for the purpose of holding us tight when she knew that she must die."

And the traveler would have taken a sharp breath, his chest caught by the mention of Death in a tale of new life. "Was it soon after Heart's birth that she left you?" he would likely have asked.

"That very night."

"And your father?"

Lark would have sighed at that point in their conversation, as both sisters often did when thinking of their ever-wandering father. "You must understand, he loved my mother so. And because of this, he left that night as well, driven away by her death. It's true, he used to visit us more often, but that has tapered off in past years. For, while I am the image of him, with my dark hair and eyes, Heart is the image of Mother. Small and contained—like a bundle of fire-sticks, ready to ignite. Her copper waves, and all they remind him of, are too much for my father, and he has stayed away in the forest for many, many months."

Heart wondered often afterward, when she considered all that happened in the days and months that followed, if a moment such as that might have been the real beginning of change between the two whispering in the woods. A moment filled with shared sorrow and shared loss.

Was it then the traveler first allowed himself to touch her sister? Did he place a hand of comfort on her shoulder? Did he wipe a tear of pain off from her cheek? Or did Lark move quickly on from what she'd said, ready to begin a new topic in their conversation? Ready to leave behind the story of Heart: what she was to their small family, and what she'd taken when she came to life.

"And you?" perhaps Lark questioned next. Heart felt certain of the query's eventual appearance in that night's exchange, certain of her sister's burning curiosity regarding the topic. "Granny is so strict with us, I have not had the chance to ask your name, let alone your history."

"Time does strange things to a man's memory," the traveler would have answered Lark, his voice low and monotone. It was the same way he responded to Heart the next morning when she took her own moment to ask about who he was, and why he dared show up inside their clearing.

"You can't mean you don't know your own name?" Lark would have replied, her tender heart most assuredly touched by such a sad reality in a way that Heart's angry heart had refused to be. "I'm so sorry! I'm sure your family wishes they might be here by your side to help you in such an awful time. They must be so worried. Is that why you travel as you do? Alone and with no destination? Is it because you can't remember any of your past?"

"Oh, I have a destination," the traveler would have said, his eyes faraway with the thought. Firm in a way required by all the traveling he did. "I don't know how to get there, that's all."

And Lark would have guessed the truth. "Home. Family." Lark understood the dreams of others in that way. She always had. A fact Heart loved dearly about her wonderful sister.

"How long have you wandered?" she might have asked him then.

"Oh, long enough," he would have answered. "I suppose I am a little like your father, in that way. I must wander until my soul finds rest. Whenever and wherever that may be."

Perhaps that was the way of their conversation, that night that came at the beginning of such a life-altering week in all their lives. A conversation about memories, and memories that were lacking.

Heart imagined the two of them there, walking among the trees she and Lark had known their whole childhoods, beginning a friendship that would grow into much, much more. In fact, she imagined it so clearly in the days and weeks that followed that she could almost believe she'd had been there to witness it all. That she'd been there to see their swift and utter understanding. That she'd been there to watch her own undoing.

When she thought about it, Heart felt sure Lark would have been troubled by what the traveler said, when he spoke of the past he did not know. Both sisters had grown up inside this clearing. The trees were their trees, filled with all of their lives and the memories along the way. They knew each knot and each tipping bough as they knew their own freckles and moles. What would it feel like to be away from this place? What would it feel like to forget it all? What would it feel like to be this memory-less traveler? And confronted with all of that, how could Lark not begin to care about the stranger? How could she not begin to draw him close for the comfort she knew she could give?

And that would only have been the first night between them. That night, and the words they likely uttered beneath its starry watch, would only have been the foundation of the remainder of the week, and all that it would eventually bring to pass.

For throughout the following days, confronted face to face with their daily interactions, Heart had the opportunity to watch the two of them grow closer. To watch them share more and become companions of the soul. She had the chance to view her future as it rotated and changed against her bidding.

Of course, all seemed simple and unimportant on the surface; even meaningless if one didn't know Lark as Heart did. The traveler chopped their wood. He mended their roof. He bundled and carried their winter goods to storage. Each task that Granny set forth, he determinedly set out to do. By night, much work had been done, and his capable hands had been the ones to do it.

Meanwhile, Heart watched him watch Lark. The way Lark came to the aid of their granny when the old woman's load was too heavy. The way Lark continued to guard Heart from the dangers of wood life—though Heart could obviously face her tasks alone. The way Lark leaned into each cool breeze at the close of a hard day's work. How she let its freshness fan the heat and tiredness from her face: a smile on her lips, happiness bleeding through from her heart.

The wood-grown girl that Heart called sister, the girl who'd hung their soaking laundry the day that he arrived, had pulled the traveler's eyes back time and time again. All while Heart looked on, convinced her own happy life had fallen to pieces. She could almost count the times the traveler watched her sister's hair to see what tint of molasses the dark waves would offer next. She could almost see the rope of adoration he threw about her shoulders as the days passed by, his own heart pulling Lark's to his. And she was certain that Lark knew he watched her. How would it be possible to not feel a look like that?

After all, it had been a few seasons since Heart and Lark had become familiar with the looks of boys and men and what they might mean. True, their neighbors lived long distances from them, but miles did not always matter when it came to the desires of the heart and flesh.

Heart knew the reason Granny spoke so forcefully to this stranger of guns. She knew why Granny warned him away from their home when it came to the dead of night. She and Lark had done it themselves the year before, with the rifle both cocked and aimed. Perhaps Lark was only eighteen, and Heart only fourteen, but in a wilderness as loosely populated as theirs, their relative youth did not keep them safe from the propositions of would-be husbands, or worse.

What surprised Heart as she stood small paces from this stranger and her lovely sister, as she watched the air tremble between them, was how obvious it was that Lark did not mind this traveler's looks. Heart knew that last year Granny had asked Lark if she was ready. She had taken Lark aside, thinking Heart would never know she made the offer, thinking Lark would never share the words she spoke.

"You are young," she had said to Lark, "but if you should want one of them, don't think you must stay here for me or your sister. You're a woman. And if you are ready for family and hearth, you must not turn back for your family that came before."

Both sisters' insides had flamed at Granny's words when they discussed them in incredulous whispers from beneath their blankets that night. Neither Lark nor Heart wanted any of the men who came to claim them. And they knew the men did not truly want them. They just wanted their skin, or their hair, or their eyes, or their hands trained in cooking, cleaning, and planting.

But as this traveler leaned toward Lark several times a day during that long week, either lifting a tub of water for her, or offering to beat a particularly dusty rug, Heart felt sure that Lark could barely remember the gun hanging on their wall, or the defense against unwanted affection that it might offer. And if her sister had needed to aim it, there would have been definite trouble in the effort.

Oh, how did it happen so fast? One week—days and nights racing by—and it was done. But no, not finished. No, not truly. Not until the end. Not until he left.

The final morning arrived, and Heart watched from the corner of their cottage as the traveler came for his last meal. Everyone knew the time had arrived for him to take his leave. Bending himself at the table, he ate the food Granny and Lark had prepared, his mouth empty of words, as theirs all were at the knowledge of his parting. While he ate, Lark gathered a small bag of hard breads and cheeses together: food for his travels past their home. As her sister worked, Heart continued to glower, impatient for the stranger to leave, unwilling even to partake of her portion of the meal. She had not wanted the traveler here all week, and this day had come none too soon for her.

Though she knew the desire was not the same for Lark. And she knew that fact should bring her sorrow—sorrow for the one she loved. Still, Heart pressed her mouth together, determined she would be pleased at his departure. She must be happy to see him go. Someone must.

Then, when he'd finished with his meal, when he'd thanked Granny, crossed the floor, and bent to take his bag from where it waited by the door, Lark remained at the table, fumbling with the food she had prepared. Heart watched her sister tie the fabric's knots with fingers that could not still their shaking. It took Lark longer than it should have to complete her task, and when she finally did, she also crossed the floor to hand the package to the traveler.

Did Lark look up to see the morning's sun glint off those yellow curls that crowned the traveler as he made his exit? Heart doubted it. Lark had watched enough as their visitor chopped their wood and worked upon their roof throughout the week. She would remember the curls, and their light, without looking again. Lark did not need another day to let it happen, for the traveler already lived inside her heart.

How did it happen so fast? How did he change everything so massively? And then the words came, the words Heart had feared since she woke that very morning.

"I'll walk with you," Lark said, unable to release the bag of food into his hands. "I'll walk with you a bit."

Heart stood from her chair, her hands clenched tightly at her sides, her voice ready to interrupt and call Lark back. But Granny held her motionless with those sharp strong eyes. Granny knew it too. How could a fact so obvious remain secret to any who watched?

"Good idea, Lark," said Granny, and she shooed the traveler and Lark out the door. "Make sure he finds a well-worn path to follow. Send him safely on his way."

And Heart was forced to watch them go, which meant that once again, the traveler and Heart's Lark walked between the trees, their conversation breaking up the future and redirecting it. But this time Heart would hear. This time she would not imagine. Even Granny could not force her hand that way.

Without further thought, Heart sprang from where she stood, brushed past her granny, and leaped through the door and into the woods. Then, free at last, and certain that ailing Granny could not follow, she quieted her steps. She stepped silently and carefully, like the huntress she'd learned to be while catching game throughout her life. This time she would know. She would know what Lark did and said to change everything.

"Thank you for coming with me," she heard the traveler say from in front of her, his voice not far ahead. "It's nice to have a companion in my travels, even if it's only for a short time. Always before I have traveled alone."

"And where will you go now?" came Lark's reply.

"Oh, I like to travel south." He laughed. "It keeps me from going in circles, I suppose, and it gives me a plan of some sort."

By now, Heart had skirted to the side of Lark and the traveler. They walked slowly in their hesitation to be parted, and she found it easy to keep them both within hearing and within sight.

"And what if you find them?" Lark said. "Your memories. Your family. What then?"

"I don't know. I don't think of it often. But I suppose I'd build a life again. Leave behind the wandering, and join whatever trade it is my family claims."

Lark nodded. "Yes," she said. "You'll find your family, and you'll remember. And then, you'll find some woman to be your wife, and she'll give you children and a home. It suits you, that kind of life. Much more than all this wandering." Lark sighed. "You did seem content this week."

"Yes," said the traveler, "I think the simple life would please me."

Lark paused, and Heart wanted to reach out and pull her away from the traveler and their dangerous conversation. But before Heart could, her sister spoke. "And are you never tempted to give up?" she said. "To stop searching for the memories, and to build a new life now? Are you never tempted to stay?"

Her words frightened Heart. They had escaped Lark's mouth so easily. And they were so thinly veiled; even Heart could not help but gather what was meant by them. How would the traveler reply? Would Heart never see the end of him?

"I have never been tempted before," he said, and his voice was solemn and slow. He grasped a nearby tree with his large hand, leaned against it. Moments ticked onward, and still he did not speak. "But I cannot stay, Lark. I truly cannot."

And it was said. The answer to a question Heart had feared would bring the worst. The greens and blues of the late summer day spun about her head. She wanted to sit down. She wanted to make the spinning stop. Instead, she stood and tried to see her sister. What would Lark do now? How had she received the news?

The traveler spoke again, this time in a different tone. "You know, last night, after leaving supper with you and your family, I found my mind began to search yet again for my past. Your kindness had touched me and had helped me dream of a time before when I had been loved."

Heart watched Lark nod. She could not see her face, or the pain she knew must lie there, but she could see her sister nod. Always listening and considerate, even when deprived of what would please her most. But the traveler continued to speak. And all Lark, and Heart, could do was to continue to stand and stare at him, to continue to listen to his words. What else could be done?

"And in that dreaming," he said, his eyes kept fast on where Lark stood. "I found I did remember something. For the first time, in I don't know how long, I remembered." And his voice broke, ever so slightly.

"What was it?" said Lark, reaching toward him. "What did you remember?"

"Really, I owe it all to you, Lark. This memory I found. I owe it to your kindness, your goodness." He paused. "I owe it to your love."

Heart tried to halt the shiver rushing up her spine, but found she could not. He'd said he could not stay, but he spoke so easily of love. Would he take her Lark with him? Would it come to that?

"You see," he continued, "I'd felt those feelings before— kindness, goodness, love—and now I remembered them again. I remembered I'd had that in a life before, from someone else. And so, you have given me a reason to continue my search. But not only that. You have shown me that the kind of happiness I've felt here, the kind of happiness and love I have faint memories of, it is worth fighting for, no matter the cost."

"What did you remember?" Lark said, her voice broken by his words despite his excitement. Her heart broken in a way Heart could clearly comprehend. "Who else's love came back to you again?"

"Lark," he said, excitement straightening him from where he leaned against the tree. "I am certain I have family. It is not only a guess, anymore, it is a fact that I know. You see, I think I have a brother. No, I know I have a brother. A brother. A brother that loved me. A brother that I loved as well. A brother who is in some kind of danger. A danger I know I must not abandon him to face alone."

"A brother?" Lark said, her voice flat.

"Yes. I can even see his face, if I think about it hard enough." He stepped forward. "You know, he does look similar to you, Lark." His hand reached out and touched Heart's sister. "Dark hair, like yours." He touched Lark's long locks softly. He brushed the tips of his fingers across her eyelids, traced his way down her cheeks. "Of course, he doesn't have that mouth."

Heart wanted to step back. Heart wanted to go home. She hated this traveler and all that he said and did. What did it matter that he laughed at Granny's jokes? What did it change that he never frowned, no matter how awful Heart worked to scare him away? Why should she care that he labored without complaint and also found time to bring a pretty flower to her sister at the close of the day? Why should she want her Lark to be happy, if it brought about her own undoing? And why could he not just leave?

"I think I should go home," Lark said, her words barely loud enough to hear, but loud enough to make Heart pause.

The traveler brought his hand down to her shoulder.

"You must see why I can't stay," he said. "I have to find my brother, now that I remember him, now that I know that he exists, and feel he faces some tragedy of sorts. I can't give up on the first clue I've had in so many weeks of traveling. I can't give up on him."

"Yes, I understand," Lark said. "You must keep looking. Maybe you'll remember more as you continue onward in your travels."

"Never before was I tempted, Lark," he said. "Never before did I think I could live without any desire to know more about my past. If you'd asked me this question last night, before I remembered my brother, I think I would have stayed. It would not have been easy to deny the ache in me for family. It would have been the most difficult thing I did each day, to keep myself from searching for my memories. But I think I would have stayed. For someone like you."

Heart stepped backward. She'd had enough of this. This world that made no sense. This world where her sister belonged to someone else.

"May I tell you one thing more?" she heard the soldier say to Lark.

And Heart froze, her curiosity holding her in place. Eavesdropping did bring sorrow, but it also brought knowledge. Heart peeked her head through the trees again, watching Lark and her love one last time. She saw as the traveler reached inside his shirt, and pulled out a rope. A rope that hung about his neck, with a smooth ring of gold glittering at its end.

"I always thought this would be the thing to make me remember," he said. "It is old, and I know it's mine. Any hint of memory from my past includes this hanging at my neck."

Despite herself, Heart inched closer so she might see the ring more clearly. She watched the traveler remove the rope from his neck, and hand it to her sister so that she might see.

"I think it is my mother's," he said. "A memory deep inside has always told me that. And, up until now, it is all I've had."

"It's beautiful," Lark said, and she ran her finger along the gold's bright surface.

"It was my only clue," he said. "Now that you've given me another, I want to give this ring to you. To thank you."

"No," Heart whispered, "not a ring."

"I will come back for it, Lark," said the traveler, taking a step even closer. "When I find my family, I will come back for the ring. I promise you that. Until then, you wear it here, across your shoulders. Promise me I'll be the only one to take it from your neck. And if you do that, I promise you—once I know who I am, once I have a real life to offer—that I will take it from this rope, and I will put it where it belongs."

And with those final words, no longer caring for the truth, Heart ran, leaving her sister and the stranger behind.

Heppson

Weeks had passed, eaten away by Heppson's anger and frustration. Day after day, he tore his way through the woods, striking out at any trees or animals that offered him resistance on his erratic, mindless path. The more he raged throughout the day, the more soundly he slept at night, and the sooner he forgot what had been lost.

There had been no instructions for existing as Bear, only the overpowering awareness of that creature. An awareness that fettered his human mind each morning as the sun rose, and that also kept him tied to the pelt once the shiny orb set. And so, he seethed and wrestled against who he'd now become, knowing nothing else that he might do. Knowing he was trapped as he had never been trapped before.

Finally, when summer had almost reached its close, as Heppson lay one night beneath his loose pelt awaiting the blessed unconsciousness of sleep for which he fought each day, a word returned to mind. A word Trickster had spoken which had offered hope when he first thought it wise to take the pelt. A word he'd thought might be worth the unknown the arrangement offered, if it truly held any power against forces like his mother.

Guardian.

Heppson's eyes blinked open at his memory of the word, sleep pushed away by the thought. What had Trickster said of *Guardian*? That perhaps the power of Guardian might assist him in his efforts against his mother. That there might be good in the form of Bear which he took. But what could that possibly mean? All he had done for days now was to wear himself to pieces in the form of Bear. Had there been any special power in what he'd done? Had he felt any more or less than an ordinary bear when his skin took on that fur? Not especially. That had been the point. He had not thought of *Guardian* for one moment, once he'd actually become this beast.

But Trickster's words must mean something. That creature of green might be a master of manipulation, but even his lies rang with some truth. *Guardian*. He had said that Bear existed as a Guardian of these woods, and that this reality brought with it certain benefits and powers, as well as specific constraints. It was why even Trickster was forced to do what he did—to offer another life-filled soul to the pelt. But what could that mean? What facts did Heppson have when it came to Bear and who that creature—who he—was?

Of course, he knew Trickster had killed the other Bear, had killed a Guardian—and that it had taken special circumstances to bring about this death. And he knew that following this fatal occurrence, it had been he who took up the cloak and became Bear. This existence as Bear required his continued entrapment within the pelt, as well as within the forest and its established confines. Which meant that *Guardian* must be something to do with that growling existence that commanded he remain and play his part.

But if this was all he knew, it seemed quite little. And whom could Heppson ask to find out more? Trickster was long gone by now, and Heppson never met another soul with whom to speak.

After all, by day, he was Bear. A frightening animal. An animal that could tear a man to bits if he desired. And by night, he was Heppson. Dirty and exhausted, his skin rough with grime and forest wanderings. Even had he crept up beside some wandering resident of these forests, even had that person known what a Guardian was, how could he ask them to tell him, a smelling, rotting, dirt-covered excuse of a wretch? Too tired at night to even bathe himself in the forest's only river, he was a far cry from the sparkling prince he'd been only months ago. They would surely think him a madman. And rightly so.

But could he really spend the rest of his existence as he had these past several weeks—foolishly exploding his way through the forest, hoping to disappear—or would he grasp at the last thing that mattered to him as a human, the chance of defeating his mother, and try to make sense of it? In the end, only one entity came to Heppson's mind as a being who might answer all his questions. And, absurdly, that was Bear himself: the snarling force that kept him chained to the pelt, and all he had agreed upon with Trickster.

Up until now, he'd fought against Bear, when sunlight streamed around him and joined his body with the fur. He'd fought the dreadful force that so easily overtook him and his consciousness by not allowing himself to think at all, and by not acknowledging the presence that stirred and grew within his mind—pressing against what "self" Heppson had managed to retain. Now he would need to submit and hear that voice. He would need to accept its presence inside of him if he wanted to know more concerning Guardian. When morning came, he would need to let Bear come.

Suddenly impatient, and hungry for knowledge, Heppson waited for the hours to pass. Finally light scattered through the leaves around him, marking the slow arrival of the day. Night itself ended in that subtle change of light, which broke the sky apart before dawn. It came in a renewed awareness of what came beyond the nearest hulking shadow. Watching, Heppson lay beneath the pelt that warmed his waiting frame. Soon enough, he felt it wrap its way around his body once again, pulling him into its frame.

This time, instead of bolting through the woods, instead of running, running, running, he remained still and quiet on the forest floor. He waited longer, and forced his twitching limbs to pause and soak the violent changes inward, without responding to the pain. He felt the pelt reach into his skin. He felt it snake its way into his bones. He felt its tendrils wrap around his innards and make him Bear from edge to core. And then, sure the Guardian presence had taken all, he waited still, remembering from that first day, and the many in between, what happened next.

First came the steady emptying of Heppson's mind. The removal of his past, and of any coherent sense of his prior self. The disappearance of who he was, or ever had been. Then came the supplanting by the force he knew as Bear. *Guardian.* But today Heppson would meet and welcome this foe, rather than flee. He would come to understand what it entailed. Today he would hopefully learn who and what he'd become. He only hoped he could carry back what he might learn, that when night returned and Heppson woke again, he'd know the truth, or more, at least, than he had known before.

The surprise, in the end, was that the truth he sought appeared as memories. Memories—not dictates or demands.

Like a library, the unopened and untouched memories were waiting for him to decide that he would find them. They were stacked inside his mind, hoping to be drawn out and evaluated, hoping to be discovered. Ready to be seen, remembered, understood.

All this time, he'd run away from Bear and what that being seemed to be: a parasite that entered from his skin and took up residence inside his mind. But Bear had only wished to offer a knowledge and comprehension of what he'd become. Bear had only removed Heppson's personal memories so he might comprehend the ancestral past of his new life, and with it, his approaching future.

Now, in his mind, as though watching the past unfurl before his eyes, he saw the first Bear, the one that came to serve as Guardian in the far beginning. A solitary human, this tiny village lass of barely ten years was drawn to the forest by the whisperings and visions which the forest flung wide into the countryside in its search for human assistance. Unlike Heppson, this young girl had dared to take the pelt and all its obligations without any Trickster forcing the matter. She had been happy to attend to the forest and the lands she loved.

For, it was as though Heppson's whole world—not just the forest where he happened to be confined, but also the further lands, which contained Alastair and the desert beyond—took strength from what the Guardians were, without even understanding they existed. It was as though the forest was the beating heart of an existence Heppson had always taken for granted, and as though the Guardians, once they were called and set apart from the rest of mankind, were the hands and limbs of that beating heart, meant to accomplish its tangible work. The village lass had been happy to become part of this endeavor, happy to take on the skin for a period of time.

Other memories, traveling from that first Bear to the many in between, told Heppson of the tasks the Bears and other Guardians had faced in helping those who arrived to claim their aid throughout the ages. There had been some Bears who offered wisdom to the leaders of Heppson's history. Their insight had helped push away marauding forces from nearby kingdoms bent on Alastair's destruction, or even helped to develop the crops of wheats and grasses that became the mainstay of his kingdom's economy. In this way, the Bears had altered the progress of politics, war, and economics—their influence far-reaching, if currently forgotten.

But the power that dwelt within them in their annual season, in their seasonal strength, was not reserved only for the high and mighty. They also changed the lives of the small and the forgotten. Hidden away in the forest, their remote location necessitated that those who came to seek their aid understand both sacrifice and effort. Both those who came were helped.

Heppson watched the Bears and other Guardians wrap the broken-limbed in their embrace and send them back completely whole, able to till a humble plot of land. The Bears that came before him were often busy in the simple business of gathering a lost child in their arms and setting the little footsteps aright. In this way, the awesomeness of *Guardian* was something Heppson had never guessed at, before the memories came. The scope of their involvement in the lives of his past and present history was mind-boggling.

No wonder his mother had stayed away from this wilderness and its Guardians. No wonder she had never spoken of the power that dwelt within the trees' confines; a power so much larger than the manipulative one she held. He could not help but think that she, or some other force, must have hidden knowledge of these Guardians from the thoughts and memories of Alastair's people. What else could explain an entire community forgetting of the one source of power that might have saved them from her evil strength?

But even beyond these larger details of his new existence, there were several smaller characteristics that applied only to the being Heppson had become and how it would affect his day-to-day existence. As Bear, Heppson realized he would be unable to die—at least normally—when not faced directly with Death or with one of his brothers. His life would instead continue until such time as he disappeared into Bear entirely, eventually becoming a simple and ordinary bear of the greater forest.

He watched this ending approach for the young lass who first took on the pelt. He watched her years bleed into decades—time meaning nothing to the role she played—until suddenly an increased difficulty in resisting the call of winter's hibernating sleep began to take its toll. He watched the lass give into this pleading and pulling of the nature of bears, her final slumber necessitating the transfer of the skin to yet another, necessitating the forest itself send visions for a new recruit to take the pelt.

Then, he watched similar scenes play out again and again with each of the succeeding Bears, the pattern revealing the order and plan of the forest's rotation through Guardians. The years of service and of otherness. The wakefulness of a Winter Bear that came with the work they did. The final descent into the ordinary call of hibernation and all that it entailed. And then, the slipping of nature to the natural world of forest life.

It was a peaceful end, he thought, though it had not come this way for some, including the Bear whom he replaced. With these Bears, not yet ready for the ending world of hibernation, Heppson saw a yanking and destructive sort of change. These Bears were torn from their Guardianship by deliberate interference of an outsider, and because of this, the forest demanded that those who caused the Guardians' destruction replace them. Trickster had faced these demands, but had somehow passed his obligation to Heppson. Though even watching it happen through Bear's memories, Heppson could not understand how.

And that explained his slow approach to Death, though being Guardian involved much more than prolonged life. For in addition to his extended life, Heppson watched the might and power of the Bears that came before him. Standing on their hind legs to face their foes, these Bears used not only the teeth and claws of the forest bears, they used also the power of the forest to strike those down who would bring harm to those they protected. Their increased strength was coupled with knowledge of the unknown, an ability to draw on the eyes and ears and senses of the natural world around them, should they desire to do so. And in winter? In the season of Bear? The power available at that time to harness the earth's strength and use it for their own was almost immeasurable.

Supplied with this new knowledge, Heppson could not help but wonder what he might have done if he'd known before of the Guardians, if he'd been taught and nurtured to trust the forest's strength? Would it have made a difference in the way he fought his mother, in the choices he made to avoid her influence? Would he have come to seek their help and gain the assistance of their power? He wondered again how she had managed to keep the knowledge of these Guardians from seeping into the kingdom of Alastair. How had he never heard of these beings and what they could do before?

Heppson felt it must have something to do with the limitations of his strength, which he also found within the memories. From the start of the memories, each Bear lived within certain boundaries to keep the power they held from overwhelming the quest for right and good, which they were meant to represent. The limitations differed slightly; some Bears more wise, others more dependent on their strength, but a few of the constraints were constant throughout the many generations of Bear. These universal limitations must have bolstered his mother's ability to influence others in such a way that they forgot the Guardian's existence completely. These constraints would have allowed her to consign any knowledge of the Guardians to the dust through constant sleight of hand and manipulation.

First, a Guardian could never leave the forest at any time, for his strength lay only within the reach of the earthy woods, which meant that if the forest were barred from too much exploration, no Guardian could escape to declare what they might do to the world beyond.

Second, a Guardian could not help those around him without them personally asking for his assistance. He could not intervene by his own decision, or make changes to the outside world based on his own desires. None of the Guardians, even had they been aware of his mother and all that she did, could have interfered with her actions, unless another came to beg their aid.

And last, a Guardian could not use his powers to fulfill his personal needs. Guardian powers were meant solely for the gain of others, and not for the benefit of those who wielded them—a fact that surely lost them merit when it came to eyes like Trickster's or his mother's. It had certainly frustrated those who came to the Guardian's powers through protracted violence. Once they had obtained their goal of Bearskin pelt, overcoming the extreme difficulty in killing what was not meant to meet Death, they had been bent beneath the forest's goals and purposes. That type had always gone to hibernation much more quickly, their dark and broken hearts contrasting with the pelt's true purpose.

So powerful, yet also so restricted. This was the world of the Guardians and their natural powers. Though Heppson now knew he had the type of strength that he might use against his mother to bring her some defeat, he also realized he had no actual way to engage her in any kind of battle, no matter how much he wished it. Only the presence of Bear inside and around him kept his own despair at bay when this final comprehension came. Only Bear and his domination of Heppson's consciousness kept him from howling in pain at the knowledge. For Bear had not finished with what it wished Heppson to discover. It had not released Heppson to himself.

Stretching past the memories, and traveling beyond them now that he'd experienced their depths completely, Heppson began to feel the edges and confines of the forest in his consciousness. He realized he now knew the forest as though he'd lived there his entire life, as if its twists and turns had been the hallways, stairs, and corners of his childhood. Within his mind's eye he saw the rivers and the glens, the ravines and clearings. He saw the pathways old and new between the trees. He saw the rare and sequestered cottages of the few who lived within the woods, far from Alastair and the life he had lived before. All of the forest's geography was laid out like a map upon his mind, information ready and available for the taking, should he need it. The forest was his. It belonged inside of him and wrapped around him as much as the pelt that joined him and Bear so tightly together. He might not ever be able to leave this wilderness again, according to all that he had learned, but it had become as familiar and intrinsic to him as home.

Time, and the day held captive by it, surged forward as Heppson surveyed the wilderness, with all its tiny details, inside his mind. He lay submissively inside his pelt and let the information feed and fill his mind, the massive amount of information passing to him requiring the consumption of minutes, and then hours. He was content at last to let it inside him, to let the forest bind him tight. After all the memories and knowledge of the forest seeped their way into his soul, then came the extended knowledge of the rest of his kind.

This was a fact he should have guessed from the beginning; a fact he thought Trickster had even mentioned in all his ramblings. Because there were three other Guardians like himself, making four in total. One for each season, four for each year. Other animals, in addition to the Bear. Heppson saw them now, and knew them by sight and by name, their names and titles slipping into his mind like well-placed bricks, lined with waiting mortar. These were his partners in his charge as protector. These were the other arms and legs of his newfound forest home.

He saw the Fish, as she sunned herself in her river, soaking up the warmth of summer's heat, a cascade of running water cooling her skin. He saw the Ant, as he stored his supply of foods and grains, as he prepared for the end of autumn in a wretched, worried way. And he saw Spring, her widely spread wings beating at the air that kept the rest of them pulled down. Almost free from the forest they all called home. Almost separate from the world they'd never leave. Guardians. All of them. And he was Bear. Denizen of winter, and one of only four. He was one of them.

That night, when he finally returned to human form, Heppson continued to lie beneath his wide and dark-furred coat. While not physically exhausted, as so many nights before, he could not move for all the thoughts flooding his mind. He thought of all he'd learned of Bear, glad that the knowledge stayed with him as Heppson, and also glad that he'd found himself again. He realized now that Bear did not mean to replace him entirely, but only had demanded to be heard. He felt sure now that even when he changed to Bear, his memories and existence as Heppson would remain. The time for the emptying of who he was had passed, at least until the call to hibernation came.

No longer frightened of his own disappearance, he thought of the life that had wrapped him close at the Trickster's insistence. Could he be happy with this life? Did he want the power he'd been given? Was it worth what had been lost? Could he forget what he'd left behind? Abandon it because the forest willed him stay within its bounds? And most of all, did it make him innocent if he knew he could not leave this place? Or did it make him weak that he could not find some way to get back to his brother and fight by his side with these increased abilities?

At first, Heppson could not say. He could only think, and think some more. But, as further nights passed, and Bear returned day after day, he realized this truly was his life. He was a Guardian. Powers and constraints and all. He might not rage against the trees anymore. He might not run until his heavily furred legs collapsed beneath him. But he could not make himself be the Heppson of old. He could not divide Bear into parts and keep only the useful pieces for his cause.

What could power mean to him when there was so much he could not do? As Bear? As Guardian? As Heppson? Although finally he knew more of Bear, and of his new home, and the other Guardians, Heppson still retained an inability to leave the forest. He was still trapped by the loneliness of this place, and the minimal vestiges of humanness left to him at night.

And he still could not fight his mother.

Moiria

With the Queen dead and both princes inexplicably absent, it fell to Moiria to keep anyone in Alastair from noting a shift in power, or from finding hope for rebellion against the crown as a result. Perhaps if her mother had been someone else, Moiria might have acted differently and ended the evil that stalked the land. Perhaps if Conrad had been there to help her in this process, then she might have taken a path that led toward rebuilding and honor. But what had Moiria seen except power held by fear and overbearance? What could she know of goodness?

The worst of it happened as soon as she stood and shakily left her mother's chamber, crimson stains coating the clothes she wore, a knife carrying the blood of both her mother and herself held in her hand. The blade was wrapped thinly in a shred of her brother's shirt, as though the flimsy fabric could hide what it had to say. After all, there was a dead queen's body to explain, and the spells and smokescreens her mother had scattered throughout her reign were unraveling in both the castle and the villages surrounding it. The people would be awakening. They would be clamoring for redress when it came to the kingdom's failures. Moiria already felt the fraying of power reaching upward all around her.

But for now, that looked to be the least of her worries. For almost immediately following her exit from her mother's chamber, Moiria had been accosted by a castle guard and accused of murdering the Queen.

"Stop," he'd said, his own blade drawn. "You will not go further."

And she had halted, wondering if this was only another horrible ending to her story; if there was no way for her to find a true escape. Inexplicably, images of her mother's knife and its strange etchings surged across her consciousness with a powerful force. Those etchings that had soaked her own blood inward, and then her mother's, now swirled before her eyes. She felt the aching of the blade inside her hand, where she gripped the knife, she felt it as she had felt them in her brother's chamber. The soldier's blade reached toward her, and all she could see were the trappings of her mother's knife.

Would she really let this guard lead her away to the dungeons below? Would she really bear responsibility for all her mother had brought to pass? Could she really trust the people of this kingdom to see the line between the Queen's evil and what had happened here today?

Or would she act to save herself, would she act as the knife so obviously thought was right? She could hear it speaking within her mind, urging her forward to keep herself from harm. And while some small part of her rebelled at the idea of the knife having words to guide her actions, another felt the surety and strength at having the knife's protection. After all, the knife was all she had.

The soldier advanced again, tilting his sword upward slightly so as not to graze Moiria where she stood. He was almost near enough to take her arms and pull her to her fate. Moiria trembled at the thought of it. At the attempts she would necessarily make to explain her mother's death. At the way the court would demand an accounting of all that had transpired. Those among the court who retained any goodness after her mother's reign would want all vestiges of the Queen erased, including her daughter. Those who had joined her mother's evil path more easily would be unhappy their leader had fallen beneath the knife. There would be none to protect her there.

The blade spoke truth, if it actually stood behind the words inside her head. There was none in this place to keep Moiria safe; none but herself. And there was only one path to be sure of her continued safety. One path open to her if she meant to oppose the many who would rise to take her life in the future weeks and months.

"Hand over your weapon," said the soldier, reaching out his hand.

This was the moment, there would be no other. Would she let him take the blade? Would she let him lead her as a prisoner before the throne? A voice inside her growled it could never be so. And so, without another thought, calling only on the anger and fear wrapping upward from her hand and into her heart, Moiria struck down the soldier, using both the knife and her mother's spells. The words and power to her actions twisted downward from her own cut flesh, stretching from her upper arm to the blade, which fell into the soldier's heart.

The soldier fell.

It had been fear that he would deliver her to her own death that made her do it, but it had been only a moment's thought that brought her to such devastating action. Part of Moiria could not believe she'd done it—the part that belonged to her former life. This echo of Moiria stared in horror at the innocent guard lying at her feet, his lungs no longer taking breath in or out. But another piece of her trembled with the force of what she'd done, trembled with the idea that now that her mother was gone, no one could ever harm her or make her cower again.

After shoving that knife into her mother's belly, after watching the awful battle that almost tore Conrad to pieces, it was strange what horrific things had become too easy for her to do. Besides, the knife's pulse seemed to confirm the rightness of her act, telling her it had been the only way. If it had not been this soldier, it would have been her. Perhaps not in this hallway, but certainly in the days to come. The swirling press of the blade repeated this truth to her time and time again, convincing her she had done what must be done.

And was there a bit of Moiria that wondered in the days that followed, was it possible to fight the witch, and then become her anyway? Perhaps. Was it the unavoidable consequence of a blade grown slick with so much blood? Moiria could not say, and did not dare to guess, but her lack of understanding did not change the consequences.

Her only tools to keep the people from turning against her and blaming her for the disorder and confusion now surrounding them were those she'd gleaned from her mother's hands: deception, manipulation, and pain. What could be done, but to use them to control the world of Alastair, a kingdom that spun about her like a compass without any pole? Spinning and seeking for anyone to offer it direction, now that the Queen was dead.

In this unexpected twist of fortune and happenstance, Moiria was forced to stop hiding and fading into shadows. Driven by the same force and insistence that demanded she kill that original soldier, she obscured the disappearances and deaths of so many others with lies and spells of her own, replacing those that fell to pieces with her mother's death. She took actions, covert and violent, to squelch the efforts of the people to rise up and become themselves again; a visible and formidable threat for both the court and villages to fear. She became a new figurehead for her mother's years of domination—a shadow of what her mother had always been before. She used her mother's tools whether it felt cruel or not; whether it felt like her decision or another's. Each time a threat arose, she acted speedily, sure that if she failed, her life would fall forfeit. A life she found that, after all, she wished to keep.

Such was the price, she told herself, of keeping a kingdom from declaring her responsible for the princes' disappearance, or demanding her head as a result. Such was the price of stamping out any hope for change, which fought to swell within the villages surrounding the castle once the witch had finally and truly disappeared. Such was the price of feeding the fury that began in her wounds and took over the rest of her being. A fury that seemed, after all these years of cowering beneath her mother's will, to have awakened with the strength of twenty of her kingdom's strongest men. What was the worth of a soldier or two, in the long run, when it came down to all of that?

In this way, Moiria's anger drove her to contain and displace any who opposed her, no matter what was required of her to make it happen. It filled her from head to toe until she could hardly think for all the tasks the pulsing power of the knife demanded at her hands. And then, after weeks of following the blade's guiding words and putting down the struggles all around her that fought to take control, Moiria realized she and the blade had come to a stasis of some sort. The court had bent beneath her authority, the villagers had returned to the simple, pointless plowing of their fields, and the further kingdoms had turned themselves away from any efforts at foolhardy invasion. All had been accomplished. And she had done it.

One night she traveled to her mother's cottage; the cottage she had visited those many days ago when her mother sent her to retrieve the knife in order to kill Conrad. Moiria did not stay long. She did not allow the pleasant memories of her childhood to encroach on all the gains she'd recently made in Alastair. Instead, when the transportation spell delivered her to the cottage's doorstep, she quickly slipped her tiny form inside. Stepping in the shadows, guided only by the errant light of moonbeams on the wooden floor, Moiria pulled her mother's blade from her side and hid it once again in the slivered crack of the floor where she had found it.

She believed now that her mother had left the blade here as a protection. It had been the source of her strength, and the Queen could not allow it to be used for any tasks except those that would benefit her desires. She could not count on the blade not speaking to others, as it had to her. Already, Moiria had begun to fear that some foolish servant would find the blade and realize the protection and strength it offered. Already, she feared it would be used against her.

And so, she had decided to do without it for a bit, in order to keep it safe, hidden from those who might understand what it could do. In some ways, it seemed silly to hide a knife when a hundred more could be found in an instant. But Moiria had come to learn of the power behind this blade, and she did not doubt it was dangerous to keep it close to her much longer.

Spreading dust and dirt over its winking blade, Moiria watched the knife disappear into the ground. She had defeated her mother. She had taken Alastair. She had protected herself from all her sought to bring her down. This must be enough for now. In the meantime, she would not think of what she'd given up to do it. She would not think of that at all.

Moiria

After all she was forced to do in the weeks immediately following the witch's death, it still surprised and disarmed Moiria when the King himself began to lift his head and once again take note of Alastair. Moiria had not considered him when it came to rebuilding the protections of her mother. After all, she did not remember much of the King's true bearing. She had been young when they first arrived in the kingdom, and her mother had kept his true character hidden away for so long. But the King's spell had been dependent on the pretended love of the witch, and with the witch dead he began again to see, though his awakening trickled slowly across his mind.

Several weeks of Moiria's dominance had passed before the King confronted his stepdaughter for the first time. He found her in the cavernous throne room, another day of her dark work accomplished and past. As soon as she saw him, she realized her foolishness in not making sure of his weakness sooner. But there had been so many actual threats that she had forgotten the useless King and how he might oppose her. Now she had hidden her knife away, her methods must necessarily be subtler.

He strode toward where she sat upon the gaudy, yet tarnished, dais, her small frame exhausted from the minds she'd bent and destroyed that day. His bearing was reminiscent of the brothers Moiria had lost so many troubled weeks before, and she could not help but feel a small, unwarranted flicker of hope that someone had come to save her from herself. A feeling she stamped out as soon as he began to speak, knowing it belonged to the old Moiria and not the Moiria she'd become.

"Where are my sons?" the King said, the now empty room echoing with his accusations. "What have you done with them? Are they dead?"

While confusion continued to shake haltingly across his eyes, moving back and forth like tides in an ocean, a force of will had straightened the King's spine in a way Moiria had not thought possible. This, then, was who he could have been, had her mother never come. This was part of those alternate possibilities of the present—those possibilities her mother had wiped away and replaced with her own plans.

Moiria stood from the throne that should have belonged to this man, and stepped downward to cross the room. Her dark blue robes, taken in replacement for the black she'd always worn before, trailed behind her on the mosaic-tiled steps.

"I have nothing to do with your sons' departure," said Moiria, her voice toneless, just as her mother's voice would have been if she had been there to face the King.

Regardless, the King pushed toward Moiria, an effort at compulsion obviously forming somewhere in his mind. "You have done everything these past few weeks that you have wished, why should I think you have not sent them from this place? The stink of your acts is all around this castle and its halls. I can feel the heaviness of it. I am not longer duped into believing it is right."

"And what of your Queen?" said Moiria, her hands gripping the fabric of her gown as she passed the King to walk toward the door.

The King's eyes grew cloudy at mention of his wife, and he halted in place. It was as though he couldn't recall whether the Queen should be missed and mourned. His head slumped onto this chest, and his shoulders caved inward beneath the struggle of his feelings for that woman.

"All I have done is keep this kingdom from falling to pieces," said Moiria, her voice harsh and cutting. "It is not my fault your sons are not here to do the same."

Moiria's back stiffened with her words. She could not fear this King. No longer would she slink away from the questioning of others. Too much had happened and she had been forced to take responsibility for it all. This King would not frighten her, no matter how he sought to shake the tendrils of her mother's curse. With the past weeks behind her, she'd become more than strong enough to face him.

The King looked up after her, his eyes imploring. "You must know where they are," he said, his words now halting and unsure.

Moiria grimaced at his weakness, sickened by the ease with which he lost his way inside their argument. He looked so small where he waited behind her, as though he were meant to be supplicant instead of king. "Leave me," she said, and turned away from the broken man to exit the room. "I do not need to answer your questions, and I will not."

But deep within her stomach, as the door swung tight to end their discussion, Moiria felt a fluttering fear that surprised her with its worries. Something deep inside her gut told her that the King would return. The blade might be hidden far away in her cottage, but she recognized the call of its protections speaking to her heart.

The King's mind would grow clearer. He would grow stronger as time passed, and as the Queen's body rotted away. The fight she'd fought easily today could blossom into another much more dangerous prospect with only a few more weeks' progression. This was another threat she could not dare to take lightly.

Which meant, a hard voice told her, that a plan must be made to deal with the man. He could not be ignored, nor could he be killed and disposed of like any other interfering, nobody soldier. Moiria had no true claim to Alastair's throne, and the people were not ready to accept her as Queen on her own merits. They had been shaken when the past Queen's spells fell to pieces, and Moiria had barely forced them to return to their fields. The death of the King would begin that whole fight once again.

Making her way through the castle's hallways and toward her mother's chambers, Moiria knew she could not think to renew the same curse against her stepfather as her mother. She would not make this King love her in the way her mother had made him love her. That idea made her want to retch across the cold stone floors she crossed. She would not play the role of wife and Queen to that old decrepit man in a bid to hedge her safety.

No, Moiria needed her own figurehead, her own link to take control of the throne and ensure her own safety. And if that link could placate and dismiss the King's power as well? Two uses for a curse were much better than one.

After careful consideration, her mind rapidly discarding any other possible options, Moiria picked out the only tool that would work in this particular situation. Prince Conrad. All Moiria had to do was locate Conrad: the stepbrother sent tumbling from the castle at the mistaken direction of her mother's last curse.

She would find broken-down Conrad, and she would force his obviously shattered shell back to this place to do her bidding. She would use the pain already inflicted upon him to keep him pliant and manageable beneath her will. Then, with him by her side, she would overwhelm this King and become Queen—just as her mother before her.

After all, Conrad was only her stepbrother. The people and the King could be made to forget such a flimsy familial connection between them, in order that they might marry and bring the kingdom to a necessary equilibrium. The King would be so overjoyed to see his son again that he would not ask too many questions.

By the time she'd reached her mother's door, Moiria knew it was the perfect plan—this idea of bringing Conrad back and marrying him. Its simplicity made it stronger than any other complicated bid to take the throne and dismiss the king. She did not need to shed blood if it was not necessary. She'd done enough of that over the last few weeks to keep her power strong. Besides, if Moiria's mother had taught her anything beyond the truth that power stood supreme above all else, it was that simple was always best when it came to a good manipulation. She must only find Conrad and make it so. If he resisted her, then she would do whatever else the situation then required.

Having made her decision, Moiria entered her mother's

rooms and closed the door behind her. Pulling her robes from her shoulder and dropping them on a nearby table, she tried not to remember how she should have sought Conrad as soon as her mother's spell had sent him on his way. If there had not been so many other tasks to do over these past weeks, she might have done it. If she had not become so much of what she'd never imagined, it might have remained a possibility. But that had not been the way of things. And so she tried not to think of what might have been different, if she had gone to find him first, if she had never met the soldier in the hall.

Moiria

Striding beneath the forest canopy, only one short sunrise later, Moiria repeatedly clenched and unclenched her hands. It had taken some time to find Conrad, even with the transportation spell. She'd never been to this part of the forest, so she hadn't been able to visualize it properly when she arranged the destination. But she had managed it after two or three separate spells and a few rough landings among the weeds. And yet, despite her best efforts, the trip had come to naught.

It had not been her intention to return to the castle without the prince, but these woods had a feel about them that made everything more difficult than Moiria had planned. It did not surprise her that her mother rarely ventured this far south. Their old cottage was on the edge of the forest, nearer to the villages than to the wilderness, so Moiria had not felt the heavy presence of the forest before as she did now. All the pressing trees in this particular area did not seem overly fond of Moiria or her intentions toward Conrad.

Still, the crown prince could not be permitted to evade her plans for their future together or his place as a tool in her capable hands, no matter where he wandered. What if it would take more effort than she had planned on in the beginning? What if all did not go as expected with her first attempts to take his will? Why should this trouble her?

She had at least managed to track him to this place, following the erratic pathway of her mother's hastily flung curse. If the Queen had been in her full power when the curse was laid, the spell would likely have been untraceable to others. But secrecy had not been the witch's primary concern.

In his confusion, Conrad had moved generally southward, further and further from his home with every step he took. He had walked for weeks prior to Moiria's search, so she'd been glad to use her powers to trace his path. She assumed he did not think to doubt the instinct that carried him away from what he sought, for Conrad would not remember the foul words that sped him on his way those weeks before.

"Excuse me," Moiria had murmured, when she'd crossed his path, as though by accident. She opted for the role of hesitant forest lass when it became clear he would not see her as his stepsister. "Could you help a lost traveler find her way?"

But even as her sugared words had glossed out into the air, Moiria had felt their inability to penetrate Conrad's will to the degree she needed to complete her plans. He might not recognize her, but that was hardly beneficial in this particular situation. Because truthfully, Moiria had not counted on her mother's curse wiping Conrad's memory so infinitely clean. She had planned on using some of the love he felt toward Alastair to draw him back with her to take the throne.

She had not thought she could make him fall in love with her deeply enough to guarantee his complete compliance in all her actions. But with his desires for his kingdom added to the love spell, she should have held enough sway within his mind to achieve her purposes. Without this natural tool, the way to begin Moiria's own manipulations became more difficult. How could she tempt with a kingdom he could not even remember?

She'd stepped closer to him then, though she could hardly see the point.

"I can't seem to make heads or tails of these paths," she'd said.

"Of course," Conrad had answered, dropping his pack to the ground. "Where are you meaning to go?"

But the words were spoken only in a kind and helpful way. Not in the protective, overly interested manner Moiria had intended to create. The infatuation Moiria had spun in the air about him did not overtake Conrad at all. In fact, he'd been impervious to the suggestion that he might fall in love with the strange forest girl she'd made herself appear to be.

At the time, her mind had moved quickly, following pathways she'd watched her mother puzzle out a hundred times before. Moiria had realized that the one impediment to this type of manipulation would be the prior existence of true love. Fake love overcoming what must apparently be that of the genuine variety would be a much harder trick to play. This had been the reason why, when the witch took the King's heart, she had chosen to kill his love before she made him pine for her instead.

Though how Conrad had managed to fall in love in such a small amount of time had been beyond Moiria's comprehension. Her world had grown so dark as of late that the idea of her stepbrother finding happiness in his exile stunned her. Leaning near him, she had breathed in the hope and happiness that hung about his shoulders. It had to be love. Nothing else smelled quite that way: like freshly grown moss, heavy with rich life.

She'd spun the air around them once again, befuddling Conrad's mind so he would not question her sudden presence or her strange interest in his past. He could not be allowed to wonder at this strange conversation with an unknown forest lass, he could not be allowed to hold back truth in anything he said.

"I see you have been helped along your path as well," Moiria had said.

"I have indeed," Conrad had answered. "I have been assisted by one whose sweetness makes me smile from morn to dusk. I suppose you see it on my face?"

Moiria had smiled, her frustration kept deep beneath the surface. "Indeed I can. You have a sweetheart then?"

"I suppose I have," Conrad had laughed. "Though I doubt you really care to know about some stranger's sweetheart. You said you needed help finding your own destination?"

"Ah, well. Interestingly enough, I have cleared up which way I need to go," Moiria had answered. "Besides, what could be better to hear about another than the love he holds deep inside?"

"I must admit she is a wonder," Conrad had said, his mind

easily disarmed by Moiria's gentle airborne pressure for more information. These were words he'd wished to speak—memories he'd desired to take out and consider. "I intend to return to her as quickly as possible. She waits in the cottage just beyond that highest rise behind us. She waits for me, kept company with her Granny and her sister. I have only one task to complete before I am worthy of the future we would have together."

"And that would be?" Moiria had prompted, pulling the tale more rapidly out of her stepbrother now that he'd begun.

"Well, I must search out my past before I begin my future, don't you see? And so, I seek the origin of my few memories, and a beloved brother I've recently recalled."

Memories. And a brother. This was what he'd sought. This was what he'd recalled with the most force of all. Moiria had walked about her stepbrother then, lightly tracing her finger across his arm, her anger coiled up tightly inside her at his mention of a past with any happy memories, a past so unlike the one she claimed. How could he have fallen prey to the curses meant for her, and still be so much better off than she? How could this be right?

"A heavy task that seems. Perhaps I can help you?" she'd said. "That is, if you would you like my help?"

"Help me?" His eyebrows had pulled together at the incongruity of Moiria's words. "You?"

"Oh yes," Moiria had said. "I think I can assist you. I think you will find me quite the helpmeet, if given the opportunity. But, of course, I will do this for you only if you wish it. I would not want to give you anything you do not desire to receive."

Conrad had squinted, and Moiria had felt his will begin to weaken beneath the offer of assistance. "If you can help me find my brother, then of course. It is the desire of my heart to find my family again."

Moiria had smiled then, and pressed her hands together, one step, at least, taken forward from the mess Conrad had created when he'd forgotten Alastair and his responsibilities and fallen in love. "Perfect," she'd said. "You will find that is exactly my specialty: delivering the desire of people's hearts."

And with a flick of her fingers, having received his permission, Moiria had grasped Conrad's mind and twisted it the direction she'd wished. She'd immediately begun the task of giving him what he wanted, just as he'd unwittingly requested.

The first step was to fling him forward on a new journey, this one toward her mother's old abandoned cottage, the cottage where Moiria had been sent to retrieve the knife meant for Conrad's death. Here he would wait in a magicked stupor, of sorts, giving her time to prepare the other portions of the future his heart so hungered to obtain. He had requested her help, and he would dutifully wait to receive it, unaware of each slipping, passing hour and day. It was not exactly what she'd wanted when she came to retrieve him, but it was something. It was a plan. And it was the best she could concoct in the time she had.

Once he'd left, Moiria allowed that Conrad might not appreciate the methods she'd use to fulfill her promise to give him back his brother and his past, but that hardly mattered. Her job was to bend his will to what she needed to survive. She would not think further, not when she had her own place in the castle to protect. Conrad was a tool now, not her stepbrother. She must wipe those memories out. She could never allow herself to remember how he had saved her when her mother attacked.

Moiria took a deep breath as she topped the small rise in topography Conrad had gestured toward when he gave the direction for his love's whereabouts. As soon as she'd left him, she'd known what her next step needed to be, known it in the pit of her stomach. She must seek out Conrad's sweetheart and tie off any useless ends he could easily do without, in whatever manner necessary. It was the only way to move forward with her original plan. If she hoped to succeed, she could have no qualms in acting both decisively and quickly.

The scrabbling current in her veins assured her this was true. No matter her doubts.

Heart

"But you're my sister!" said Heart. "Does that mean nothing to you?"

Oh, how she wanted to stomp her feet like a three-year-old child. Why had this happened to her Lark? What had that awful wanderer done? Butting in and cutting their sisterhood apart. He didn't even bother to actually take Lark. Instead he left her here, alone and empty, her twinkling eyes grown dim with waiting.

"It's ridiculous," said Heart for what she knew must be somewhere near the twenty-fifth time that day. "He could be a crazy loon, you know? He could give trinkets to any girl he meets on his way. When we first saw him he was only dirt and grime. Do you really mean to sit here and wait for a pile of dirt and grime?"

The two of them stood near the river that ran just beyond their cottage, the late summer wind teasing both their hair. Heart, the shorter of the two by several inches, pushed her fists into her hips, elbows sticking outward in irritation. Lark leaned with one open hand against a tree, her patient eyes calm upon her sister's anger.

"I hardly think he was only dirt and grime," said Lark.

"Oh, he was handsome," Heart conceded, "with those golden curls atop his head. I suppose I'll give you that much. But he is gone, Lark. And you've your whole life left to you to lead."

"As long as I do it your way?" asked Lark, her eyebrows raised.

Heart sighed, and both arms fell to her sides. Ever rational, Lark was, even when it came to her own irrationality. But couldn't she see what her choices did to Heart? Couldn't she see that the path she insisted on choosing brought changes to their dear family in more ways than one? Changes the rest of them were made to bear? Changes Heart was made to bear?

"It had to happen someday, Heart. Things couldn't go on forever in the same old fashion. That's not the way of anyone's life."

"Well, it should be," muttered Heart. "We were happy before he came."

"Yes, we were happy," said Lark. "And we will be happy yet again. You'll see."

Heart's eyes narrowed and she looked intently at her sister. By now, Lark had left the tree where she'd leaned earlier and walked closer to the river. Her bare toes absentmindedly rolled stones into its grasp.

"Did you let him kiss you?" Heart said suddenly, though she wasn't sure she really wanted to know the truth of it.

"Heart!" said Lark, looking up at her sister in surprise. "You said so yourself, I only knew him a week."

"So? Time didn't seem to matter too much to you in any other regard."

"You make me sound cheap when you say that."

Heart shrugged. She knew her manner of speech hurt her sister, but somehow she wanted to cause her pain. She wanted Lark to feel the fear that rumbled in the pit of her stomach whenever she thought of her future, now that the wanderer had changed it all. She wanted Lark to understand what she did when she placed her affection and loyalty with another. What it meant to be the abandoned one, the one left far behind.

Heart looked pointedly at the ring around her sister's neck, and asked again. "Did you let him kiss you, when he gave you that?"

Lark sighed. "Tell me this, Heart . . . ," she said.

And Heart knew her game with those four words. Those words that said she'd done it, but would never admit to the deed. Lark had used those words so many times when she kept something back from Heart as a child. And because of that, Heart couldn't help but understand what they meant. The words were a code for lies. Lies meant to protect Heart from the truth, but lies all the same. Lies about dead pets. Lies about missing fathers. Lies about kisses given to new loves.

"Tell me this, Heart . . . ," Lark said.

And before she'd finished, Heart already knew the traveler

had kissed her. Kissed her well, and that she'd liked it when he did.

But Lark continued with her transparent words anyway. "Why would I kiss a boy I'd never seen before in my life? And why would I let that boy kiss me?" she said.

Heart opened her mouth to speak, to finally call her sister on the long-overused ruse, but then a rustle came from beyond the trees directly behind them.

Heart turned, her hand instinctively going to the bag at her waist and the small blade she kept inside. Lark jumped where she stood, and reached for the band hanging from her neck, her eyes filled with hope.

But it was not him. It was not Lark's long-lost wanderer. Not this time.

Instead, it was a witch.

Heart knew the girl emerging from their friendly forest was a witch, knew it on sight, knew it in the deepness of her bones. From the moment the girl stepped into their gazes, she saw the interloper's heart and the darkness and Death it held. Seeing people that way was, after all, one of Heart's gifts. Lark would not understand who the girl was, not with the clarity Heart had. She might be the older, wiser sister, but she could not see the innards of strangers in the way that Heart could.

And from the outside, it was not obvious who this stranger was. After all, the girl did not dress as a peasant. She did not stoop over a cane. She did not have gray wiry hair, and she did not cackle. She was a young witch—almost the same number of years as the sisters themselves—but a witch all the same.

But whatever Heart knew, at that moment, in that meadow, it did not matter, not one bit. She was not a player in this particular game, a fact made apparent by the witch's solid concentration on Lark's lone figure where it stood. This confrontation was not about Heart at all, and her knowledge of the witch would do nothing to change what happened in this place. She could feel that truth as well, no matter how she wished to deny it.

"Who are you?" said Lark, after a small moment's hesitation. Her hand still held the ring at her throat.

"Who am I?" said the witch, her voice almost slender in the near silent way it reached Heart's ears. "Who are you?"

The witch's dark hair—coal, not chocolate—hung behind her in a stiff sheet, a strange almost-mirror to Lark's. Her eyes, not like Lark's at all, ate up the light around them. Those eyes swallowed the light whole in deep and endless caverns of blackness, as though they gobbled at the world around them to fill an always-empty hole.

"I am . . ." Lark took a breath. "I am nobody."

Startled laughter fell from the witch's mouth. At first, Heart did not think it could be her laugh, even if her mouth had opened to release it. How could laughter from one as evil as that be so complicated? So tinged with broken dreams?

"Nobody indeed," said the witch. "And yet you stand in my way. Which is why I've come. Which is why it was necessary to find you."

"Heart," Lark turned from the witch and locked her eyes upon Heart's. "Hurry home. It's not safe here. Go find Granny."

Heart was not surprised her sister thought to send her from this place. Lark didn't see she had nothing to fear from this witch. This trouble came for Lark, not Heart. Lark was the sister in danger.

"No," said Heart, her breath beating wildly inside her at what might happen. "I won't go." For how could she leave Lark alone to face this shadowed girl and her manipulations?

"Heart . . . ," said Lark again.

But the witch did not let her finish the command. "Oh, leave your sister," she said. "I don't think your Granny needs anyone to check in on her just now. She wouldn't tell me where you were when I asked, and her old age made my powers of persuasion rather heavy to bear. It wasn't what I wished, but it's the result all the same. Besides, every act of power deserves a silent witness. Your sister does not wish to leave. We should honor this request of hers."

"Granny," whispered Lark, her voice horrified and broken. "What have you done?"

But the witch only flicked her eyes away and sighed, as though Lark could never actually understand. Heart stilled her inner pain at what that meant, determined not to lose her way in the battle just before her. If Granny were well and truly gone, she must concentrate on what was left of her family. She must concentrate on Lark and how she might possibly be saved. She must think of Granny later.

The witch had not banished Heart, or killed her yet. So, taking these statements and actions as a somewhat backward invitation, Heart moved to join Lark by the stream.

Her feet cracked sticks beneath them as she moved, the noise a dissonant reminder of how simple life had been only minutes before. Still, at least she and Lark would face this witch together, as they had faced so many other struggles before. As sisters. That must mean something here. But before Heart could reach Lark and take her hand in support, the witch's fingers flicked out sharply, and Heart's limbs and body froze mid-step.

"I said witness," said the witch, her gaze hard as stone, "and that is all I meant. What I have come to do here is between your sister and myself. You may watch from there, and that I give you only because you've shown some loyalty by not running away for your own safety."

Heart's mouth struggled to speak, her mind desperate to track the girl's strange words or their intended meaning. But her lips were frozen, along with her legs and arms, and the words would not fly outward.

The witch turned back to Lark, done with Heart now that she offered no further challenge. "I suppose it was the blond curls?" she said, almost conversationally. "They always were the talk of any girls allowed around him. Did you think your babes might have the same, when they came along? Quite the happy family, I imagine."

"What are you doing here?" said Lark. Her voice was quiet, and her eyes stayed firm upon the witch-girl as she spoke. Heart knew Lark well enough to know she would not let the witch use any personal weakness to achieve her evil aims. She would not shake at what had happened to Granny or Heart, knowing the fight at hand was all she had the chance to win.

The witch answered, her words like a snake upon the forest floor. "Did you think it would be as easy as that to get your dreams? Did you not count on a struggle of some sort?"

As the witch spoke, and Lark waited for her words, Heart desperately tried once more to move even one portion of her body. Perhaps if she could move her toes, she might understand how she could possibly move the rest of herself. Perhaps then she might get to Lark. In the meantime, why didn't Lark run? The witch had not frozen her in place yet. Why did she not move?

"Run," Heart wanted to yell. *"Run from this place. Go now."*

But Heart could not say the words, just as she could not move her toes. She realized, her stomach sinking with the pain, that no matter how her insides screamed to be let loose, she could do nothing, nothing at all, to help her sister. Meanwhile Lark did not even move her eyes from the witch, let alone her feet. Instead, she spoke, her chin lifted, her eyes unfailingly defiant.

"I am not afraid of you," she said.

Heart heard Lark speak and wanted to laugh in desperation. Not afraid? Not afraid of this witch-girl and her endless, light-eating eyes? How could Lark be so foolish? Especially with what the witch had said of Granny!

"Not afraid?" echoed the witch, her words as amazed as Heart's thoughts. "Then you must think your love will save you. You think you can't be touched by the power I hold? You think all will come out right, in the end."

Heart watched Lark step forward, her movements closing the

distance between her sister and the witch, despite the idiocy of such an action. "You may have made him forget," she said angrily. "His family. His name. His past. And you may have harmed my granny in some horrible way I could never imagine. You may even hold my sister captive so that you might strike me down at your will and whim. But I will not quiver before you. I will not fear your weakness. For it is only weakness that creates such pain."

The witch flinched, and Heart strained at the invisible binding that continued to hold her still. What was Lark doing? Didn't she realize the danger in this witch-girl's heart? Why did she not leave this place at once? Why did she bait their captor so? Was this all some bid to keep Heart safe? Was that the reason Lark had engaged so fully in this fight? As though she might distract the witch and keep Heart safe? If so, Heart only wished she would stop. She only wished Lark would care for herself.

In front of them, the witch pulled herself upright beneath Lark's words. She coughed and began again. "Even should we dismiss your foolish assumptions about my power, there are flaws in your logic." The witch leaned forward, her face within a breath of Lark's. "And not even a kiss between you, I think you told your sister. Not even a flicker of love to shield that pretty face of yours."

Lark's hand clutched tight at the ring about her neck, her fisted hand the only sign of her concern. The rest of her stood firm and steadfast, as though by will she might shake the evil that this girl had brought.

"What is that you hold?" said the witch, her eyes leaving Lark's and narrowing themselves at the glimmer of gold shining through Lark's fingers. She reached toward Lark, and then drew her hand back, as though from a fire. "It's that ring, isn't it? He gave you the ring. I would not think he'd part with that. Of course, that complicates matters here. It seems his only goal is to make things more difficult for me."

"Leave him be," said Lark, the words biting and hard. "Leave us be. You know I will not leave my sister where you've frozen her in place, and you know I have no weapons that would strike you down. But whatever you try to accomplish here will not lessen the love between him and me. It cannot give you what you want. You might as well leave. For in that regard, you have already lost."

"I would not be so sure of that," said the witch, her eyebrows raised.

Heart, sensing a change in plans for the witch—now that the ring had been discovered—returned to her efforts at moving her body. She must break free of the witch's hold! She must meet Lark halfway in her misguided efforts at confrontation. What would her defense be at that point? Could she guess what the witch would do next? None of this mattered if she remained trapped in place, if she still could not move one finger of her own volition. Lark would not leave her here, which meant she must break free. At least then they both could run.

And yet, no matter what Heart tried, no movement came. Though she could not understand how this had happened. How did that witch wield such complete power over her? With one small movement, she kept Heart from running to Lark's side. Was the sisterhood between Heart and Lark so tiny, when it came to this witch's magic? Was it truly not enough to break this spell? Heart found herself dismayed that this might be true, dismayed that she was running out of options.

"Oh, little bird. Lark, I think your sister called you?" The witch raised her eyebrows and glared at Lark, remaining completely uninterested in Heart, or the great and useless efforts she continued to make toward escape. "You will see that you cannot stand against me quite so easily," she continued. "Though courageous, you can do nothing. I do not even need to bind you in place, not with your sister waiting just beyond."

By now the witch had leaned forward, and she held herself close enough to speak directly into Lark's ear. Heart choked on the bile rising in her throat, wishing she could force out her own words and draw the witch's attention from dear Lark. Wishing she hadn't become part of that witch's strength, part of her threats.

You dark-sludged vermin, thought Heart toward the girl. *You scheming prattler and cool-faced liar. You ugly girl-witch, with a putrid, smelly heart. Get away from us. Leave us and go.*

But Heart's mouth spoke no words. With all her effort, she could not even move her tongue. She could do nothing to save her sister or to resist this horrible girl. She could only watch.

"I think I have it," said the witch, taking a small step back from Lark, her eyes triumphant in a horribly sinister way. "I think I have the way to bring it all to pass, even in this forest, with its damp and heavy power. And you will sit there and take it, since there is nothing further for you to do."

Lark shifted beneath the witch's sight, but just as the witch had spoken, she did not move or speak. She was not one to attempt a useless escape. She was not one to back down from a foe. Even if it meant her life, she would not cower beneath this witch's feet. And Heart was proud of her sister in that moment, even if she found her behavior both irrational and tragic.

"You wear a ring of promise, which ties you to your fate. Even you can tell the truth of that," said the witch. "Tell me, what is stronger than a promise? Shall we tie that band on tighter to keep your promise whole and firm? What forest, no matter its feelings regarding my methods, could complain of my fortification of such love?"

The witch lifted her fingers into the air, her index finger and her thumb held slightly apart, ready to act. Lark watched every movement she made, her eyes darting to Heart's only once in all that time, as though to bid her sister fond farewell and send her love. Heart melted at the thought, and watched as well, her spirit aching to do more.

"We will bring that band of gold so tight," said the witch, "that only he who put it on may take it off. We will make certain you will be his, or belong to no one at all. Then you will keep your promise to your love, the very deepest of your desires, and I shall keep all of my promises to him as well."

Tightening her mouth, the witch pulled her fingers closer

together, as though she held and squeezed an object between them. Across from her, and quite suddenly, Heart's sister fell to her knees, her eyes growing wide on the witch. Heart watched as Lark clutched at the band, and the rope it hung from on her neck. Her sister's face turned white. Then, from Heart's frozen vantage point just footsteps away, she watched as the rope suddenly disappeared. She watched as the ring widened and came circling around her sister's neck instead.

The witch's fingers continued to squeeze inward, slowly but insistently contracting. "I cannot bring you Death, with a ring such as that around your neck, with this forest watching on, but it often happens that a smaller curse will serve as well as the larger one would have done."

Lark's brown hair began to fill with streaks of white. Her golden band, her golden collar, wrapped tight about her neck. Heart trembled at the pain broadcast from her sister's face, and sweat dripped into her eyes from the renewed efforts she made at moving. The efforts that brought no results at all.

"Lark," said the witch. "That is your name. Tell me, shall we make the name more apt? I think it might lessen that tightness you feel."

Lark's red lips pressed against each other. Her fingers wrapped about the shrinking bit of gold. Still, she did not pull against it, not against the ring her love had handed her. Instead she seemed to grasp it, like a chain that held her tight to him, despite the witch's curse.

Meanwhile, the witch's other hand reached up, tightened into a fist. She twisted it outward and let her fingers open, slow and halting in their movement. As she did so, the last of Lark's dark hair turned white as snow. Heart stared in horror, her muscles limp as she finally gave up on reaching her sister in time. It was much too late.

"I hear," said the witch, "that a desert lark sings low and mournfully, when it opens its beak. And perhaps you will be glad of this, as that mournful tune will be your most constant companion now. Perhaps you will find life as a bird more forgiving than the life you've lived till now. I must admit its benefits appeal even to me."

The witch's hand came closed.

Heart's eyes blinked shut, shocked by a resulting light so bright she could not bear to see it. She heard, as though from miles away, a long and piercing scream, and then, following close behind it, a hesitant and aching birdsong to take its place.

Heart struggled to open her eyes, struggled to force the lids apart, struggled to regain even that small portion of control over her own body. When she finally managed it, when she finally felt release from the spell that had held her so tightly before, the witch she hated so dearly stood right in front of her. Waiting, her dark eyes watchful of Heart's own. In one hand, the witch held a bird—a white and brown-flecked bird. She reached out to Heart's hands, lifted them, and placed the bird inside her palms.

The witch's empty pits of eyes narrowed and became, for a moment, the eyes of an ordinary girl.

"Guard her well," she said, "as a sister should guard those she loves. She could fly and be lost to you in a moment, if you do not keep her close. You have already failed to protect her once today, and this is all you'll get for how you tried." She stepped away.

Heart looked down at her trembling hands, finding she did not care what happened to the witch beyond this moment, or where she went, not now that this reality had become her own. The little bird's small heart thumped rapidly against her fingers. Heart kept one hand to hold it close and, with the other, lifted the feathers nestled at its neck. Would she find it there? The band of gold? Yes. Of course she would.

A band of gold. A ring of promise. A prison of love, which held her sister tight.

Moiria

Up until then, all of Moiria's actions, however horrific, had come following a threat. Her mother, directing Heppson to murder. Her mother, again, ready to kill Moiria herself. The soldier, sure Moiria must be jailed for the Queen's death. Lessers in Alastair's court, threatening Moiria's place of safety in association with the crown. Villagers, blustering for rebellion. Even the King, seeking to blame her for the evil wrought by her dead mother.

All of these threats resulted in a necessary response from Moiria, her blood crying out for her defense. But all of that changed when she'd gone after this girl whom Conrad loved. She had become the offender, instead of the besieged.

First, there had been the grandmother, her small figure standing stalwart in the cottage door. Moiria had pressed her for information regarding her granddaughter's location. And when she'd refused, Moiria had pressed harder, determined to get what she needed for her quest. She had not thought to drive the old woman to her knees. She had not counted on her heart giving out under duress. It had been an accident of sorts, but she had done it, and she had left the woman there to feed the flies.

Then, there was the Lark. That girl had stood there, so resolute. She hadn't wanted to hurt Moiria. She hadn't known about the kingdom or its politics. All she'd desired was the return of her one true love and the safety of her sister. All she'd desired was happiness, a family, and a future. And yet she'd still stood in the way, she'd still kept Moiria from her efforts to obtain Conrad's submission. And Moiria had decided that offense was enough.

Strange that, looking at that girl, Moiria saw herself, or at least who she was before she went to trap her mother. Confronted with such innocence, she suddenly remembered hesitant Moiria, hiding in the shadows as she watched her brother escape. She saw the relative weakness of her past self; her complete ineptitude in fighting the Queen. She felt her old fear, and she saw her past failures. She saw these things, and knew the girl she'd been had trembled beneath those burdens. She'd been like Lark, wanting and unable to obtain.

But she could be that girl no longer, not if she wanted to live. Not if she wanted to succeed. She would have to act, in any way she could think of, regardless of the cost. And so, she did.

Afterward, she could see that changing Conrad's dearest love into a feathered creature, with little memory or rational thought, blew that old Moiria far, far away in a way that cursing her own evil mother never had. Consigning that innocent life to a point-less existence and the finite lifetime of a bird, separating her from all that she held dear, made all the difference in who Moiria became at her core.

And though there was a moment, as she handed the fluttering fowl to her sister, when Moiria recalled what her original efforts of rebellion had been intended to bring about, the memory and feelings soon left her. The change had come, when she'd decided and made the bird, when she'd put the ring about that innocent's neck. And with that change came power. Which somehow made it worth it. Or so she must believe. The rest might have been in defense, but this had been her choice. And once she had made it, there was no use in denying who she'd become.

Now, all that remained to assure her complete success was her final manipulation of Conrad and her taking of the throne. This would be simple enough, when the bird had sung its last trilling note and fallen to the ground, its life spent. Moiria could not bring Death to the bird herself, not with the ring about its neck, not with the forest looking over her shoulder, but she knew that Death would come on its own much more quickly in the bird's new circumstances.

How long could a desert lark live inside this forest? Especially one untrained in avoiding danger or foraging for food? Not long at all. Moiria would wait for the bird's death, and then she would go to Conrad and make him hers. This was the path she had chosen.

Heart

Initially, the bird tried to fly from her, its wings beating against her sweating grasp.

It was a small lark, colored much more lightly than others she'd seen, though some brown remained and whispered its way through the feathers. This plumed pigment was all that remained of Lark's chocolate curls. Sister of Heart's heart, gone in a second.

Overwhelmed, Heart dropped to the ground, her knees and skirts slapping into the mud that stretched from the river's bank. Inhaling a ragged breath, she hurriedly swallowed her sobs and stared at the bird clasped between her hands. She gazed at what had been left behind of Lark. And though seconds ticked by, and the day moved along its course, the bird remained, nothing more. A simple lark . . . a simple lark was all she held.

As evening drew close, Heart remained in the mud. She didn't know what to do. She couldn't go to the cottage. She couldn't go seek Granny. She knew what she would find there—the witch had been clear in that regard. And she couldn't handle the pain of losing Granny without her sister by her side. She could only block it out, a weak attempt at not accepting all she had lost this day. It was too much to carry the burden of that much death.

Meanwhile, the sun trailed its light backward as it fell into the horizon, as worn out by the day as Heart. Luckily, it could leave this world behind. It could forget what happened to dear, sweet Lark. It could forget what had happened to dear, sweet Granny. Heart, on the other hand, could not. All she could do was stare. Stare and stare.

What's done is done, said a disconsolate voice inside her mind, pity and anguish breaking against her heart.

Heart startled at the words, her hands tightening on the bird she held. It was as though she had heard the sister speak whom she had never thought to hear again. The sister she'd failed to protect from that horrid witch and her dark spells.

You can't blame yourself, said the voice. *Neither of us would wish you to do that.*

Her Lark had always been there to guide her, so much so that Heart almost swore she heard her now, speaking in her mind. What would she do to face this trouble with the sister who'd always waited at her side? What would she give to imagine she was not alone?

"What do we do now?" she said out loud, aching for the conversation to be real, allowing herself to pretend that it was. "There is no one to go to for help. Granny is gone. And none of our neighbors would understand or believe what I have to say. But you cannot remain a bird forever!"

You are right, said the voice that should have been Lark. *And because of that, we must act quickly. I believe that every curse has its loophole, and you were there to see this one made. Think what was done. That will tell us the way out.*

Obediently, thinking it the best plan that she had, and dreaming of her Lark, Heart closed her eyes and tried to think of what had happened with the witch. She watched the footsteps of that evil girl once more, the image playing over inside her head. She saw that dark one's eyes take in Lark. She saw her hands reach toward her.

"The ring surprised her," said Heart, opening her eyes.

There is love inside my ring, replied Lark's voice. *Love protects us all, you know. It is a saving power so deep that even Death cannot sever it without a fight.*

And Heart did know it. After all, it was her sister's love that saved her, that terrible night she'd been born. The night Death should have taken her as well as her mother. Heart's eyes filled with moisture at the memory and the strength of their love. But then she shook herself from her past to concentrate on what might be done now, with today's particular tragedy.

All she could think of was her sister. Lark's dark hair turned white. That terrible flash of light which forced Heart's eyes to close at the all-important moment. The ring of gold about the bird's feathered neck. Then, as her mind considered that gold band, Heart heard the voice again, inside her.

Only he can take it off, it said.

Heart's head snapped up. The words hung in the air around Heart, ringing with a certain truth. "Only he can take it off?" she asked. "But what can that mean? What can that matter? It's not like I even know who that boy is, or where he might be."

Only he can take it off, the voice repeated. *And he must. He must take it off.*

Heart's shoulders slumped down again as she considered the bird in her hands, as she considered the strange words in her mind. Was she mad? Was she so completely unhinged that she thought to speak with a bird that used to be her sister? Did she honestly think to follow the course this pretended conversation, which took place within her mind, directed her to take?

He must take off the ring, said the voice again.

Heart leaned her head forward and pressed against the bird's feathers. She felt their cutting smoothness, firm against her skin. The bird's heart trembled against her fingertips.

"Of course," said Heart. "The ring is what holds you as a bird. And only your wanderer can remove it. But what does that mean?"

It means you and I must leave this place. You must find him. He must remove the golden band. It is the only way to freedom. The only way to happiness. We cannot go back; we can only go forward.

"But that's impossible," said Heart. Her head lifted up again and her eyes searched the trees around them. "How would we ever find him? The wilderness has hidden him far away."

Loopholes are almost always impossible, said the voice. *It is the way of things. Granny always said the same, when she would tell us tales 'round the fire. We must only be thankful there is a loophole, and that we know what it is.*

"But how?" said Heart again, wanting certainty, wanting to

be sure all would come out right, wanting the words to be real. "How can I find him? He could be anywhere."

You're right. He could be anywhere. And the truth is, you could never find him on your own.

Heart felt a heat inside her belly, angry at the puzzle she'd been left to solve. "Make up your mind, my imaginary Lark. You say I must go. You say we must find him. You say it is the only way to save you. Don't tell me there's no actual way to do it."

The voice inside her mind laughed. *Imaginary?"* it said. *Are you so certain? Listen. I will fly to the wanderer. Make no mistake of that. My heart seeks my love. And you will have to watch me closely, so you can keep up and protect me as I go.*

"Keep up?" Heart said. "I cannot fly! I cannot skim over tree-tops, or float over streams. I have no wings to carry me. I am not even sure it is you I hear. This may all be a silly effort I've created to hold you close!"

Yes, sighed the voice, *it will be difficult. But I can think of nothing else. The wanderer is the key. We must find him. And I must not go alone. There are too many ways that I might die along the way. You would never see me again. You would never know what happened. These are the truths we have. We must make do.*

"And what if I lose you?" Heart whispered. "What if I lose you, the way I have lost everyone else? Mother. Father. Granny."

It is a possibility. You may lose me. I may die. But that does not change if we stay.

"Lark," Heart said. "Suppose we do this thing. How can I keep up with you? How will we stay together? Can you even wait for me?"

It took some time for the voice to answer. Heart supposed the voice that claimed to be her sister must be tired. For what would it be to find yourself suddenly changed into a bird? To feel another heart inside your body, beating much more quickly than yours had ever thought to beat before? To find your stomach wanting worms, and your breast adorned by feathers?

Heart, Lark's voice finally said. And Heart heard the words roll slowly across her mind. *I will leave you feathers. One in the morning.* She paused. *One at midday. One in the evening. Follow the feathers. Look for where they fall, and follow me.*

And that would be their plan? Oh, how she wished that she had more to carry forward with than that. But Lark was gone, made into bird. And Granny could not give her any wisdom for the pathway forward. Which meant this was all she had. Words with her imaginary sister. An effort to find a wandering traveler. A forest stretched before her without any tangible goal in sight. Feathers on the ground, blowing in the wind.

"Follow the feathers," repeated Heart, her mind scrambling at the thought. "Follow the feathers," she said, as she haltingly stood to take her path. "Follow the feathers."

PART III

Heart

Heart kept the feathers as they fell. She carried these offerings of her sister in a small brown bag she'd had with her the day the witch changed both of their lives. Most of the feathers Lark dropped were white, but some of them were brown. The brown ones, of course, were much more difficult to find on the forest floor. When Lark dropped those, Heart searched among the dirt and stones and weeds of the wilderness for seconds, minutes, even hours, before she knew the way to follow her sister. And then, once she'd found her clue, she walked on.

Along the way, she foraged for berries and nuts. She dug for roots to fill her empty stomach. On occasion, she pulled out her sling and aimed for a squirrel to roast when evening came. She could not bring herself to eat bird, not now that Lark had taken that form as her own.

Steps and steps of following made up each never-ending day. This was Heart's role now. Led by a bird. Searching for a stranger. Hiding from the probability of her sister's likely death. Moving forward to she knew not what. The voice she imagined to be Lark's rarely came to her now, and Heart understood her sister's silence. Lark was, after all, a bird. The effort to seek her love must be hard enough as it was without worrying over her trailing sister.

And so, Heart tried to be glad her sister continued onward and dropped the feathers as the voice had said she would. That she did not take to nesting or searching for worms all day. She tried to believe she did not miss having a companion to share words with throughout the day. But it happened, eventually, that it became too much.

Heart had stopped by the stream to lift water to her lips, to send drips of coolness down the sloping sweatiness of her neck. She had picked up a feather recently, and she followed its point, knowing from experience that whether or not Lark flew in her immediate sight, she would find her sister in the direction the feather demanded she walk.

She needed a break, so she took off her shoes and sat down to dip her toes in the shallow wetness of the river. She felt the roundness of the stones along the bank—brushed, rubbed, and broken into smoothness. She fingered a rock beside her, one not yet beaten to submission by the movement of the water. Its edge and grittiness chafed against Heart's palm, scraping white lines into her skin. The pain reminded her of all that roiled inside.

"Blast them all," she said.

Anger flaring inside, she threw the rock against the water, cutting its smoothness into prisms of liquid that burst upward from where the rock had fallen. She kicked her feet against the water, disturbing even more the smoothness of the river's gentle path. Oh, how she wished to yank each drop of water from the depths of that river and throw them at the trees surrounding her. Oh, how she wished to stop the ever-constant stream of water from slipping past her as though nothing at all were wrong.

"Stop," she yelled. "Stop moving forward. Stop gurgling and wandering, going whichever way you're pulled."

Couldn't it be stopped? Couldn't it be made to stop? She picked up another rock beside her and pitched it into the stream. She threw her arm sideways to give it more power.

"Stupid witch!" she growled. "Stupid boy! Stupid ring!"

With each angry burst, she threw another stone at the sparkling water, though the river did not heed her. Despite a splash, despite a plop, despite a momentary reflection of what she'd done, the river went along its well-worn way, with or without Heart's rock-made missiles. She picked up one more stone and held it in her hand, her fingers pressed against its grooves and edges. Then, stretching out her arm, Heart held the rock over the flowing water, wondering if she'd truly let it drop.

A moment passed. She took a breath.

"Stupid Lark," she whispered.

And she let the rock fall down, gravity doing most of the work for her. She did not have the energy to throw her weight behind the bitter missile this time.

Heart dropped her head into her hands. How could Lark do this to her? How could she care so much more for someone else that she dragged the both sisters into this trap? If only she had stayed as she was before. If only she had let them remain the same. Two sisters. Complete in themselves, with no need for outsiders. If she had done this, the two of them would both be home, and the witch would be elsewhere, turning another person's sister into a useless bird of white and brown who couldn't even speak.

How Heart wished to throttle Lark for what she'd done. As if it would do her any good.

Heart dragged her head upward and looked into the water. Light danced between the surface of the stream and the stones below. It moved back and forth through the currents and eddies of the water. Bits of grass and straggly weeds wove their way from front to back, drawn ahead by the pull of the water, yanked backward by the pressure of their roots. Dirt and bits of matter bobbed along, heading downward with the river. The scene was so natural, so normal. Everything Heart wanted. Everything Heart didn't have.

But then, another movement, distinct from all the streaming, came. A fish moved in the depths. A fat, round fish of red. Heart watched it tweak from side to side, its body pressed tight inside the pressure of the moving water. Forgetting Lark for one blessed moment, the hunter inside Heart woke. She considered the taste of fire-scorched fish and rolled it about her tongue. What a change from what she'd eaten lately!

Heart reached for the knife kept always at her belt. True, she would do better with a spear, or even more so with a well-prepared dam. But as she did not have either at the moment, she hoped her skill might make the knife serve well enough. She watched the pathway of the fish. She considered where it might go next, so that she might wait a flick of fin ahead of its progression. The fish's way was leisurely—a careful and unhurried advance to its destination.

Which way? thought Heart. *Which way?*

She held her knifepoint ready. Then, she watched as the fish turned itself to face her. It hovered for a moment, not moving with the stream. It held itself in place, its nose pointed to Heart's waiting form. Motionless in the water right before her.

Perfect, she thought. *Stay a bit more, dear.*

She pulled her knifepoint back, ready to strike her dinner.

If I were you, a bell-like voice rippled forcefully in her head, *I would not bear that knife into my flesh.*

In a flash, Heart screamed and dropped the knife into the river. Her first unfiltered thought was that she'd found someone else's sister whom the witch had enchanted and left to brave the forest's depths.

"Bother and blast," she hissed, when any breath returned, and she'd grabbed her knife again from where it'd fallen. "I will never eat meat again."

Her second thought, following quickly on the other, was that she'd lost her mind. This seemed fairly likely, even if the first was true as well. Meanwhile, the fish—as though a fish could possibly do such a thing—wriggled its way to the bank of the river, pushed its mouth up to the surface, and blew a few bubbles along the water. Its shimmering scales caught light and flipped it sideways, frontways, backways, and some into Heart's gaze.

You have been touched by evil, the fish said, when it spoke again.

A shudder took Heart's shoulders in its grasp and shook. Hard. It did speak! Or at least she heard words it supposedly had to share. And what a thing for a talking fish to say!

Why you've decided to hurl rocks in my river is beyond me, it said, the words full of rebuke. *Do you think it will solve your problems?*

Like a magnet flipping inside her stomach, Heart's fear,

which had blossomed inside her at the fish's first words, disappeared. Instead, she wanted to throw another rock, and this time to aim it for the fish's head.

"It makes me feel better," she said, "to hurl rocks. What is that to you?"

You are lucky you didn't hit anything, said the fish, its voice sounding once again inside Heart's head.

"You mean you're lucky," Heart retorted.

The fish hiccupped, and Heart realized it had meant to laugh.

You are not afraid of me? said the fish. *Even though I speak?*

"My sister speaks that way as well," Heart said. "At least I hope."

Your sister?

"She is a bird now. A lark. She flew past here earlier today. I travel with her."

Your sister is a bird? How interesting. She cannot be a Guardian. I know our lot well enough to be sure of that.

"Guardian?" asked Heart, confused. "I don't know what you mean by that. Lark is just a bird. A witch made her so."

Ah," said the fish, *"and that is the touch of evil on your head.*

"I suppose you could call it that," Heart answered, her head turning to the side at the thought.

How interesting! And what do you and your sister plan to do about this curse that she's acquired?

Heart hesitated and wondered for a moment about the oddity of conversing with a fish. What would a stranger think, if one came and crossed her path? What would she have thought, only a few weeks ago, to see herself talking to this fish? Then she shrugged. It had been so long since anybody cared to speak to her. And Lark's voice was not anything she had ever been certain was real. At least the fish existed.

"Well," she said, answering the fish, "there is only one who can break the curse. So, we search for him."

I see. You seek the cure. Much luck yet? said the fish.

"Not particularly," said Heart. "Anyway, I only follow my sister. She is the one who knows where he is."

Does she now?

"Well, shouldn't a person's heart lead them to their love?"

The fish blew a bubble or two more, as though it thought as well. *I should think a person's heart should. And for what reason do you join your sister on her quest?*

Heart dropped her eyes to her hands. They fidgeted in her lap. Even the fish understood she was the expendable portion of this quest. "Lark wished me to protect her," she said. "Our sisterhood has always meant much to us."

And rightly so, said the fish, its nose almost bobbing in a nod. *This is my river, you know. I live here season in and season out. There are not many who know of the Guardians now; there are not many who come to seek my help. Usually, I am alone. It is a difficult way to live. The solitary life is not the best one, I think.*

Heart looked up.

I agree you are right to accompany your sister. But do you not wish to do more than follow?

"All I have ever been asked to do was follow," muttered Heart. "And what else is there to do in this case anyhow?"

Perhaps you think I am an old fish. Or a crazy fish. Or both, said the fish. *That I dawdle off in conversation. You do not understand me at all—me or my talk of Guardians and my river. But despite this, and despite others like you that insist on misunderstanding, I wait here in my river, so that every summer, when my powers reach their peak, I am available for those who need me. After all, I am the Summer Guardian, and it is my purpose to wait.*

The fish looked at Heart. It gulped down a breath of water. Heart wondered if it meant for her to speak. Did it think it spoke sense? Did it think she cared about its river or these Guardians it mentioned? It spoke in riddles, and then asked if she wanted to do more than follow her sister. What was she meant to say in return?

"What does any of that have to do with me?" she said.

Heart, isn't it?" said the fish. *"Heart would be your name?*

Heart pressed her mouth together and nodded, not wanting to know how the fish knew her name.

Heart, I swim up and down these banks—day in and day out—and I watch for any who seek my counsel, who seek my gifts, and who seek my power. I swim and swim, and normally—the truth of it is—I see no one. As I said before, I am usually alone. Stories of my kind and our seasonal gifts are not shared around fires these days. Even here in the forest, the truth of our existence has been shuttered and veiled. After all, you have no clue what a Guardian is, or what one can do for you, am I right?

"No, I don't," said Heart, suddenly impatient at the fish's confusing words, suddenly ready to be done with the madness of their conversation. She brushed her skirts before her and moved to stand and leave the river and its fish.

Going already? I hardly think, said the fish, *that you'd abandon such a chance to help your sister. I hardly think she would wish to stay a bird forever.*

"Of course not!" Heart looked at the fish again. "Who would want to stay an animal forever? And what wouldn't I give to help her? But what does any of that have to do with me listening to you any longer? Some silly red fish, bobbing in a mediocre river, mumbling words that make no sense."

The fish harrumphed, if such a thing were possible. *That temper will not serve you well, I think*, it said. *After all, temper mixed with witch hardly ever does one good.*

"My temper serves me well enough," Heart snapped again.

Not if it means I leave you here to solve this problem all alone, said the fish. *It will not serve you well enough then. After all, I am the only one around to help you in your predicament. For even should your sister find her love, there is still the witch to be defeated. You cannot think she'll let you off so easily. You cannot think you will not need some further tools to fight.*

Heart's breath caught inside her as she remembered her last

encounter with the witch, as she remembered her inability to do anything to help her sister when she became a bird. What would it be to live through such a moment again? To have her hands so tied that the witch could cause them sorrow yet again.

"You are a fish. In a river. What good can you do?"

The fish gulped down water once more. *What good can I do, you say? Do you not remember my mention of the word 'Guardian' earlier in our conversation?*

"I'm afraid I think only of my sister," Heart said. "Other details do not keep so well."

Yes, the fish said. *And for your unfailing love of your sister I will help you now, despite your horrid temper, and despite your forgetfulness that I am, in fact, one of those animals you so despise your sister being.*

"Really?" Heart laughed. "You promise to help me? Tell me, what do you plan on doing, little fish? Do you plan to swim your way to the witch and make her turn my sister back?"

This is my river, said the fish. *"My place is here.*

"Yes, you've said that. Several times. But I hardly think escaping this river would be the trickiest part of dealing with a witch. All she would need to do is eat you."

It might surprise you—my power. The fish blew bubbles again. *It might surprise you—her weakness. Anyway, despite my continued repetition, you fail to ask the most important question.*

"Do I?" said Heart. "And what would that question be, little fish? Why don't you enlighten me? You insist I stay to be saved by you. Why don't you tell me how such a thing is to be done? For truly I should be moving on to look for feathers."

The fish went still and spoke clearly and distinctly in Heart's mind. The words were slow and dropped upon her consciousness like stones would plop into a calm and waiting sea—if Heart's mind had been anything near calm and waiting.

I said I was a Guardian. Do you not wonder what a Guardian does?

Heart sighed, willing to take the bait if it meant the fish might explain herself. "All right, little fish," she said. "What exactly is it that a Guardian does? How can you help me?"

The fish's belly swelled in size. Its fins flapped against the stream. *Where does the sun sit now?* the fish asked with an excited, hurried gasp of words.

In exasperation, Heart looked above her to the sky. "I would say there are another four or five hours to nightfall," she said, wondering why the fish did not answer the question it insisted she ask in the first place.

Go, said the fish. *Gather your sister and return to my river after dusk. I will tell you then about this thing you've asked.*

"You will answer me then?" Heart said. "First you insist I ask you this question, and then you say I must wait?"

Yes, said the fish. *That is the way of things now.*

"This is ridiculous."

Go, said the fish. *Gather your sister.*

"And I suppose I have no choice?" said Heart.

Of course you have a choice, said the fish. *You always have a choice. You may continue onward and never return to my banks. You may remain unprepared for the battle ahead. You may follow your sister and whimper as you have done for the past several days. Or you may act. You may move forward with preparations and tactics of your own.*

Heart felt trembles up and down her spine at the fish's words. Would she give up a chance to face the witch and conquer, no matter how insane the scheme might seem?

"All right. I will find my sister," she said. "And I will return. And hopefully it will do me some good. Otherwise I may very well find it wise to eat you."

The fish laughed. *It will do you good*, it said. *I promise, it will do you good.* And it sank into the river and swam away.

Moiria

Moiria paced the empty throne room, the King's eyes following her every step. She had sent the courtiers away from the long and drafty hall, not needing their fawning agreement in this particular situation. She had sent away her supposed advisors from where they cowered uncertainly near the curtains—the curtains she herself had lurked in long ago. She could not, of course, send away the King. Technically, and now actually, this command was beyond her.

"I will not be put off this time," he had whispered, as he swayed before the throne just moments earlier. His will was an unused muscle, and it shook at the effort required of it, but he held it tight.

With his words, Moiria had stood and asked that they be left alone. The Lark was not dead yet. Moiria had reached with her mind and felt the bird's wings flapping through the air. Strong, powerful, full of life. Seeking Conrad, where Moiria had hidden him away. With the bird alive, Moiria's plans to circumvent this King were not substantially in place.

And so, left alone with the old monarch, as he'd requested, she paced.

"I do not understand what you want of me," she finally said. "What do you mean to accomplish by coming here and making these sorts of demands? It's not as though you are ready to take on leadership of the kingdom yourself. You barely manage to keep your feet as I speak to you now."

"I want my sons," said the King, his voice an echo of what should have been a powerful demand.

"And I tell you, I have nothing to do with their absence. The eldest I am seeking at this very moment. I have sought him since you last came to demand his presence of me. The younger left of his own volition and is beyond my reach."

"I do not believe you are so weak. I do not believe it would be so difficult for you."

Moiria halted in her pacing and stared at the old King. His robes were tattered and fit him poorly, as though nothing new had been made for him for years. His gray beard reached down to his collar in rambling tufts, like dripping stalactites in a cave. One shoulder hung lower than the other, and his hands were clasped in front of him, shaking with uncertainty.

"You look awful," she said.

The King blinked, but did not contradict her.

"You look nothing like a King."

"I know. But I will grow stronger. I already have. I feel my health returning. And if you continue to provide no explanation, I will assume my sons are dead and that you have done this horrible thing. You will pay for such treason with your own life, once I have the means and power to take it."

Moiria turned away from the King and walked again to the farthest end of the room. Here, the throne sat on its tiled pedestal. Moiria turned and sat down upon the stones, her hands pressing on her knees.

"I know you will," she said. "And I assure you, I am seeking Conrad as a result. He is what you want, and I work now to bring him to you."

"And what of Heppson?"

"He left on his own. I cannot help you there."

"You cannot?"

"I will not."

The King pressed his lips together, as though considering how hard he could push Moiria. "How long until Conrad arrives?" he said.

But as he spoke, Moiria felt a memory of her mother's gaze upon her. What would that woman think of the way Moiria sat upon the throne? Of the manner she adopted in answering the King's questions as though he had the right to ask them of her?

Of her efforts to keep trouble at bay, regardless of the cost? Would she have ever let a conversation like this go so far?

Straightening her spine and standing, Moiria looked angrily at the King. Purposefully, she reached for the pulsing that lay sleeping and coiled in her belly. The knife might be in the cottage, and it might not speak to her as forcefully from such a distance, but she could call upon its strength, if she wished.

"I have had enough of your questions," she said coldly. "Do not come here and embarrass me in front of the courtiers again as you did today. You do not have the ability to dress yourself, let alone care for this kingdom. And your demands for your sons will be met when I decide it is time."

As the King made to interrupt, Moiria lifted her hand. "I said it was enough. Go now, before I do worse than send you away."

Of course, he did not have to listen. He could have laughed at her words and swept her from the room himself. Moiria knew she held no particular power over the man. All that held him now were the vestiges of her mother's past curses. They had been strong and powerful, but they were frayed and broken. If he had thought to flex his strength against them, it would have been easy enough. Her own plans to replace the bindings were not complete.

The King had said he did not believe she was so weak. Well, that was foolishness on his part. Foolishness that Moiria would be glad to take advantage of to keep her place. She breathed in relief when the King dropped his gaze and began to shuffle toward the doors.

"At least I will have one son back," she heard him mumble. "At least there will be Conrad. With him at home, I will find a way to make things right."

Moiria, more concerned about the man's increasing will-power than she would have liked, turned from him and pressed her hand against the cool metal of the throne's copper-hued back.

"Conrad," she said. "Conrad. Conrad. Conrad."

The King's insistence on his son's speedy return meant the

Lark must go sooner than the laws of nature seemed to require of her. That was obvious. Moiria could not alter Conrad's will until this last impediment was entirely removed, and she could not wait it out any longer.

"It was silly of me to let her sister protect her," said Moiria to herself. "It was silly of me to give them each other. I will have to change everything, if I mean to accomplish what I've set out to do. I will have to get rid of the sister as soon as I can."

At least it would not take much to set the forces in motion and begin the process that would end the sister's life. And she would not have to be personally involved again. She would not have to see it happen. She would only have to give the orders to make it so.

For her task, Moiria chose a young soldier of the kingdom who had little will of his own to overcome. She called him to her mother's chambers that evening, where the curious eyes of the court could be kept from understanding.

Once he'd arrived, he stood there in the darkened room, his legs almost trembling beneath him. What kind of boy had he been, to think he could serve as a soldier? One pressured to do so, likely by the opinions and desires of those around him. Now, she would use this weakness to overcome him and bend him to the course that she required.

Of course, to complement such useful weakness, a slight transformation was necessary. After all, the soldier must be formidable enough to end the sister completely. The two girls must speedily be separated by Death's final hand. He could not bring this about without a large dose of help from her.

"Shall we make you stronger?" she asked him, coming to stand immediately in front of where he waited.

The soldier shifted in his boots.

"You would like to be stronger, wouldn't you? Not so easily kicked about by the others in your unit. I could do that for you, you know."

The soldier lowered his chin and shrugged his shoulders upward. "If you wish it, your highness," he mumbled.

"No," said Moiria, her voice cutting and harsh. "If you wish it. Tell me, answer me now, would you like to be stronger?"

The soldier raised his eyes to hers, tried to hold her gaze, and, failing, dropped his sight down to the floor again. "Yes," he said, the word almost a whisper.

Moiria was not surprised that the soldier desired such a change in might, or that he was happy to accept the curse she offered to drop upon his head. She had chosen him for this purpose, and she had chosen well. She did wonder briefly, once she'd changed him, what the sister would feel when she met the beast he would become: a giant dog with sharp and wild teeth, manic and crazed from the change wrought upon his body.

She supposed it would be fear. Terror and pain at what the wild dog would inflict. But the girl should count herself lucky that this transformed soldier would kill her so quickly. After all, she would never see her beloved sister's final demise as a bird. Death would be a quicker fate for her.

In the end, the sister Heart would be the one to leave, and not the one left behind. Moiria had given her that.

Heart

Gathering Lark was not such a difficult thing to do. When evening came, the bird hovered above Heart's head momentarily, as if in recognition, and then landed on a nearby branch to sleep away the night hours as usual. Perhaps this was not the way of an ordinary bird, but Lark had not changed completely yet, and this was the pattern she'd held throughout their travels so far.

Heart went to her sister, once she'd landed, and folded her hands around the bird's form. She lifted the bird off of the branch and pulled her inward, to her chest. "We must go to consult a sage," she whispered, the irony she felt at the idea seeping out into her words despite herself.

The bird's heart fluttered, and Heart felt a ghost of a breath wash over her mind.

Why? Who?

"You will understand later," said Heart. "Until then, sleep in my arms. I will carry you and you can rest. We'll continue our travels tomorrow."

The bird settled calmly between Heart's palms, no other questions floating from its thoughts. Its feathery breast grew large and small with each breath it took. Her sister Lark had gone for now, and all Heart held was sleeping bird. What craziness she would believe to make this truth untrue! What craziness she meant to take part in by consulting some strange fish about the matter!

At least it did not take long to complete the action and find the bank of the river again. Heart had not bothered, once she had her sister in hand, to backtrack and find the exact bend of the river she had met the fish at before. She only sought the water's edge. This would be enough, she thought, as the fish had insisted that the entire river belonged to her—in all its parts. If that being could not meet Heart here, then how could it even begin to help, when it came to Lark's difficulties?

When she arrived at the bank of the river, the sun had begun its last descent. Golden and rosy, it fell away from the sky, its last parting rays giving light to the stream. Heart searched the water's depths with the last of the day's light.

"Where are you, fish?" she murmured, somewhat afraid she had concocted the entire conversation in an effort to control her own fate and take part in her sister's irrational quest.

No answer came to Heart, and the sun continued to dip downward. Dusk reached out to grasp the river's flow, as Heart's inner timepiece clicked forward. She felt impatient and annoyed by how this all seemed destined to turn out.

And then, the most marvelous thing of all happened. That is, it would have been the most marvelous thing, if Heart had not watched her own sister become a bird so recently. For, as she watched, the fish appeared. And, almost immediately upon her seeing it, it burst before her. With the burst, the fish disappeared amidst an exploding cloak of fog and steaming water.

The entire alarming process was so sudden that had Heart not been holding Lark, she would most certainly have pulled her hands to her face in order to block the gusts of water and light. As it was, she turned to the side and squeezed her eyes shut as tight as possible.

When she dared to look again to the river, Heart found in the place of her glittering fish a gleaming maid, as human as herself and clothed in a long red cloak of fish scales, which stretched from head to foot. The fish-maid smiled, apparently unfazed by Heart's widened eyes.

"I am so glad you asked for help," she said, as she grasped her hands tightly together. "It has been so long since I've seen another in my human form."

The maid's voice was clear, and it reached across the forest air, no longer a sound heard only in Heart's mind. Heart's hands shook, and she tried to calm them so she would not upset Lark where she waited in her grasp.

"What are you?" she choked.

"I am a Guardian," said the being. "But I already told you that."

Heart continued to stare. "Guardian?" she said. "What is that supposed to mean?"

"It means that long ago, when the previous Guardian left this life, I took her place inside the fish. I swim by day. I walk by night. And I wait to help any who might seek my assistance. Once I was merely a maid, like you. Now I have powers to help any who come my way and request my assistance."

"I have never heard of any Guardian," said Heart.

"Yes, the old ways have been lost. They often get lost, I think. Which is why I am usually alone when nightfall comes, no crowd of supplicants ready for my patronage." The fish-maid let out what might have been a young girl's laugh, many long years ago. "It is very lonely, you know. Especially since I see the other Guardians so rarely."

"The other Guardians?"

"There are four of us, and we all reside here in this old, thick forest that came from times before. This forest you have grown inside, and never once realized was meant to be much more, all because time keeps passing. We Guardians are seasonal, you know, our powers accentuated by the changing of the year. You are lucky to find me here in summer, at the height of my influence. So, in addition to my offer of guidance, I can also give you a gift."

Her words kept coming, falling out of her mouth as a waterfall plummets over a cliff, but Heart could not grasp them, or make them carry sense.

"What," she finally managed to say, "could you possibly be talking about? And how is this meant to help my sister or me? I never thought you would be a girl. I never thought you were real."

The girl stepped out of the water, her robe of scales trailing behind her. She laughed as she touched Heart's arm and brushed the robe's hood back from her head. Heart looked into the common face that this action revealed. Simple blue eyes, a turned up nose, and a sprinkling of freckles on her cheeks.

"You're so ordinary," Heart said.

"You will be hard to convince, despite your sister's own change into animal," the fish-maid answered, her eyebrows raised. She linked her arm in the crook of Heart's elbow, and pulled her from the river and further into the darkened woods.

"I have thought about your purpose much since we last met," said the fish-maid. "And I must admit I have not seen this boy your sister seeks. An oddity, when my river is so central to this particular wilderness. Perhaps some spell has carried him past my sight? I would not put it past your witch. Regardless, I know nothing of him or his whereabouts."

Heart trembled at the wet skin of the fish-maid where she held her and concentrated on appearing untroubled. Within her hands, the bird breathed normally, completely unaware of their exotic companion. "Is that what you have to tell me?" Heart asked. "Is that why you asked me to come back and speak with you again?"

"Partly," said the maid. "But in the absence of any truly useful information regarding your quest, I want to offer this instead . . . a knowledge of the Guardians themselves, and the aid each of us might offer you. And my gift, of course."

She dipped her head to Heart, her eyes searching for some recognition of what she'd said.

"I think it important that as your sister seeks her love," said the maid, "you seek each of the Guardians of this forest. Not only may the others know more of your sister's love than I do, but they will also offer you gifts to assist you in any final confrontations you may face. Yours cannot be a simple role of bystander, if good is to conquer. You must feel this deep inside."

The fish dropped Heart's arm and crouched near a large, mis-shapen tree. Its branches reached downward to the forest floor, and the fish-maid bowed beneath them, her arm stretched out before her. Soon enough she bowed outward and stood again. In her hands she now held a loosely wrapped package.

"What is that?" Heart said.

But the girl did not answer her question immediately.

"You know now somewhat of the Guardians, since I have told you. And before I give you this gift, I implore you to search for the others of my kind, along your travels, and to see what they might know of your quest. It is my best and truest advice, as I both desire and am compelled to give."

Heart shook her head, struggling to follow or believe the maid before her. "But how would I find them? How would I do as you say?" she asked. "It's not as if I meant to find you. It's not as if I don't already follow my sister."

"I can help you recognize them on your path. From that you must take hope. With this aid, it is very possible that you might find them."

Heart couldn't help her gut from responding to this strange advice. What did it matter that this maid had been a fish and Heart had seen the girl transform? What did it matter that she made strange claims of powers and even membership in a clan of other similar beings? What did it matter that she spoke of giving much-desired assistance? Heart couldn't help but make a face at what she said, at the limitations that she voiced.

"It is very possible?" she repeated. "You really think I should spend all my spare time searching for these comrades of yours from the corners of my eyes just in case they might know something about my quest? You think I should believe a scale-clad girl that spends her day as fish? You think I should do this, instead of finding another more reasonable avenue for helping my sister?"

"Yes, I do," said the fish-maid, without a blink of her eyes. "The powers of the Guardians are great, even if they are forgotten. You should not let this opportunity slip through your fingers. It could very well make all the difference. Even should you gain only the strength of our gifts, they will still be useful to you in whatever battle you must eventually face."

"And what if my sister should die in the meantime?" Heart asked. "What if this little bird heart of hers gets tired? What if someone shoots her while I seek these Guardians of the forest you speak so confidently about? What if we never find her dearest love?"

"It's true that I would keep her hidden from guns," said the fish-maid, "but other than that, I would not worry too much about her death. Usually an enchantment gives its victim a little time to find release. It is the nature of the balance between good and evil—a side of things the evil never wishes to acknowledge. There must be a chance for her to succeed, you see?"

"No, I do not." Heart gritted her teeth. "In fact, I was entirely unaware there was such a rule book to enchantments."

The fish-maid shook her head. "There is much you do not know, dear Heart. Much that witch of yours does not understand. This forest was built as a protection against the negative encroachment of evil in this land. And though our powers are constrained and hidden, they are much more useful than you would ever imagine. Which is why you must search out the other Guardians. They can help you. Just as I help you now."

Heart wasn't quite sure she wished to follow the fish-maid's logic, or that she agreed the fish-maid even helped her. But she supposed she must play along now that she'd returned here, if only to find out more about the bundle the girl held. If only because she feared this might be the one way to avoid falling before the witch once again. If only because—other than Lark and this maiden—she was all alone.

"What and who must I seek?" she asked then, swallowing her complaints as she would have done for Granny or for Lark in days now past.

"Well, autumn follows summer. Which means you must seek for Autumn next." The fish-maid suddenly looked quite concerned. "Of course, he will be quite difficult to notice."

"And why is that?" said Heart.

"Well," said the maid. "She is an ant, by day. And they are rather small, and troubling to tell apart."

"I must find an ant?" said Heart, disbelief exploding around her once more. "This is your suggestion for my efforts?"

"Yes, you must find her, even if it will be hard. Please understand, Ant is very diligent. She knows much that goes on in our forest. And it is likely she has heard of your sister's love, even if the wanderer has traveled beyond these woods. The network of ants she associates with is large."

Heart did not want to think of how one set out searching for an ant—or a large network of ants— in an attempt to find a missing person, so she left it at that, and moved on to the remaining Guardians.

"And Winter?" she said. "What form does he take?"

The fish-maid pressed her mouth together. She pulled her hood again over her head, veiling her eyes in the shadows of darkness. "He will be most difficult of all to encounter. You see, he barely understands his role as Guardian himself. And in some ways he still fights against his daily imprisonment." The fish-maid squared her shoulders. "Find Ant first; she will help you search out Winter. By then Winter's ways may be more settled, and you can plan how you might reach him best."

"Dare I ask of Spring?" said Heart. "Or is she some buzzing bee who will sting me to death before she discovers what I wish to know?"

Here the fish-maid smiled. "Oh, Spring will find you," she said. "As it always does. After all, you cannot make Spring appear before it wishes."

Heart took a breath and nodded, resigned that she must be content with answers such as these. What else had she expected when she came to seek the wisdom of a fish? What else had she expected on a journey following a bird? Why did she suppose she would find sense and order, or a world that read from left to right?

If only this supposed Ant might speak to her on her own as

the fish had done. It would make the process so much easier. It would make it seem more real and arranged by fate. Still, perhaps these gifts the maiden mentioned truly would help Heart in a future fight against the witch. Perhaps it would make all the difference. Regardless, it was all she had, other than the strange and wind-like words of her lost sister. And the fish was right. She had to do something other than follow Lark and bide her time.

"With that said and understood," said the fish-maid, "I shall give you my gift."

She held the bundle out to Heart, but Heart's hands were full of Lark. Before she could take it, she stepped toward a tree nearby and woke her sister so she might take the tree branch between her tiny birds' feet. She placed her there and stroked her smooth and feathery head.

"Oh, the things I do for you, little Lark," she said. "Look at me, talking to this fish."

Never before had she called her sister *little*. That was the term most often applied to her. After all, Lark had been Heart's caregiver since her birth. She had been the one to guide Heart's steps, not the other way around. How had everything changed so quickly? How had the world flipped upside-down?

Turning from Lark, Heart reached out to the fish-maid. She took the bundle from the girl and unwrapped the gift inside from all its rough-clothed coverings. She draped the hemp-like fabric over her arm to use again later. When she finally held the bundle it'd contained, she could see it was a box.

A simple box, without decoration or color, it had been built of green wood, and cracked slightly as a result. But it held its shape firmly enough, considering the unprepared wood. The box was long in shape, almost twice as long as its height. It could have held an old man's pipe—the long-handled kind, preferred by old and pudgy men. Or it could have held an instrument, one smaller than a flute, but narrow in like manner. The clasp that kept the box shut was the most ornate bit of the whole business. This clasp was filigreed, carved with twirling leaves and vines. Heart moved her hand toward the clasp, wondering what was inside.

"Oh, you must not open it now!" said the fish-maid, her voice sharp and quick. "It is for a time of trouble, when you truly need it. Do not waste it here."

"But what is it?" said Heart, her eyes searching the shadows for the fish-maid's blue ones.

"I cannot tell you that," said the girl. "Only that it is fitting, as a Guardian, that I send it where it will be rightly used. I could not give it up to serve the Guardian's own purposes, but I can give it up for yours."

"Then how will I know what it is?" said Heart. "What does that even mean?" She shook the box, but heard no sound.

"You do not need to know what it is."

"That's ridiculous," Heart said. She looked up from the box again. "How will I know if I need it, if I don't know what it is? The box could be empty, for all I know. And there I'll be, opening it with a grand flourish in the face of an attacking witch, to find absolutely nothing to help my cause."

The fish-maid smiled. "It will not be empty when you need it. I promise you that."

"Where did you get it?" said Heart.

"From the bottom of my river."

"You mean some fool threw this in your river—probably because they didn't need it anymore, probably because they thought it garbage—and you're giving it to me as a magical gift?"

"You should trust a little more," said the fish-maid. "After all, I used to be a fish, and now I am a maid. That is something."

"Perhaps I'm crazy," said Heart smoothly. "Perhaps I have made all of this up. Perhaps you are a figment of my imagination."

"Perhaps," said the fish-maid. "Or perhaps you are lucky. To find me in summer, when I can give you my gift. And yet, it is almost autumn. So, if you do find Ant, you'll get a gift from him as well."

"Lucky?" Heart said, anger washing over her chest like a quick and unheralded storm. "Lucky to have my Granny fallen at the hands of some overzealous witch? Lucky to have my dear sister made a bird before my eyes? Lucky that I hear my sister's voice less and less as time passes, as though the bird would swallow her whole by the time we are through with all this?" Heart took a ragged breath after her long speech. "You call this lucky?"

"Yes," said the fish-maid, still unaffected by Heart's anger. "I do call this lucky. For, despite it all, you have the heart to keep going. Because you are now armed with truth, and with the gift of another. Because there is hope for success. And that is much to feel lucky for, even considering your dismal odds."

Heart lowered her head, not because she agreed, but only because she was too tired to fight the fish-maid's words. She was tired of trying to make this all seem simple and devoid of strangeness.

"Do not be afraid to ask Ant for his gift," said the fish-maid. "He is an ant, and will be loath to give away an item he's stored away for keeping. But he is supposed to give the gift. If you ask him, he will do it."

Heart looked at the fish-maid standing in the forest. Her robe of fish-scales caught the moonlight and flashed it back at Heart. Her face had grown more and more veiled by the night's dark gloom and her cloak. She no longer seemed an ordinary maid.

"And what of you?" said Heart. "What will you do, now that you've given your gift?"

"There are other gifts for other travelers. And until they come, I shall wait here, as I have always done before."

Heart wanted to ask the fish-maid how long she'd been trapped as fish. But the words did not come. She could not bear to think of Lark as a bird forever, and she did not want to know how it had happened to this maid. But the fish-maid seemed to catch her thoughts, despite her.

"I am human in the night, and it is enough. So many years

have passed since the family I knew passed on; it is not as though I could return to them anyway. Besides, I decided to pursue my life path here. This is what I wanted. Do not worry. I believe you will complete your journey successfully. Never fear. It is your task to do. And when tasks come along that are meant for us, we usually find ourselves capable of completing them."

"And your gift will help me with that?" said Heart, almost jokingly, almost in complete disbelief.

The fish-maid narrowed her eyes and pushed her lips together. "My gift will help you save the one you love," she said.

And with those words, she left Heart in the forest glen. She disappeared into the night.

Heppson

Who would have thought that a forest, filled to its topmost branches with every form of life imaginable, could feel so empty? Predator cannot have companion, not in the wild wood, which meant Heppson was alone. What of the awesome power of Guardian in the face of such a solitary existence? Nothing. Nothing at all. Without the whisper of another human in the air, Heppson could not even flex his Guardian powers and attempt to help another. He could not gauge the costs against the gains.

True, a few cottages and thrown-together half-villages graced the woods he lived each drawn-out day inside. If he'd wished, Heppson could have crossed inside their boundaries to find some measure of interaction with humankind. Still, if he went that way, he could only go at night, in human form. And then, such night hours would necessitate the use of a tavern haunt—dark, and smelling of filth and wastefulness. Even there he must carry the hide with him.

What village, though small and dark, welcomes an outsider: dirty and covered with the hide of a bear? What friendship could be built by a traveler who appears only at night, with no purpose or story to claim as his own? Certainly no brotherhood as Heppson had claimed before with Conrad. Meanwhile, he did not dare to search out the other Guardians. Not when he remained so uncertain of who he himself wished to be. As such, Heppson found his prison of solitude complete and all-encompassing, unbreakable within the forest limits.

It happened when the summer days drifted firmly away: time passing, as it always does. The coolness of autumn arrived.

He first saw her bundled form where she curled against the ground, covered by a simple cloak, asleep. Her form lay near the shuttered and fading light of a heap of fire-devoured logs.

Heppson found he could not help but stay to watch her, this human girl he'd discovered deep within his forest. The hours of his time as human silently slipped past him while his gaze took in her, hungry for the kind of life she lived.

A human. A girl. And one quite near his age, it would seem. Sleeping right there, in his empty, mindless forest. As though such an act were normal and of everyday occurrence. As though young girls with long manes the color of flame often traveled alone and slept beside half-collapsed fires.

Captured by the simple, inescapable fact of her existence, captured by her humanity, Heppson paused his aimless night-time wanderings and—almost hypnotized—watched her breathe. He watched her sleep. He watched the embers of her fire as they glowed against her pressed-closed eyes and wrapped-tight self. When morning came—and with it Bear—he managed to make himself slink away, if only because he promised himself he would find her again when night returned, and she slept once more beneath the open air.

He would never have done such a thing before: watch a stranger from the shadows while she slept. Perhaps his sister, Moiria, had chosen to hide from their mother and the world she created, to slink about in her attempts to live a life unnoticed, but Heppson had walked through his prior world with head aloft, as a prince of the kingdom was intended to walk. As though by pretending his will did not cower beneath the Queen's, he could make it so.

Now, things had changed. Now, he was not half himself any-more. The prince he'd been had disappeared, along with all the counterfeit bravery he'd dragged about with him. So when night arrived and Bear detached its hide from skin, Heppson found that those few blessed hours when he could watch another live were the most prized of his day. How could he not stay, even within the shadows, if it meant he might escape his utter loneliness for one brief moment?

Night after night, cross-legged beneath his momentarily detached hide of fur, he sat still and quiet, a few paces from her camp. She would not guess he waited near, a bulge within in the shadows of the night. She would not guess he watched her, and envied her life, her freedom, and her human form.

Each morning, before daylight arrived, Heppson took himself far away. He could not make his trundling burden of Bear keep quiet in the sticks and weeds that surrounded them both. And he did not wish to scare her in the way a bear must always frighten travelers who stumble across its path. Only when night returned would Heppson earnestly slink back on quiet feet, to wait once again outside the glowing ring of fire the girl had built. And before she slept, as she spoke out loud, he could not help but listen to the words she whispered.

Who could blame him if he pretended she spoke to him? Who could blame him if he pretended he was human too?

The first attack came after almost three weeks of nights spent near her fire. Three weeks of listening as she recited half-remembered poems into the flames. Three weeks of watching her roast her meals and thank the squirrels that fed her body with their own. Three weeks of hearing softly spoken memories of a remembered sister and life gone on before. This night, the sun had not yet set, and Heppson still hung several paces back from the girl's camp, anticipating his return to human form, wishing he could shirk his heavy cloak immediately and on demand. He knew she would have finished her meal by now and that she would be hunkered by the waning flames, waiting for sleep. But he could not come too close to her yet. He still waited for the night's arrival.

The attacking wolf, as Heppson saw it in that startlingly clear moment, was strangely alone, unaccompanied by a pack of any sort. The creature smelled differently than other animals of the forest he'd encountered, and Heppson found himself thinking it could not be an ordinary wolf, though his understanding of the puzzle halted there, with greater things at stake. The wolf had not approached the girl's camp yet, but his paws were already bent on a sure path. Heppson saw in its tightly focused eyes what it intended. He gathered its intent for the girl without another second's pause.

What purpose for Guardian—for Bear—if Heppson could not protect her now? What purpose for his claws, if not to tear the wolf's throat before it tore hers? This was a task he was meant and prepared to take on as his own. Without waiting for the wolf to tread closer to the girl's camp, without waiting for her to discover her own danger, without allowing night to bring his human form, Heppson attacked. Bear's claws and teeth ripped outward.

How easy he found it to end the creature's life, once he'd decided to move. Heppson found the fight with wolf not much different in feeling than the hunts he and Conrad had taken part in as they grew to men, though his success as Bear felt more assured, more rightful. There was a hunger inside of him that demanded to be fed. This was no game. This wolf would not harm the girl while he watched her camp. She would never even know it came.

Just as she did not know a bear chased her tracks and watched her camp as regularly as the moon.

When all was finished, the wolf lay at an angle, its neck broken from the shaking Bear had done. Blood had pooled and matted in the fur about Bear's snout; a witness to the acts of violence he had only just completed. Heppson's breath heaved with the exertion of the battle.

Convinced his work was done, and that no other predators lingered near, Heppson dropped to all fours and abandoned the wolf to the forest floor and the critters hidden in it. He moved away from the battle and toward the girl's fire, intent on ensuring she was completely safe. He no longer wished to think of the wolf, or what he might have wanted, for the sun had begun its final descent.

Unfortunately, separating mind from Bear took longer than

usual that night. When the sun sunk downward the Bearskin loosened on Heppson's back as it always did, but it took effort to release his mind completely from the grasp of Bear, from the hunt, and from his necessary awareness of every subtle movement in the woods. It took hours before Heppson became completely human again.

Only when the change was complete could Heppson untangle the truth: that engaging in his fight as Bear had welded the two of them more closely together. That by taking on Bear's powers and abilities, he had become, for that moment, more Bear than himself. This then must be the way the other Bears slowly became more animal than man. The way they trod the path toward their eventual hibernation and sleep.

But it had to have been worth it, in the end. To save the girl. He knew he would choose such a thing again, if it were required of him. Heppson crouched beneath his bloodstained pelt and stared toward the girl's fire—his eyes trapped by the burnished copper of her hair, by the slow and steady movements she made to stir up the flames before her.

She sat up late this night, considering how long it had taken to settle himself following the wolf's interference. Normally, she would have slept by now. But autumn had left enough dead leaves and fallen branches for her fire to be strong, and tonight the girl had made the structure tall. Perhaps she'd feared for her safety that particular evening? Perhaps she'd guessed at danger's reaching hand?

As Heppson's awareness returned, as his mind began again to track the words she said and tie them down to meaning, he realized in surprise that she railed at those shooting flames. At first he found it difficult to pick out all her words—to escape Bear's thoughts of dangerous beasts and a thirst for domination—but when comprehension did finally dawn, Heppson almost laughed with the absurdity of how much he agreed with his new charge's words, even considering the task which he'd just finished.

"Stupid Guardians," the girl shouted, as she threw a loose stick into her flames. "Stupid. Irritating. Useless. Guardians."

The branches sparked and tumbled where her projectile hit.

"What use are you to anyone," she said, "if you can't be found? 'Find an ant,' she says. Find an ant? I've probably stepped on the creature by now."

Reaching to her side, she threw another branch onto the fire.

"What am I thinking," she said, wrapping her hands tightly about her middle, "wasting my time with this ridiculous task? I should give up, I should try something else. Anything else. I will run out of time. I will lose her. Or that witch will come back, and I'll have nothing to use in a fight."

At these last words, the girl dropped her head into her hands, her shoulders heaving in the manner of gulped breath. Concerned, and even more interested now that she had mentioned Guardians, Heppson wrapped his pelt closely around his back and moved with practiced tread closer to the girl's camp.

When he had halved the distance between them, he stopped and dropped low once again. He crouched behind a large tree, his Bearskin and the dark shielding him from accidental discovery. He could see and hear the girl much more easily from this vantage point, even if he had snuck much closer than he'd dared before.

The girl continued in her silence. While he waited for her to speak again, Heppson's eyes were drawn upward to a branch above her. Here, he noted a speckled white bird which almost glowed in the moonlight where it perched. It had tucked its head into its feathers and apparently gone to roost for the nighttime hours. The yelling below obviously meant nothing to this animal, for it never stirred with all the girl's rage or stick throwing.

Strange that the creature should choose a site so near a loud and noisy human being for its night's rest. How unlike the ordinary actions of the forest animals Heppson had grown used to over the past several months. They startled at the slightest whisper of his paws upon the ground.

Suddenly, the girl's words broke the silence again, and Heppson's gaze returned to her, his thoughts leaving the bird behind.

"Now Lark has grown completely mute," she said, "with no help to offer me at all. I am all alone, and I have failed."

Heppson's brow lowered at her words. What did she mean? And what could it possibly have to do with himself or the other three of his kind?

"I must accept the fact," the girl said then, almost in a whisper, "that I cannot find this ant. It is impossible. It is a waste of energy and effort."

Heppson's mind gathered and rearranged all she had said, and then, amazingly, it leaped. He struck finally upon some meaning to her words, putting together the pieces of what she said. Guardians. An ant. Her search. As she went silent again, her shoulders curved forward in desperate upset, he found himself wanting to step forward, to ask her more, to verify that what he thought was true. She sought for Guardians? She sought for Ant?

But I can find the Ant, he thought mechanically.

Of course, it took him a moment to realize this was fact. To realize that, as Guardian, he felt a constant pull toward the Ant—as he did to all the other seasons. That while he could not name a location or offer the girl turn by turn directions, he could heed the pull of his bond with Ant and travel toward him.

And since Ant lived within these woods—the only boundary given for his bear-shod feet—he could easily take this girl there if he wished. He could easily follow those pulls and find the Ant she sought.

What would it feel like to join this girl and make himself a companion to her travels, instead of an unknown drifter clinging to her wake? Heppson did not want to acknowledge the satisfaction such a thought gave him, knowing that it could never be done as he would have done it once before. No, if he meant to help the girl, Heppson felt certain it must be as Bear. Not only was it a

Guardian's purpose to help others, but his disguise as Bear would also prevent any unanswerable questions. If he determined to do this, Heppson could give the girl no clue of his ability to take on human form.

Besides, what would a strange young man say, arrived at a girl's fire? How could his sudden appearance as Heppson fail to frighten her? Not to mention his necessary disappearance when a new day began? How could he convince her of the knowledge he held as an ordinary man, dirty and carrying an old fur?

Look over there. I see an Ant. Just thought you might be interested?"

The possibilities of such a conversation were completely insupportable. It had been so long since he met another as a human. He could not think how to do it again, especially not with her. At least as Bear the girl would assume Heppson could not explain the path he forced her to take. She would not think it possible to argue with the path he pressed her to follow.

Which meant all he needed to do to further help her was to wait until morning. To wait as her fire burned down. To wait as she finally fell into restless sleep. To wait for the sun to rise and for his furry pelt to melt against his skin.

Only then, when Bear came, when the sun rose and human form disappeared inside the pelt, would he join her camp. It had felt right to vanquish the wolf. It would feel right to do this as well. Winter. Bear. Heppson. All three of them would act.

Heart

One shouldn't scream at bears. Heart knew this. But never did she think to find one hovering over her as though it wished only for its dinner to wake and look it in the eye before it feasted. Heart's screams at the confounding sight pierced the air and shook Lark up to the sky in confusion. The bird's wings beat both fast and hard as she startled from her roost and winged away into the distance. Which meant that Heart's next yells were for her fleeing sister.

"Lark," she shouted, not caring what a bear might think of such an outburst.

But the bird was already gone. Heart reached toward the sky despite the danger, but she could not fly. She could not leap into the sky and bring her escaping sister back. In fact, she could not even stand and give her chase upon the two feet left to her. Not with a bear hanging over her and eyeing every movement she made, his dark and muddy coat filling her sight. But at least she marked a feather fall when Lark took flight, and she knew: if she could find it upon the ground, if she could follow its direction, if she could live beyond the bear, she might find her sister again.

Perhaps, she thought wildly, shutting her mouth from the screams, her mind grasping at any straw available, *perhaps this bear might even speak. Perhaps he could be made to understand.*

It was not as though the thought of talking animals felt strange to Heart anymore. After all, she was overrun with talking animals, when it came right down to it. Why couldn't this lumbering animal, with his hot heavy breaths puff-puffing against her face, be one that spoke?

"What do you want?" she ventured, her voice barely crossing the distance between them, bound as it was by her fear.

But the bear did not move.

"Do you speak?" she said, and then she faltered before

continuing. "Are you truly a human, trapped as a bear? Is this some masquerade you're playing?"

Her words sounded downright absurd, even to her, as the bear remained motionless and unheeding. As any normal, flesh-and-blood, human-eating bear would. And yet, the creature had not moved in for the kill, he had not sought to tear her skin apart with razor claws or teeth.

Willing to try anything, Heart slowly pushed her way back-ward. She slid from beneath the bear, and came to a sitting position. Then, magnetically drawn to the only thing that connected her to Lark, she slowly angled sideways so she might inch toward the feather. Her eyes remained on the beast, calculating whether he meant to move at any point and continue his efforts to devour her. Maybe he would just let her leave, if she went slowly enough and gave it no fright.

Becoming more courageous as the bear remained still, Heart shuffled forward on all fours, her arm stretched toward Lark's clue to where she fled. She must have the feather. What would she do without the feather? The feather meant everything. It *was* her sister, in so many respects.

Still, inside her mind, trampling along beside the thoughts of Lark, a fearful question darted to and fro, over and over again. Unable to settle or subdue the energy that pumped inside her veins, the query spun around inside Heart's consciousness. Again and again, it threw itself at her, refusing to disappear.

For what would she do if the bear decided to eat her?

But no! Granny had always said to think only of the problem at hand, to leave the others until they forced you to carry them along. She had said it did no good to fear for what you could not change, which meant that until the bear whipped his teeth into her flesh, Heart could not waste her time with worry over how it might feel when he slashed apart her life. No, she would only worry about the feather. She would only worry about Lark.

When she finally reached the feather, finally saw it resting carelessly upon the forest floor, she reached outward and took the shaft into her palm. Breaking her sight from the bear, she looked down and made sure to note the direction her feather pointed. Her link to Lark regained, Heart breathed out quickly at the relief that came from having solved her first problem. In her mind, as she always did, she trained a compass in the direction it identified.

Northeast, she thought. *We travel northeast.*

If only she could leave the bear. If only she could avoid being eaten.

The bear remained motionless where he had stood since she woke. He did not attack, but only watched her movements warily, his eyes shifting with her every movement. Perhaps this was a place of his, this bit of forest floor. Perhaps he wished to sun himself or eat some berries growing nearby. Perhaps he only wished Heart to leave. To leave and go about her day. To take her feather and her supplies, and disappear forever. This, of course, she was more than willing to do. Haltingly, Heart came to her feet.

The bear watched.

Bending to the side, Heart gathered her things from where she'd left them while she slept. If she left them here, it would not take a bear to kill her. The upcoming chill of winter. The loss of flint for fire and knife for food. The disappearance of cloak and blanket, which she had filched from a cottage she'd passed when it grew cooler. And, of course, the box she'd received from the fish. She could not turn her tail and run without gathering her supplies first. She knew better. She needed all she carried.

And since the bear, for some odd reason, was content to stand and watch her movements, she kept to her hesitant steps and snatched at the things for her bag. She tried to slow the beating tumult of her heart, tried to stop imagining the beast's teeth against her bones.

Northeast, she repeated in her mind, the word like a mantra with its repetition.

The direction was all that mattered. The direction and leaving this bear behind. Within a few minutes, even with her sloth-like steps, Heart had gathered all her things in her arms. She checked to be sure of her feathers, and then slid her footsteps backward, her eyes upon the bear. All she wanted was to leave this place. Was that too much to ask?

She pushed her way backward once more. Her heels pressed into the more dense foliage of the forest. She wondered when she should run. Should she wait until those eyes no longer trained themselves on hers? Would they ever move away and leave her to escape? For an animal that did not speak, his eyes seemed so aware of all she did.

It was then, in this last moment of consideration, that the bear finally moved. He picked up his heavy feet and lumbered toward Heart with pressing intent. He advanced, lifting and placing paw by massive paw as he came forward. His nose came closer to hers, where she had suddenly turned to stone. On all fours, he stood at almost her same height. Once again she felt his breath puff warm and heavy on her cheek. In and out, in and out.

A shiver began at Heart's head and traveled down her back. Her knees began to buckle, but she frantically pulled them tight.

Running is most certainly not an option now! she thought, her mind snapping backward at her fool-headed efforts to flee.

For now she did not dare move, but imagined instead the crunching and snapping of the bear's jaws, the death that would come to her while Lark flapped her wings farther and farther from her side. She tried, once again, not to think of her own blood spilling on the ground. But what was left here to imagine other than that final scene?

Her foot slid backward in renewed fear at the possibilities. But this movement was apparently unacceptable, for the bear stepped forward again, this time with a larger step than hers, a step that only brought him nearer. The beast was close—oh, so close. His shoulders were wider than her frame, and she dared not think of his massiveness should he choose to stand. She was small, and he seemed to be a larger bear than any she had seen before. What could he possibly want besides tearing her up into bits? What other purpose would he have for stalking her so closely?

Then, suddenly, the bear's snout angled upward into her face. His eyes—not human, but focused in such an un-animal-like way—bored meaningfully into hers. When he was apparently convinced she watched him closely enough, the bear began to shake his head side-to-side, side-to-side, until finally his nose pointed to the west. It took another step, and came to the side of Heart. It came between her and any possible path that went northeast, toward her sister. It leaned toward her frame, its bristling pelt inching inward to her skin.

And Heart stepped sideways to avoid his touch. Sideways. To the west. And away from Lark.

She'd not expected the loss of ground, and when she realized what she'd done, she went to move toward Lark's path again. But the bear stood in her way, its paws and claws a threat she could not easily dismiss. Then, it moved in closer, and leaned toward her yet again. Heart stepped sideways.

"No!" she cried, and leaned back to the place where she'd just stood.

But the bear had already moved into that spot. Not only that, it had begun to lean again, and now—despite the insanity of it, despite the sense she should have had—Heart tried to hold her ground. Against a bear? Against its size, and teeth—so sharp? Against its evident desire that she walk west? This, she tried to do?

But why should a bear concern itself with where she traveled? She could understand if it ate her, if it crushed her form between its jaws to find its dinner, but why should it care to push her westward? Why should it care which path she took? Yet over and over, the beast leaned into Heart again. Pushing, prodding, coming so close she could do nothing but step where it wished, or find herself pressed up against a wild bear.

Away, and away, and away. Away from her dear Lark. Heart looked beyond the path, looked beyond the bear, looked to where her sister had flown, and then, no matter how her soul broke inside her at the thought, she walked where the bear bade her walk. Step after step, she walked.

Moiria

The soldier had failed. The sister's heart still beat. As did the Lark's. Thump, thump, thump. Life pumping onward. Moiria growled in frustration and swept her mother's books from the table and onto the floor. They clattered to the ground, a loud reminder of how little she had managed to accomplish. The King demanded Conrad show his face. He demanded. Well, what was to be done when that blasted bird simply would not die?

Sure, she had sent another assault of soldiers. Three of them this time. Three wolves with fangs meant to rip apart the protection she had mistakenly given the bird. But it was not enough. It would not be quick enough. Not after what had happened today. Not after the King appeared, shaven and well dressed, to make his appeals to the court. Not now that the councils required Conrad of her as well. They had finally dared to step beyond the curtains to join the King's cause. And soon enough they would gather the people to stand behind them.

Moiria gripped her hands on the table, her fingernails digging into the wood. What was to be done? She couldn't give in. If she allowed them to take back the throne, to take back the governance of the land, then they would kill her. It didn't matter the charges, she knew some evidence would be found. She would be made to bear the weight of all her mother's evil, as well as her own. Her life would end. She had been the only one not to disappear, and that would be proof enough of her guilt.

"I will have to bring him back," she whispered to the emptiness around her. "At least it will buy me more time."

Moiria lifted her head and lowered her shoulders. She took a deep breath and calmed the racing of her heart. She had sent the wolves early this morning. They would kill the sister. How could they not? One solitary maid could not think to fight such a fearsome foe. And soon enough the bird would be dead as well, freeing Moiria to return to her original plans. Freeing her to use Conrad as the pawn he was always meant to be.

Meanwhile, she would gather Conrad from her mother's cottage. She would bring him here—overwhelming amnesia and all. She would show him to the King, blame his weakness on her mother, and insist that she could cure him of it all. She would become a servant of the King, seemingly bowing to his will as she prepared her further plans. No one would harm her. They would need her knowledge to help Conrad recover.

Moiria straightened herself completely and wiped her sweating palms down the length of her gown. She kicked at her mother's books where they stood in her path.

"I will bring him here," she said to the empty room, knowing her heart spoke to her mother, and the pulsing of the knife. Knowing she spoke to that witch who would never have found herself in this horrible mess. "I will bring Conrad here only because I wish it. And soon enough, I will have everything I want, everything I need. Soon enough, I will be safe."

Heppson

There was, of course, the problem of the night. When evening threatened its approach, Heppson realized he must make the girl fear him somewhat if he expected her to stay and make camp where he left her. He had already decided he would not guard her as his human self. He did not feel he could make those sort of explanations. Still, he could not chase her down each morning if she chose to run away in his absence. They would never reach Ant with those kinds of setbacks to fight. Which meant that boundaries must be set, boundaries necessarily born of fear.

He began by leaving her in a clearing and backing away from her sight. With a low menacing growl, he disappeared backward into the foliage. And then he waited, for he knew she would make the attempt. When it came, when she darted into the trees, feet flying and arms flailing at the branches around her, he bounded after her. He opened his mouth to the bear sounds that signaled attack. He batted her sideways with a paw, driving her form into the ground as gently as he could. She did not rise once she had fallen, but stared at him, her mouth open, her breath rapidly moving her ribcage up and down.

Heppson closed his jaw and hid the teeth, which frightened her so. Once she rose from the ground, he guided her to the clearing where it had all begun. Then he backed away, retreating from her sight again. Of course, he knew she would try once more. And he knew he would have to drag her back when she did so. He only hoped she would lose her desire to run before the sun dropped completely downward. Before his form became a man's, and his hands were tied into inaction.

He'd found that being kidnapped by a bear had produced a wary silence in the girl. A silence very different from the running monologue he had grown used to overhearing at her fire. Even with one small day behind them, Heppson regretted this silence. Regretted the loss of fiery courage that came the more he cowed her into submission. After all, he did not wish to harm her. He did not wish to scare her. But he meant to help her find her Ant, and this was the way he had determined to do it. It was what he had to offer. It was what he had to give, considering his existence as Bear.

"You know," she finally hissed, when he'd pulled her back the fourth time, when the sun's last rays barely held his pelt together with his skin. "It is very wrong to abduct strange lasses in the woods." Her word choice did not veil her tone, and Heppson felt acutely the anger she directed toward him.

"Where are you taking me," she said, more raggedly, as her breath heaved in and out, "that it matters so little where I wish to go?" The girl's voice broke sharply with those words, and she pulled in a loud and choppy breath. She sagged into the ground.

And this time Heppson knew she would not run. He saw the broken spirit she carried within her breast. After all, he had seen that look often before, when his mother was nearby. That look that meant the fight had gone, to leave only defeat. With her this way, it would be easy for him to leave her to the night. He would watch her from afar, and he would not fear that she might run. He had frightened her enough.

And with days of this repeated, it became an ordinary part of their travels together. His leaving her to a nighttime camp, her waiting for his return in the morning. Eventually it became so regular she had regained a bit of her prior dignity. She'd stand waiting for him, her pack gathered and ready, her fire banked and covered with dirt. And they would continue, walking onward the way he chose.

One day she glared at Bear as he entered the clearing, apparently unsurprised to see him there, though equally and obviously unimpressed.

"And so you are back," she said, "to continue your herding. May I dare ask why we travel as we do? Westward always? Perhaps another direction would suit me better. Did you ever think of that?"

Heppson stared blandly at the girl, his bear eyes undeviating in their lack of response. He must appear as a primarily dumb animal, unable to communicate or give the explanation that she sought. He would wait here as long as it took for her to accept that reality, to accept his inability to give her any answer to her words.

Finally, the girl sighed, her shoulders caving downward with desperation. Convinced she was defeated by his silence, Heppson advanced again toward his new companion. Arriving at her side, he nudged his nose into her side. He was ready to begin their journey for the day, and he must get her walking.

The girl no longer shuddered visibly at his touch, a fact that both heartened Heppson and absolved him of a small portion of his guilt. He may have frightened her enough to keep her with him, but she obviously no longer believed he would eat her at any given moment, which meant he could guide her movement with a gentle touch, instead of with Bear's roaring or bared teeth. And so he pushed at her frozen form, forcing her onward in movement yet again.

"West, west, west," said the girl, quiet this time. "Always we go west."

Heppson pressed his snout into her side more firmly, as though to emphasize words he had not spoken.

"Yes, I know," she said. "I'm going. Although I did have my own plans, before you took me prisoner. I had a companion I preferred to your hairy demanding self."

Heppson hesitated slightly at her words, but stifled the pause as quickly as possible. He did not wish her to guess he understood. He did not want her to count on any comprehension from the beast he allowed her to see. And so he shoved her again, hoping she would tell him more as they walked, but not allowing himself to ask.

"There was a bird I traveled with," said the girl, her voice accusing. "And I am very sorry to have lost her with your persistent efforts at leading me astray." The girl reached out to press a branch away from their path. She ducked her head slightly, and sighed. "I was meant to stay with that bird. I was meant to follow her."

Heppson nudged his way through the undergrowth, his nose tipping downward. He'd noticed the bird she spoke about, of course, perched above her fire. But he'd not thought at all of the feathered creature when he made his plans. He'd not noticed that she mattered to the girl, or that they were meant to stay together. Silly, really. He'd been taught to be more aware than that. He'd been taught to consider his surroundings. But when he'd found the girl, she'd been all he could see. The bird had slipped to the bottom of his consciousness. As unimportant as withered leaves beneath his feet.

"Now I have no idea where the bird has flown. Now I am lost," said the girl.

She paused in her advance, one hand coming to her brow, her other hand clasped onto her side. Heppson turned to look at her, this girl he had meant to help in her search for an ant. How many times had he watched her at night? The fire lighting her hair and making it its own. How many times had he wished to be the prince he'd been before? To speak to her as a boy would to a girl. Now he realized that in all his imagining, in all his pondering, he had missed what really mattered. And to think that it had been a bird. A fairly nondescript and forgettable bird, as far as he remembered.

The girl dropped both hands to her sides, her eyes wide, her voice trembling. "She flew away," she said. "She flew away from me without a backward glance. And she's not coming back. She's not searching for me, as I would search for her if I had my freedom. What will I do? My Lark is gone!"

Why would she care so deeply for some creature that had flown of its own accord, and left her far behind? Why would it matter when before she had only spoken of finding the ant?

But before he could finish his thought entirely, Heppson

caught movement in his peripheral vision. His mind jumped rapidly with animal instinct—only slightly tempered by his human heart—and Heppson threw the girl roughly to the ground, batting her soundly from the side with his massive front paw.

The girl's mouth opened as she fell, and an incomprehensible and half-finished scream spilled brokenly outward. Any words of complaint, which she might have spoken, were trapped by the dirt, which now cradled her head. He watched her push upward on one hand, but she quickly dropped down again, disoriented. Haltingly, she rolled to her side, and pulled her legs inward, the action instinctual for one who feared a bear's advance.

"Now you are going to eat me," she murmured, her gaze falling sideways in apparent dizziness and confusion.

But Heppson's eyes lifted from where she'd fallen, leaving her to herself. He heaved his massive frame until he stood tall and resolute above her fallen form. He was full of barely bridled energy, his hind legs pushed into the dirt, ready for an attack he felt but could not yet see.

At least the sun stood high above them both. At least his bear pelt wrapped him close, so he could fight the creatures that lurked only paces away, hidden in the foliage of the trees. They had come for her; he could tell. Their wolf eyes trained themselves on the girl, their tongues lagged out in breathless hunger for her blood. They did not know they faced a Guardian.

When they attacked, Heppson's paws fell swift and heavy. His teeth tore sharp and quick. His lumbering form moved quickly—more quickly than he would have thought possible—as he worked to keep the wolves' dancing frames from reaching where the girl had fallen. One wolf flipped backward awkwardly to the ground, its legs no longer pressing an advance.

In his mind, while grasping at the neck of another beast, Heppson trembled, fearful he had hit the girl too hard when he forced her to the ground and out of the fight. She had not been able to rise afterward, and he hated his strength for what it might have done to her. He hoped she was not hurt, and wondered, as he snapped his jaws, at this strange attack of wolves he faced as her protector.

For even now, injured, missing two of its throttled companions, and faced with sure defeat, the remaining wolf continued to strike out against Bear. But why? Why would any of these wolves attack prey so near a bear? Why would they risk such a fight when there were plenty of other choices running about the forest?

Why did they want her so?

Heppson's paws continued to swing, unbothered by his inattentive thoughts. Left and right, left and right. His claws raked across the beast that thrust its way toward him. His teeth raged outward, swiping for a handle of flesh, for a grip on bristled fur. Still, the wolf came forward. It never ran. It never slunk away or admitted defeat. And so, Heppson fought and fought. He fought until, at last, he'd killed the wolf. Until all three of them lay lifeless on the forest floor beneath his feet.

Dropping to all fours, Heppson's breath heaved in and out. A taste of tainted blood trickled down his throat. There had been more to these wolves than met the eye. These wolves that would not give up on their attack. No, he did not need to be a Guardian to understand that. And if he had not been here to beat them back, he was certain the girl would be dead by now, if not from them, then from the prior attack.

One wolf, in the beginning. And then a bird left far behind. Now another three wolves had sought the girl's throat. There was so much Heppson had not understood when he watched the girl by the fire. So much he had not thought to question. Now he served as her protector, though from what he could not dare to guess.

It would be so easy to ask her and gain the particulars of her strange and dangerous situation. But he could not take that path. He had pledged to remain Bear to her, to keep his words and human self far hidden from her gaze. Which meant he would have to pay careful attention to all she said and did, if he meant to make sense of the girl and the world she carried with her, if he meant to protect her at all.

Which he most certainly did.

Heart

A bruise ached along her middle from where the bear had swiped at her, though she found she did not mind. Despite the terror, despite the confusion, she had heard the jagged, ripping sounds of the bear against the wolves. And now, when it was over, and she had finally managed to sit, she saw the evidence of the wolves' attack on his bleeding hide. With such proof borne into the bear's flesh, she was more than happy to cradle her purple side.

He'd been hurt by the attack. He'd stood over the three dead wolves, as her jostled mind came slowly back to her. He'd panted as blood dripped from his face and into the dirt at his feet. Some from them, and some from him. She realized then, that she'd never touched the bear by her own choice before. Only been nudged and prodded and wrangled into submission. But after watching him fight, after watching him save her from those beasts, she knew she must reach toward him.

Picking herself up, and clumsily ripping a stretch of fabric from her underskirt, Heart moved toward the bear. Cautious. Slow. He winced when she first touched him. Winced when she pressed against the welling gashes on his back-most legs. It seemed an odd thing to do, especially to her. Certainly a bear doesn't normally obtain doctoring following a fight. But she did it anyway, until the cloth was soaked, and she could do it no more.

"Thank you, Bear," she said then, and patted his sweaty hide.

She let herself lean against him for a moment, afraid she might fall once more into the ground. But soon she'd recovered herself, and the two of them, with unspoken communication, moved onward—both ready to leave the wolves where they had fallen.

From her youth, Heart had been taught to never let a useful meal go un-gathered. But she did not harvest any meat from those wolves who'd tried to eat her. Their unnatural persistence against the bear disturbed her. Something in it all reminded her of the witch who'd changed her sister to a bird. A thought that troubled her more than she cared to admit.

Before the sun had even traveled another hour's path, Heart and the bear reached a bend of the forest's river. Here the bear allowed her to stop, apparently aware of the tremors which still traveled up and down Heart's legs and spine. Leaving her on land, the bear moved into the water unhurriedly, letting its flow wipe the remains of the morning from his hide. Heart also washed her hands at the bank, and pink bled from them both downward through the river. Before her, Heart watched the bear hang his head. Fatigue balanced on his shoulders. He had been shaken by the wolves as much as she.

Heart stood and moved backward from the bank. "I will make a fire here," she said. "We both will rest for the remainder of this day."

Of course, it was true that when she saw the weary bear hang down his head, Heart thought of running. Perhaps now, after the bear's awful fight, she might be able to escape and seek for Lark once more. Perhaps now she might be allowed to disappear, and leave the huge beast's side. But how could she leave, after what he had done for her today? He had saved her from those wolves, for some reason unknown. And so she stayed. Besides, there might be more beasts thirsty for her blood.

She built the fire, and Bear watched her from the river. Heart wondered, as his eyes followed her movements, if he would stay within the ring of light her flames created when the sunk sank beneath the horizon. Or if he would leave, as he'd done all the nights before, after she gave up on her escape.

She found she wished that he might stay. It did not hurt her to admit she was afraid, not after the morning she had faced. Yes, she was afraid. Of wolves, and whatever else might wish to eat her in the night. Who wouldn't be?

But as the sun began to lower itself, taking refuge in another world for the hours of night, Heart watched the bear move backward from her camp.

"You're going then?" she said, but of course he didn't answer. And of course she couldn't make him stay. What was she to the might of a bear?

Once he'd left, Heart found she could not keep still. She could not make her camp, and fall to sleep, and let the day brush past her like a shadow. No, like a nettle caught between two folds of fabric, thoughts of the wolves grated up and down through her mind. Unwilling to be forgotten. Unwilling to be left behind.

Finally, no matter the idiocy of such an action, Heart left her fire's safety. She carried a stick full of flame for light and for protection, as feeble as it seemed. Moving slowly, she traced her way backward to where they had left the wolves' empty, lifeless forms. Her feet tugged at vines and branches along the way, but she did not trip or fall. She was a forest lass, after all, even if she was foolhardy.

She wished it had surprised her, what she saw when she arrived. She wished she'd truly thought to find three dead and rotting wolf carcasses awaiting her in the woods. But she found she could not gasp with surprise at the human soldiers lying on the forest floor. She couldn't say she hadn't fully expected to find them. After all, was she not clearly aware of the witch's propensity to turn her captives into animals? And did she doubt that evil one would try to stop her in her quest to help dear Lark?

The lifeless forms lying mangled in the dirt were boys not much older than Heart. Each of them wore a soldier's garb. Each of them bore the wounds of an attack inflicted by a bear. Had they wanted to kill her? Had they wanted it really? Or had they merely been bent to follow the witch's command? Killed by a bear they did not truly wish to fight. Heart could not bring herself to want to know more. She could not bring herself to wonder what innocence had been lost in the fight for her protection that morning.

She only knew they had come, and that they'd wanted her, not Lark. Which meant the witch was after her as well. Which meant she'd been marked. Heart turned from the bodies before her, flung herself into the trees she'd only emerged from moments before. She must find her fire. She must wait for the bear. For she could not stand to be alone.

It took hours to wipe the images of the bodies from her mind, and when she finally slept, morning was only breaths away. After the restless night, and when she woke, she found her Bear waiting. He watched her, patient for her eyes to open. He lay on his belly beside her, his head dropped between his front-most paws.

Heart took a deep breath at the sight of him. Perhaps he had taken her from Lark, but the wolves would have done the same—in a much more drastic way. Perhaps her Bear had come to help her. Perhaps they'd make things right together, as a team.

Lark had been gone so long, and Heart was so lonely at her loss. Gone first to the wanderer who'd taken her heart. Gone next to the bird that had taken her body. Perhaps the problem would mend more quickly with this bear, who actually cared if Heart breathed in and out for a new day.

Heart rose and prepared for their departure. She ate old roots she'd gathered weeks before; roots she'd kept within her pack. She stamped out her fire and washed its remains away with water pulled from the stream. She did not wish to stay here any longer than necessary.

When she'd finished all she could, she walked toward her Bear. He rose from where he'd waited on the ground. Heart remembered his true standing height as he fought the wolves the day before. So massive and so angry as he fought against his foes. She looked at him closely to see how his gashes fared with a night between him and the fight, but she could not find the marks of his last battle. His heavy fur obscured them completely, and the stream had long ago washed away the blood.

"I'm sorry I don't understand you," she said, "or why you've taken me. I still can't guess your purpose in dragging me on through the forest. But if you had not been near yesterday, I would be dead. And for that reason, I must trust you."

By this point, Heart had given up on his understanding her. Throughout their time together, he had merely watched her words with his eyes. After all, he was only a bear—ordinary in every way except his herding her. But she spoke to him now anyway, feeling a need to state her purpose, to let him know what had changed when he'd fought her fight.

"I'll go with you now," she said. "I believe you mean to help me with my task."

And then, as she watched, the Bear dipped his head. Down and up. Down and up. As though nodding in agreement with her words. His eyes were steely and strong, trained on her face with force, trained on her face with meaning. And she knew he understood. Her Bear. Taking in her words.

As this realization came, the Bear moved toward Heart and closed the gap between them. He nudged at her hands with his nose, brought them up to touch his thick fur. Her hand ran along his nose, over his head, and up to his shoulders. It was the second time she had touched the bear of her own volition. And she did not shake. They were partners now, friends against the grasping of the witch.

Her Bear leaned toward her again, and now it was she who understood.

"You want me to climb your back?" she said.

Bear bent forward to his paws, closer to the ground. Heart grasped his fur between her hands, tightened her hold and pulled herself upward to sit atop her Bear. Awkward and uncertain, she attempted to settle herself onto his wide and muscled back. She wrapped her hands more tightly in his hide, and leaned down into his hulking and warm form.

"I'm ready," she said, as she felt him prepare to spring forward. And she was.

Moiria

Conrad did not recognize his father, even when the old man wept upon his feet. The witch's curse had been powerful, and it remained unyielding despite Conrad's return to loved ones and familiar sights. Moiria was not surprised by his lack of improvement. Perhaps the Queen's other curses had begun to fray and fall to pieces, but this particular vendetta had been sealed with the witch's last breath of life. It would not be easy to circumvent, should Moiria even care to do so.

Before her, Conrad stood above the King, confused and unsettled by the turn of events. His eyes flickered between his father's head and Moiria's silent form, almost as though he expected her to make sense of the situation. The only other occupant in this abandoned room of the castle, its location specifically chosen for its remote and uninhabited location, Moiria stared at the two of them without concern. She remained silent, distant, and untouched. She might be playing at mediator here, but it was not her true purpose to bring the two to rights. She would not provide Conrad any explanation, no matter how earnestly he asked.

True, Conrad had lost himself in her defense, those many months before when her mother had meant to end her life. True, he had borne the brunt of a curse meant for Moiria's mind and protected her from a horrible demise. But that had happened so very long ago. Before her hand was forced to inflict pain. Before she'd given up on overcoming all her mother's wishes. She could not think about his sacrifice, not now.

The King, his tears apparently spent, finally looked to where Moiria waited. "He does not know me," he said.

"I told you it would be so," answered Moiria. "I told you time and time again. That is why I insisted on bringing you here to see him, away from the court and their troublesome eyes. They would never accept him as your heir if they saw him so befuddled and useless as this."

"You mean to say they would blame you for his sickness. That is why you've kept his return a secret."

"Perhaps I mean both," said Moiria. "The point is he does nothing for either of us, as he is."

The King shuddered at her words. "And why should I not have you locked away? Why should I not call my guards and let them see what he has become? Why should I not blame you for this all?"

"Because what will you have then? A damaged heir? I tell you I have nothing to do with the state he is in, and you have no choice but to believe me. After all, I brought him back to you. That should buy my own life, I think. And as for circumventing my mother's curses, you must give me time to make any changes in his current state. You must pull back pressure on me and let me try to heal his mind."

"Why would I give my son to your care?" said the King. "I do not trust you."

Moiria walked toward Conrad. She pressed his waiting form into the chair where he had sat before the old King entered. Her control of him reiterated, she turned back to the King. "That you have made perfectly clear," she said. "But I am your only hope to get him back. I am the only link you have to the old Queen and her dark ways."

"My own physicians might . . ."

"Your own physicians could not make head or tail of what has been done to him, and you know it. You cannot even comprehend what has happened to you over the past many years, let alone depend on other mindless drones in this kingdom to solve this particular problem."

"I still cannot believe you will help me, whatever your fancy arguments. And what of Heppson? What has been done with him?"

"Heppson left of his own accord. I'll have nothing to do with him. I've told you so from the beginning. But I promise you this," Moiria turned slightly and let her eyes fall down on Conrad's waiting form, "I will work upon Conrad's memory. I will make him fit to take the throne. I will do all of this if you give me time, if you help cushion my acceptance in the court, and if you stop fighting against me. It is a fair agreement. I give you what you want, and you give me safety in return."

Conrad had remained silent throughout the conversation, Moiria exerting just enough pressure upon him to keep him wary and cautious. Now she released her force a little, allowing his mouth to join their own, and tempt the King into action.

"You speak of memories," said Conrad. "Is this a place I have been before? I should like to know more."

The King reached toward his son, drawn by a voice he could never forget, but Moiria remained standing between the two. Around them, the stone floors and walls of the relatively empty room pressed tightly on both men's damaged spirits.

"If you push him the wrong way, his mind will shut like a trap," said Moiria. "Your contact with him must be limited until I remove the damage my mother has wrought. He must be completely in my care, if we are to bring him back at all. You wouldn't wish to harm him with your probing, would you?"

"Completely in your care?" said the King, and she could tell he ached to hear his son speak again.

"Completely in my care. I will begin to work upon the curse, and I will keep you apprised of my success. Until then you will leave me, and all my other methods concerning this kingdom, alone."

Moiria knew the King could not help but agree at that point, not if it meant his son might truly return. It was a small spell for Moiria to bring about, his giving in to her in order to save the one he loved.

She had been right to bring Conrad here. He made an

excellent bargaining chip. Besides, it would be easier to control his future, once the bird died, if he was already in her grasp. It would be easier to turn his heart to hers if he remained within her sight, instead of remaining holed up in that cottage. And how could the King resist her explanation when she told him of their engagement? All that time spent together in rehabilitation. Why would he not love Moiria for all that she would do?

Of course, Moiria could not think how she might actually break her mother's curse. She did not truly have the power to give him his memories back, no matter what she told the King. She had tried, briefly, in the forest, when she had first come across Conrad in his wanderings. But she had failed then, as she was sure she would fail should she try again.

In fact, she wondered how he even knew of the brother from his past. What had awakened that small tendril of recollection? What had circumvented her mother's powers even that precious little bit?

It didn't matter. She could fake his memories for him if needs be. She could make him Conrad enough to fool the King and all the kingdom. And once they were married and she was Queen, she would be finished with the both of them. They could require nothing more of her at that point.

Heppson

By the time they came anywhere near where Heppson felt the presence of Ant, the leaves of the forest were almost fully on the ground rather than in the trees. If the girl had not finally trusted him enough to climb atop his back, he knew they would never have made it in time for her to find Ant within his season.

From time to time, as they traveled, Heppson thought upon the snatches of words he overheard the girl speak. He thought about the bird she'd left behind, about the sister she missed so dearly. He tried to understand the connection between the two, and wondered if he had done right to carry her away on a single night's whim. But in the end, he gave up on weighing the good or bad of what he'd chosen.

What was done was done. He had to believe this. He could do nothing but move onward with his present task, and make the best of where he traveled now. If he'd learned anything from the twisted path he'd taken since running from his mother's knife, it was that even when decisions turn out differently than you would think, it is not possible to take them back.

He'd thought it best to leave his brother. He'd thought it best to take the Bearskin. Was this true? Who could say? And how could he now debate the rightfulness of dragging off the girl? He could only be glad she was alive. That she was with him. And that he had the chance to make at least one part of it right.

The morning they arrived in Ant's domain felt chilly to Heppson, even beneath the Bearskin. The girl trembled against his fur as the wind whipped past their moving forms. He wished he could better keep her warm as they traveled, but their speed was necessary if they wanted to succeed. Of course, winter would be even harsher when it arrived, despite the little bag for fire that she carried, despite the cloak across her back. Perhaps Ant would give her wisdom to end her journey. Perhaps she'd be ready to leave the forest, and go along her way. Heppson drove himself harder at the thought of it, not wanting to remember how it felt to spend his days alone. Not wanting to think his use to her might end.

When afternoon arrived, Heppson slowed his gait and halted. He lifted his nose and smelled the crisp air around him, centering his concentration on one particular strand of energy. He was right. Ant crawled nearby; near enough that he dared not move for fear that he might step on him. Now, he had only to make the girl understand.

Of course, Heppson knew he might speak to the girl if he wished. Even in Bear's form, he could use his mind to reach hers, a fact very apparent from his memories of other Bears and their interactions with humans. But he had never done this, not in all their days spent traveling together, not even after the attack of the wolves. He had known that some level of separation must be kept between them, now that he was human no longer, now that his world had nothing to do with hers. And he had not trusted himself to stop speaking to her, if ever he started.

If he'd spoken to her, he might have forgotten what he'd left behind, and what he'd become. Funny that even if he were a human still, he could have had no contact with the girl who rode on his back. Not with a mother like the one he'd left behind. Which meant it was good he did not speak within her mind. Which meant it was good that he remained an animal to her.

But how does a bear that does not speak tell his human companion that she is very near the creature that she seeks?

Heppson rippled his back, a sign between them that the girl should dismount. She did so, and stretched her legs and arms.

"We've stopped early today," she said. "Are you hurt?"

Heppson made no move to answer her.

The girl sighed. "Really," she said. "I know you understand me a little. No ordinary bear would carry me onward day after day, making sure I find a respectable place to camp, with water nearby as well. No ordinary bear would fight wolves to keep me safe. The least you could do is nod once or twice and offer me companionship in my travels."

Heppson turned from her without a sign, a dumb animal instead of a man. Why had he thought it would be so easy? To come so close and stay so far? Every day the girl spoke something similar to him. Every day he ignored her entreaties for further communication. Instead of nodding, he sniffed along the ground and followed the faint but steady trail of Ant's movements. The girl watched.

"What do you look for?" she said. "Are you hungry at this time of day? I suppose we are nearing winter. Perhaps you are seeking to increase your girth?" She laughed a little, then wrapped her arms around herself and shivered. "I must say I don't much look forward to that season, myself."

Heppson continued his progress, acting oblivious to her words.

"Well, it's not as though I couldn't do with a rest myself," she said.

He caught the girl's shrug in his peripheral vision but continued to nose about the ground. He pushed aside the twigs and dirt and fallen leaves that covered Ant's erratic path, following him purposefully, despite the nonsensical direction of his steps. And then—after all the weeks of travel—there Ant was, yanking a bit of fallen plant matter from the ground, pulling it toward some den he'd created for herself. Ant. Guardian of Autumn. So small and unnoticeable that Heppson could hardly believe it. At first, he did not know what to do, now he had found him.

I bring you one who seeks your help. He spoke into Ant's mind, opting for simplicity.

I'm busy, said Ant. *Leave me be.*

Heppson lifted his nose from the ground, surprised. *As Guardian you must listen to her,* he said. *It is your place.*

Only if she's wise enough to ask me for herself, said Ant, *which she obviously is not. Besides I don't see you letting her in on your royal-Guardianship either. I must continue gathering for winter. This year's season will be colder than most. No surprise, since you can't properly control it yet.*

Heppson's anger grew inside him at the Ant's uncaring attitude, and his comments about Heppson and his own behavior. Who exactly did this Ant think he was? Behind him, the girl brushed at her skirts and looked into the sky. She ignored the Bear and the creature at his feet.

How would she know you are here? said Heppson, gritting his teeth. *You are, after all, a minuscule ant who no one rightly notices or cares for. But she has sought you, I assure you of that, and in this way has fulfilled the requirements of speaking with a Guardian.*

I told you I was busy, said Ant. *Leave me be, and in a few days she can speak to you instead. Winter has almost arrived, you know. Or then again,* and the ant chuckled, *maybe you don't.*

Heppson let a hot breath escape his flaring nostrils. It knocked aside the ant. *You,* he said, *forget that you're an ant. This girl wishes to speak with you, and speak to you she will. Climb aboard my nose immediately.*

I have a feeling you will not let me alone until I talk to this human of yours.

I have a feeling you are right, answered Bear within Ant's mind.

Fine then, said the ant, and he climbed aboard his nose. *But I'll have you know that even an ant, with the assistance of his friends, could do wonders of damage to that thick, shaggy hide of yours.*

Heppson did not reply, but gave him the petty victory of words. What did it matter as long as Ant spoke to the girl as he asked? And besides, he was too busy trying not to think of the way his breath had caught when Ant called the girl his own. If only it were so, and if only meeting Ant would not bring their travels together to an end.

In actuality, it took the girl several moments to notice what

Heppson offered. First, she batted at his nose, asking why he wished to smell her, as well as the ground. Then she complained of the dirt spread across his snout. Finally she put her hands upon her hips and glared at Heppson where he stood.

"You needn't drive me any further in that fashion," she said. "Aren't we beyond this type of forced travel?" It was only then, in her righteous anger, that she finally looked and saw the six-legged insect where it waited impatiently. The girl gasped, her hands flying to her face. "The Ant!" she said. "Autumn's Guardian. You've actually brought me to him."

And before Heppson knew it, the girl had taken Ant from his nose, and lifted him upward that she might speak with him. It was almost as though she'd forgotten Bear right where he stood. It had been true she needed this Ant. It had been true this was what she wanted when she spoke to that fire so many nights before.

"Please," Heppson heard her say, the words falling over themselves as they hurried out of her mouth. "You must help me. For all its ridiculousness, you must. Now that Lark is gone, you are my only chance. You're all I have left of the quest I have started."

While the air stayed silent on Ant's side, as the Guardian spoke with the maiden through her mind, Heppson could not help but eavesdrop on the words his recent charge uttered. He had brought her here for this moment. Perhaps now he would understand what it all meant?

"You must help me break this curse," said the girl. "You must help me find my sister. You must help me find the wandering man who can solve it all."

She paused.

"I did not mean to leave her side," the girl said. "I would have stopped it if I could."

Heppson saw her glance toward him when the words were spoken. He saw the sorrow in her eyes. Feelings of guilt rose to the surface again, despite his recent determination to keep them away. What did it matter that he had brought her to Ant? What in the scheme of things did that do for all that had gone wrong, both with her life and with his own? Did it matter than none of his decisions had been simple? Did that mean his deficiency wasn't real? He still had failed Conrad. He had failed himself. He had failed this girl. What could he do to make up for all of that?

The girl nodded at Ant as she listened to another mind-spoken speech, agreeing with what had been spoken. A few moments longer she listened, entranced by words Heppson could not hear himself. He supposed he might have listened in, if he truly wished to make himself part of the conversation. But it seemed wrong to use his Guardian powers for the deception of spying and he did not do so.

Finally, the girl crouched to the ground and let the ant crawl from her hands. She continued to stare at the insect, hands on her hips, as though still listening to several important details Ant felt pressed to offer. Her face was calm and grave, and her mouth pressed flatly together in consideration. Lifting her head, she turned to Heppson.

"He says you must dig beneath a nearby tree for me. He says his gift was carried by many of his kind when he first obtained it, but that he cannot retrieve it on his own, due to its weight and size."

From his small vantage point, Ant cocked his head toward Heppson. *I suppose you'll let me go about my day, Bear? If I give her my gift, which she's been taught to request?*

Heppson harrumphed through his bear nose. *I only bid you do what you are meant to as Guardian. Do not make me out to be some ogre.*

Well, we'll see about that. Though I think you'll be glad to know I have kept your little secret. I have not told her you are Guardian of Winter. Though why I should offer you that courtesy is beyond me.

Heppson lowered his head. *I thank you,* he said. *For both that and the gift.*

Ant nodded almost imperceptibly. *This gift, I do believe, will be of some use to the girl,* she said. *Especially with you along her side. The forest called me to it in a way that rarely happens anymore, which was why I made such a concerted effort to drag it to this place. It did not wish to come.*

What is it? said Heppson.

The Ant laughed. *I cannot tell you that.* And then, impatiently, he presented a detailed picture in Heppson's consciousness of the specific wildwood tree he had hidden her gift below. Once Bear nodded in understanding and recognition, he quickly turned and skittered away before Heppson could ask more. Ant's mind was full once again of smells and food and other useful items laced throughout the forest floor. He no longer cared about the Bear or the girl.

It seemed this particular Guardian had served as Ant a long time and could not help but be driven by his animal instincts. Heppson understood that would happen to him eventually as well; that Bear would come to be his full existence. But even if he knew the theory, he did not like to think of it, not here at his beginning.

Paces away from him, the girl stood and stared at the trees surrounding her. For several minutes, neither Bear nor the girl moved, though Heppson kept his eyes tight on the girl's still form. If there had been any time he wished to speak to her, this was it. What would she do, now that she had spoken with Ant? But he did not speak to ask her what she thought. He moved instead to a tree, several yards beyond her, which looked exactly like the image Ant had introduced into his mind, only moments before. Purposefully, he dug with his clawed paws beneath the boughs until he came upon a cloth-wrapped package nestled in its roots.

Once he'd stopped his efforts, the girl turned and walked to Heppson's side. She let her hand lift to his head and brushed back his thick and heavy fur as she might have stroked a common kitten, were she an ordinary village lass. Heppson found himself, oddly enough, wishing he could purr, to give her the comfort a simple animal might. Instead, he nosed at the object below them, hoping it would be enough.

"Thank you," she said. "Thank you for bringing me. I understand your purpose in dragging me this way. I would never have found him on my own, and Ant has answered many of my questions." The girl sighed and reached down to take the package in hand. "I cannot open this, Ant says, although he was kind enough to tell me it was a blade—a little more helpful than the fish in that regard. Of course, Ant does not know where Lark has gone, since my bird is a feathered creature and flies above the forest floor, far from Ant's eyes or the eyes of his comrades. But he has seen the wanderer. And he could direct me toward where he last saw him."

Him? thought Heppson, trying not to purposefully lean into the girl's hand where it cupped his massive, beastly head.

True, he had known of a bird, which occupied the girl's most inner thoughts. He had even known of a sister. But not of a 'him' that played part in this quest. Of course, why should a Bear such as he care that his companion sought a 'him'? What should a fact such as that have to do with the Guardian of Winter?

"I suppose the best thing to do is to seek the wanderer out," said the girl. "Perhaps Lark continues to do the same. Perhaps we will be reunited when we find him. He must be my goal now, as I have no other path to follow. I always knew it would likely come back to him."

The girl leaned into Bear, her forehead resting against his hide. "Ant says there is only one path I can follow to help my sister. She says I must take this path, find the wanderer, and conquer the witch who holds him captive. I suppose the fish was right in that regard; there will be an eventual replay of the battle the witch and I fought before."

Hearing the word 'witch,' Heppson's fur stood upward along his back. The muscles of his legs tightened, and his lips pulled back into a half-shown snarl. Of course. A witch was involved in all that happened with this girl! Though why a witch had not occurred to him before this moment, he could not fathom. All those animals, lusting for attack, lusting for the girl's blood. Who else but a witch could bring such an unnatural act to fruition?

And there was only one witch who Heppson had dealt with personally; only one witch whom he had watched hurt others in this way. Could it be that his mother had caused this girl's pain? Could it be that his mother had sent out those wolves to rip the girl to pieces?

This forest may never have been under her attack before, but perhaps she had vanquished Conrad after Heppson's departure. Perhaps she sought to increase her power even further, or even to find her long-lost son. Was this all part of the same battle he'd thought he'd left behind? He had no inkling of it, when it came to his Guardian awareness, but it was difficult for him to understand much of that world anyway, or what he ought to know. He could have missed the signs of the forest facing attack. He could have become so caught up in this girl that he was unaware of his mother's influence.

The girl had not noticed Bear's edginess, so caught up was she in her thoughts, and she continued speaking. "Ant says I must seek out the Guardian of Winter," she said. "He agrees with Summer that only with the assistance of each of the Guardians can I be prepared for this battle." She stopped her patient brushing of Heppson's hide and looked off into the trees once more. "But he would not tell me what form Winter takes. He would not tell me whom to look for. He only said that you might help me follow the path toward the wanderer, and that he guessed we would find Winter along our travels."

Heppson pointed his snout toward the trees, not wanting to hear more of Winter and his possibilities. Ant had told Heppson he protected his privacy in this matter, but for how long could things remain as they were? This girl expected Winter to appear and provide some sort of direction—some sort of gift to help her in her quest. She expected Winter to have wisdom of some sort.

Heppson barely knew himself as a Guardian, let alone how to guide this girl to success. He had served as a guide in the search for Ant, but that was all he could think to do.

"You will help me travel northward, will you not?" said the girl, pulling slightly on his fur, as though to get his attention. "That is where Ant bid me find the wanderer, and I do not wish to make the travels alone."

Heppson felt her watch for some reply. Felt her eyes trained on the side of his head. Felt her willing him to turn. Finally, he did. But he did not speak. He would travel with her. He would keep her safe from any enemies. He would seek to discover if his mother had sent them. And he would help her find this wanderer, this 'him' whom she so desperately sought. But he would not reveal himself as Guardian, not as Winter. Not yet. Not when it would only bring her disappointment. Not when he could give her nothing that she actually desired.

After all, there was not much use in letting her despair of Winter's help, not much use in being who he was. Slowly, he bent his head toward the ground, and then lifted it in agreement.

"Good," said the girl. "I shall take that as a 'yes,' and consider it settled. I know you like to pretend you don't understand me, but it is fairly obvious you comprehend each word I say."

Heppson stared solidly back, not flinching. Neither did he allow his bear's mouth to turn upward into some sort of convoluted smile. The girl grinned at him anyhow, breaking the dark and frustrated moment just behind them. "Fair enough," she said. "Fair enough."

Moiria

As far as Moiria could tell, the wolves had separated the bird from her sister. Each of the girls still lived, a fact stranger each day it remained true, but they were separated. And at least the separation made the Lark weaker. Of course, true to her purpose, the bird continued to move through the forest and toward Conrad. She resolutely sought her love, and find him she would; Moiria and all her plans be hanged.

Watching within her mind, and wishing it were not so, Moiria saw the bird advance. How odd that such a little creature should stand in the way of all she did. This must have been how her mother felt when she watched the child Conrad, toddling about in his princely shoes, seemingly without a care in the world. The Queen could not kill him because of the protection held in his mother's ring. And Moiria could not kill the bird due to the same aggravating emblem. It must have made the Queen feel powerless to be contained in such a way. It must have made her fear defeat, though she had hidden it well. Certainly Moiria feared defeat.

Yet, day after day, the bird flew onward, apparently unchecked by nature's move to cold. She stopped to peck at insect-infested bark. She stopped to tuck her head beneath a wing and rest. She blew aside in storms of wind, and sheltered herself when hard rains fell. But then, when morning broke, she flew yet onward. Always toward Conrad. Unknowing, mind-beleaguered Conrad, who was now kept in a cell-like room in one of the lowest levels of the castle.

He had been relegated to simple basket weaving, and also, rarely, the cleaning of rusty armaments. Anything to keep him busy. Allowed no visitors, and fed only with trays carried in by Moiria's hands, his days passed idly and without point. Little did he know of the heart full of memories which sought his empty one in so determined a fashion.

After several weeks, Moiria realized the bird would arrive at the castle before it met Death. Curious at the strength of the bird, she allowed herself to wonder what would happen were she to stand aside, and let the creature come. What would happen were the bird allowed to alight on Conrad's shoulder? Would his own heart tell him how to release her from the band about her neck? Would Lark's sudden appearance do anything for the nobody that Conrad had become in both mind and soul?

Moiria realized that while her mother had taught her the ways of magic and schooled her well in the manipulations which made another's will your own, she had never given Moiria a true understanding of what occurred in the process of a spell. And she most definitely had never educated her on what might happen in the case of a witch's defeat. According to her mother, such a thing could never happen and was consequently of no concern. Moiria could not help but think about what might happen, were the bird to find success.

Even if it could not be. Even if she must not allow it to happen.

She remembered, in some small form from that time before, how she had often dreamed of happy endings, like any other girl born breathing. In tales sung 'round hearth fires, a bird like Lark would most definitely have found her love, and both would have been released from the chains which held them tight.

Were such things possible in reality? What made them come to be? Now that the King no longer actively fought to take the kingdom, and now that the court accepted her presence as inevitable, Moiria had time to think about the possibilities of an alternate ending. To imagine what she might have hoped for, if she had been somebody else.

But in the end, when the bird arrived at the castle walls, Moiria acted as duty demanded. When the bird arrived, she did her witchly part to make certain the spell remained intact.

It was morning when the Lark flew in and the bird's wings lagged in strength. For every push of its feathers upward, there was a breath of almost falling that followed close behind. Moiria knew that in the forest there had been many places for the bird to stop and regain her strength in safety. But nearing the castle, the Lark had needed to continue onward with her flight when night arrived. After all, the villages between the castle and the wilderness had neglected any efforts at growing trees in the pursuit of staying fed and housed. Add to this the presence of mouse-catching cats who dabbled in birds, and it was obvious such places were not meant for those with wings. The Lark had traveled beneath the moon by necessity, and her wings were labored from the effort.

Bewildered and exhausted, Lark spent her last energy in flapping at the castle walls, trembling for admittance. Moiria imagined she could feel the presence of Conrad, but the bird could not reach him. This had been the reason she was meant to keep the sister as her companion. Not only for protection, but also for those tasks in her quest which required human hands. After all, Conrad's tiny room had no windows she might bob her head inside. And he slept soundly, unaware of his dearest love's presence. Doors did not open for birds all on their own.

Moiria, however, was clearly cognizant of both Lark's presence and the spell she'd placed on her. Seeking her prey, Moiria stalked the bird with well-practiced feet. Her slippers were used to staying silent on the paths of the castle's garden, so the bird did not startle at her wary advance. In her hand, she carried a gilded cage: a pretty thing to hold the jittery bird while she determined what to do with her. She could not kill her outright, but she could keep her trapped and far from any food supply. In the end, it did not take much to get the drained animal into the contraption. Lark's beating heart was frantic, but she had nowhere else to go.

"And here we are," said Moiria, her fingers latching the cage's door, her hand pulling it upward so she might see the bird more clearly. "Together again."

She looked into the beady eyes of the trapped fowl.

"You've not managed to die yet, I see. Well, perhaps I can help to make that happen."

Behind her, the sudden sound of crunching rocks made Moiria whirl in guilty surprise. She'd thought she was alone with the Lark when she spoke to it, but her eyes now narrowed on the King's interloping figure. He leaned upon a staff of middling height, which he'd taken to carrying recently, but he was an imposing barrier all the same. Especially since he stood between her and the castle doors she wished to enter. His eyes were much clearer than she'd seen them look before, a fact that caused the hair on her arms to stand on end.

"Ah, Moiria," he said. "So interesting to find you about. And what do you carry in that cage, pray tell?" he said.

Moiria took a breath, smiled, and walked toward him and the castle just beyond. She made every effort to act unconcerned by his presence. "A common bird I found about the grounds. I've decided to make a pet of it."

"A bird for a pet? That seems an odd thing for you to spend your time with, I think. Come closer, if you would. I'd like to see the bird you've chosen."

Moiria pulled the cage closer to her side, hesitant to let him see. "It's rather a personal project, you see. Not one I wish to share."

As soon as she'd spoken, she realized her mistake. The Queen had never allowed others to know what she really wanted or cared for, at least not until she played her hand completely. After all, it is hard for your enemies to fight you when they don't know what you seek. By telling the King she cared for the bird, Moiria had given him that tiny smidgen of power he needed.

"I am still the King, Moiria," he said. "And growing stronger, I dare to think. Bring the cage to me."

Moiria walked along the path and lifted the cage into his sight.

"A rather ordinary creature," said the King.

"I told you it was a common bird."

"And yet, it is a personal project of yours? Tell me, how does my son do? After all, it is because of him that you are free to walk about and gather birds, instead of living out your days inside a prison cell."

Moiria lowered the cage, her eyes narrowed. "He has made some progress," she said. "I need more time."

"More time to play with birds?" The King lifted his eyebrows. "I understand you have learned much from your mother, and it is true I want my son returned to health. When it comes to regaining him, I am willing to play according to your demands. Still, I am remembering how this world of politics used to belong to me. I am remembering the balance of power needed between alternate sides."

"What do you want?" said Moiria, all efforts at pretense gone.

"I will take that bird from you. It is true I see nothing but an ordinary lark inside its bars, but you have thought to put it in a gilded cage for a very particular reason. It will be my collateral, for my son. I will return the bird to you when my son regains his memories."

Moiria stared at the King, her mind unable to supply a worthy response. To think he'd had this kind of ability in him all along. Her mother must have truly veiled his mind with her curses to make him seem so addled in all of Moiria's memories.

The King walked toward Moiria and pried the cage's handle forcibly from her grasp. "Never fear," he said, as he bent his frame to look directly in her eyes. "I am not a cruel man. I will feed the bird, and care for it. It shall not die on my watch."

Moiria's mouth opened to speak; yet she stayed silent.

"Thank you, Moiria," he said. "I'm sure you must be off to assist Conrad. Time is of the essence, you know."

And then he turned and walked away.

Heart

Snow had fallen regularly for a month. In heavy, settling flakes, it slowly drowned out the world Heart traveled through until she could not remember summer's existence anymore. No longer did the sounds of the forest play cheerily against her ears. Where before the birds had twittered and the river had run, now there was only the rare and solemn clomp that came when a bough released its heavy load of crystallized moisture onto the ground below.

"I am cold," Heart whispered into the frigid air, which held her tightly in its vise.

Her hand rested on the shoulder of her Bear, and she leaned against the heat he radiated as they traveled. Recently she'd dropped from his back and returned to her travels by foot. Her body needed the extra exertion to keep itself warm, to keep the blood pumping through her veins. Of course, even if the effort of walking kept her heated and misted with sweat for the majority of the day, night's approach would change all that. When the sun no longer edged its way between the empty branches and onto Heart's shoulders, her sweat would turn chilly on her skin.

"We should make a fire," she said, "while we still have light."

The night before she had barely managed to fan her flames to any worthwhile height, and she began to fear that soon enough she would fail completely. Finding any useful wood for such a venture became more and more difficult each day. And since her Bear continued to leave her at night—doing she knew not what—her efforts to survive until morning rested solely in her own hands. It wasn't as though Heart had never been taught to survive the chill of winter. But before, there'd always been a home and a well-stocked pile of firewood to see her through.

Add the problem of night to her essentially doomed search for Winter, and the entire venture bordered on hopeless. Her previous search for Autumn may have seemed terrible at the time, but at least then she had known she searched for an ant. Now she and Bear journeyed forward and merely hoped Winter would appear along their path. That Winter would reveal itself and offer up its gift without any action on her part. The entire effort had become insurmountable when Heart thought much about their odds.

Bear halted in his progress forward, aware always of her requests for rest or shelter. He swung his head from side to side, nosing his way through the snow-laden plants crowded about them. At least he always found Heart a corner to make her camp before he left. Heart liked to think he did not truly leave her; that he waited just beyond her camp in the wild woods. Perhaps he kept guard in case another wolf arrived to wring her throat. Perhaps he sought answers to their quest for the wanderer and Winter. She did not like to think she was truly alone at night.

Bear dipped his head beneath the branches of a particularly large snow-bedecked tree, and led her into a sheltered alcove of the forest, trees ringing 'round a small opening to the sky.

"I never imagined the forest was so large," said Heart, bending in beside him, "when I lived so happily in my own little cottage glen. I never knew I could walk its length for so many days, and see so much of the same."

Her Bear watched her face, but he did not answer her, not even to nod his head—as he had but twice before. She could not help but debate how much he understood of what she said. In some moments it seemed he knew so much, but in others like this, her words felt dry and useless in her throat. What was conversation without any answers?

Heart sighed and began to work on her fire. She pulled together nearby sticks, dusted them of their icy coverings, and pulled out a bit of dry kindling she had gathered earlier from the underskirt of a bush along their path. Pulling out her flint, she hit it sharply to produce a spark. Heart blew, willing the flames to catch and grow. But the fire did not come easily, the last dumping of snow more damp and full of moisture than other flakes this winter had produced.

Heart leaned back onto her feet, breathed in deeply, and worked to calm her fears. It would do her no good to get upset. She rearranged her tinder and struck at the flint again, determined to produce flames. But despite her continued labors over the next half hour, the fire refused to catch. Heart's fingers trembled. Her legs, folded stiffly beneath her, began to feel the ache of deep cold. She tried again and again at her flint, but to no avail. Her efforts met only with failure. Finally, the sun began to sink into its bed. To her side, Bear watched, his gaze intent on Heart's lack of progress.

Quivering now, Heart brushed her hand against her brow— as if any sweat dripped down her face—and tried once more. If the fire would not light after all she had done, she had no further ideas of how to force it into existence. If only it would catch this time. But nothing came. Her hands fell to her knees, the fingers curled in a frozen grip about her flint. She huddled by the unlit fire, her stomach tightening against the shivers, which threatened to begin there and travel throughout her frame.

"I cannot make it start," she whispered. "All is too wet. My fingers cannot work any further. They are too cold. I am too cold."

Bear came closer and nosed at the sticks before her. He lifted his head toward the setting sun, as though to watch the orb's last sliver beam its parting glance. Heart watched him as he stood there, wondering what he might do. He had no hands to start the fire; he had no way to solve this problem. But would he leave her alone, as he had always done before? Heart hoped he would not, for if he did, it was likely she would never see him again. Not after a night without fire. Not when she already quaked with cold, with the day not even gone.

The sun sunk deeper, moving downward as it must, and Bear hesitantly began to back away. His heavy paws crunched crisply in the icy snow as he moved backward. Heart eyed him, but did not say a thing once it became apparent what he planned. What could she do, but sit and let him make his own decisions? He was a beast, and she was only a girl he had not yet eaten. He should be sleeping by this time anyway, his warm round form well hidden in a cave.

Her Bear looked again toward the falling sun before swinging his head once more to Heart, but she closed her eyes, shutting out his gaze. She did not want to see it happen. She did not want to believe it. By the time she'd opened her eyes, Bear was gone.

Heart gathered her cloak more tightly about her middle and scooted back to huddle at the base of one of the trees, its trunk providing a vague shelter from the elements. She pulled her knees into her chest and imagined the warmth of her Granny's cottage. What would she give to be there! So many days had passed since she'd left that place, but the memories were alive as ever. The way the three of them sat about the fire. Granny snoozing. Lark humming. Heart busily building some contraption. Then her sister had fallen in love, and all had changed. All had disappeared.

Heart pulled at the bag at her side and clumsily brought out the gifts of the Guardians. They were both bound in bits of cloth, and it took time to free the box from its wrappings. Her fingers would not move the way she wished them; there was no quickness or ease in the sluggish digits. When she finally held the box, Heart found she did not know what she should do with it.

Perhaps I should open it now, she thought. *Perhaps it will save me from a death of cold this night.*

But Summer had said she would use this box to save the life of one she loved. Did she truly only love herself? She cradled the smooth contours of the box in her hands for several more minutes before placing it once again inside its wrappings, and then placed it back inside her bag. She would not throw away this gift to fight winter's chill, even if Death took her in this fight. Besides, she would be cold again tomorrow. And there would be no box for her then.

Next, Heart fingered the wrappings of her second gift. It also remained a mystery to her, as far as what its' worth might be. A blade she'd been strictly charged to leave wrapped. She could feel its length through the fabric, its weight on her palm. But what could a knife do to start a fire?

Heart sighed. Sent to find the Guardians. It seemed she had failed in her part of the quest. She could only hope that Lark would succeed without her and manage to vanquish the witch on her own. That she would find her love and that he would free her from her prison. Lark might wonder then where her Heart had gone, but she would find happiness with the wanderer, and the past would be necessarily forgotten. Heart had been angry at Lark for so long, for giving her devotion to another. But she realized now it was the way of things. Time cannot stand still.

Heart placed everything back in her bag, and pulled it all close into her belly. Then, she began the wait. Her shivers, with time, grew smaller, and a tight warmth within her chest began to snake its way outward. Not a good sign, she knew. Heart watched the shadows move through the forest. She watched them bend down and reach up, stretching about the dead plants to cover the ground until at last, in all their length, they disappeared completely. The sun must be entirely gone now. Twilight had passed. Night had officially come. Warmth and calmness gathered and drifted from the tip of Heart's head to her trembling feet until she fell completely still.

Would Bear find her in the morning? Or would her lack of breath make her a stranger to his life-searching nose? Perhaps he would lumber away to his sleep, glad to be freed from this useless quest. She blinked slowly, perhaps for the last time. A shadow loomed large in her vision.

"Death," she meant to whisper. But her mouth was still.

Heppson

He had to leave her. He would not let her watch the transformation from beast to man as it occurred. He could only imagine what she would think of such an experience; of the terror such a sight might give. Which meant there was a time, albeit brief, when she must wait it out alone. When she must think her Bear had abandoned her.

When the sun went down, Bear's skin became loose about Heppson. His fur hung heavy and slack on Heppson's bowed shoulders. He knew now, of course, that she would see him for the failure he was. A Guardian without a purpose, without a plan, and without a gift. But he would not let her die to keep his secret. He, at least, would not do that.

Shakily, Heppson stood from where he crouched beneath the pelt. Today he could not give himself time to recover completely and become his most human self. She needed the fur to keep her warm, and he needed to start a fire with his limber and warm-blooded fingers.

He took the pelt in hand, suddenly aware of the state of his human body beneath it. He had not cared for himself as he should. A half-hearted beard hung ragged from his chin, his clothes were dirty and unwashed. Still, it did not matter. He could not allow himself to care. What did it concern him what she thought of his human form? As long as she lived, as long as she made it to morning again, that was all that mattered.

The girl barely moved when Heppson approached her where she'd hidden herself beneath a tree. In another moment, she may even have been gone from him completely. But Heppson acted quickly, bending down and wrapping the Bearskin about her shoulders without further hesitation. Firmly, he tucked its furry folds around her limbs. He held Death back and moved to build a fire for more warmth. He would not think; he would just do. It was the only course of action.

Only when he'd finished, only when the flames shot skyward and exuded well-established heat, only when the girl's breathing had become more regular, only then did Heppson dare to look to where she crouched. New tremors of shaking racked her body as it awoke from the cold she'd felt before. The heat of the fire, the heat of the pelt, the heat from his body that remained inside the fur: all of it wrapped around her and forced her body to tremble its way back to equilibrium. Her eyes, of course, were already locked on his by the time he met her gaze.

"You are the Guardian," she accused, sure now that he saw her. Her words popped across the embers of the fire, spitting all she felt toward Heppson. "You are the Guardian of Winter. You have been the entire time."

"Yes," said Heppson, the single word all he could manage in the face of her indictment.

"And you've understood my words every day we've walked together," she said. "Every time I've spoken. Every moment I've asked for help. You could have spoken into my mind, just like the others. You could have been more than a bear for the whole journey."

"Yes," said Heppson again.

He could feel her anger boiling toward him, almost as though she reflected the heat from the flames of his fire back at him. He could tell she would come to hate him for the empty days of waiting for Winter's appearance. All those hours of travel that he'd been there and never spoken. She would hold it all against him—all the things he hadn't done right. As well she should. In fact, he imagined she wished to throw his pelt back in his face, if it were not so necessary to keeping her warm and alive. Who would want a gift such as that? One offered only with lies and pretended friendship?

"Why?" she said. "Why didn't you tell me who you were? All that time I hoped for Winter!"

Heppson shrugged helplessly at her questions, and squatted down upon his heels. Why did he ever do anything? Because he did not know what else to do? "I did not ask to be Guardian," he finally said. "It is not a role I undertook or even grasp. I had nothing to offer you, not like the others who you sought."

The girl choked out her words, her indignation increasing as she came more and more back to herself. "You did not ask to be Guardian? As though that makes it better? Well, I did not ask for my sister to be turned into a bird! And I did not ask to be attacked by wild wolves! And most of all, I did not ask to be abandoned in a frozen wasteland; left alone to die by the very person who should be saving me."

At her last attack, Heppson stood again quickly, his voice gruff and pointed. "I did not leave you," he said. "You are not dead, and you are not alone."

"Am I not alone?" came her quick reply. "You are nothing that I thought you to be. You have hidden and kept yourself back from me for this entire trip."

"And what was I supposed to do? Fabricate false answers to your queries? Spontaneously produce a gift to help you on a journey I know nothing about? I've done what I could, considering the options open to me. I took you to Ant. I've led you toward this wanderer who will supposedly solve all your problems. And now I've kept you alive when winter and its storms would claim your life."

"Winter!" laughed the girl. "Winter and its storms! And why should winter even seek to claim my life if you wished differently? Why should the wind blow like cutting ice? Why should the sky dump continued flurries of white onto my head? Aren't you supposed to have some control over all this?"

Heppson did not answer. What could he say? He had known she would see through him when she knew the truth. After all, that was why he'd not revealed himself to her before now. That was why he'd hidden himself away inside the skin of an ordinary bear and denied the creature who he truly was.

"So that's it?" she said. "You simply pretended you weren't

Winter because you didn't *mean* to be him? Because you didn't know what to do? Because you had no better plan? That was your solution?"

"I may not have acted as you'd like," said Heppson, his finger pointed at her. "And I may not have had some grand plan to help you defeat this witch of yours, or find your bird, or whatever else it is you need to do. But I did not keep away, no matter how often you say it. I did not leave you alone. I never could have left you alone. I've learned that much at least."

"And yet you've failed to help me in the one way I needed," she said. "What was the use of staying, if you had no plans to help me?"

Heppson's hand dropped and he turned away from the girl. "You will see it as you must," he said. "Perhaps I shunned a fight I should have fought. What's done is done." He reached to his side, and threw another of his gathered branches into the flames. "Anyway, I've always known you'd be disappointed when you learned that it was me," he said. "From the very beginning, I've been well aware of that fact. Becoming Bear has made me a failure in more ways than one. I suppose I should be used to it by now."

The girl sighed noisily, her breath rushing out, as though to gut an unnecessary candle. "You are a fool in more ways than one," she said. "Don't you see? You're my Bear. You've saved me from wolves and carried me endless miles on my journey. You've been my companion for days on end—the only one I've had to trust. Now you are Winter as well: the very being I have sought all this time."

Heppson held himself still at her words, unsure of what her words might mean.

"Can't you see, Bear? I'm not disappointed you're Winter. I'm only horrendously angry that you did not tell me who you were. Horrendously and incredibly angry. You kept a secret from me that will change everything. You did not trust the two of us to figure out what it might mean." The girl went silent, and bent further inside the pelt. Slowly she turned from him, wrapping herself neatly in the fur as she closed her eyes. "I'm going to sleep now," she whispered back at him. "We will speak again when morning comes. Perhaps then this might make sense. Perhaps then I might forgive you, and know at all what I might say."

Heppson opened his mouth to question her further, but then thought better of it. Instead, he watched her fall asleep, making sure each breath rose again, every time it fell. Making sure his fire kept her breathing in and out. She had been angry, yes, but she had not wept at who he was. That must mean something. Mustn't it?

Heppson

Before the sun rose, Heppson took the pelt back from the girl. Part of him feared the fur would take to her, instead of him, if he did not wear it across his shoulders with the sun's first rays. And part of him still cared that his transformation take place hidden and out of her sight. He did not know about the transformation, from the outside looking in. And he did not want her to know either.

He did not speak to her, when he took the fur from where she waited. He was not ready to feel her anger again, or resume the debate she'd ended the night before. He was not sure she'd decided to let go of all the mistakes he'd made, and he didn't know what he would do if she did not. He realized he could have touched her as a human then, for the first time, if only by accident, but their hands did not meet, and he quickly stepped away. He went away to become Bear again, away into the woods.

When he returned, paws tramping through the snow that had almost cooled her heart to silence, he felt himself hold back. While he'd been gone, she'd packed away her things —as usual— and tidied up the majority of the clearing. She waited by the remnants of his fire, her eyes on the ground and her hands twisting a twig back and forth between her fingers. Thinking he knew not what. He waited for her to speak.

The girl lifted her head and looked at him. "What now, Bear?" she said. "We seem to have found Winter, you and I. In fact, I think I've received a gift of sorts from him."

She rose then, and walked toward him. When she'd come close, she reached out and placed her hand upon his head—as she had done so many times before when she thought him a mere animal. "The fact is," she said, "that I'm alive now. And I would not be if you had not stayed with me all this time."

Heppson held himself still beneath her. Her fingers brushed

at the thick hair that had kept her warm the night before—the same as they would have done before she knew of his betrayal.

"I will not lie and say I don't feel pain. That the sight of you as a human, instead of Bear, does not remind me of who you might have been this entire time, of what we could have accomplished already, if you had only trusted me and revealed the truth. But I will remember what you've done for me. I will honor that, and we will move forward. It seems the best possible path open to me at this point."

Heppson lifted the snout of Bear. His large eyes found hers and he knew she spoke the truth.

"I don't know what to do, Bear. Ant spoke of you in such a way that I truly believed you'd have some all-important clue to help me on my quest. And yet, you seem as confused as I. You've turned out to be both more and less than I could ever have imagined. What options do we have? Have we already failed?"

Heppson remained silent, having nothing to say.

Roughly, the girl put her hand beneath Bear's jaw and lifted Heppson's face to hers. "You must speak to me now, you know. No more of this dumb animal silence you've carried along with so far. I know from both Summer and Autumn that you can speak into my head, and I will not have you pretend you cannot help me anymore. That, at least, I will demand."

Heppson straightened his back and pulled his snout from her hand. *Demand*? he said, speaking into her mind, a bit of his old self rearing its head.

The girl smiled, dissolving any righteous anger he might have felt. "And there it is," she said. "Your voice. After all this time."

He huffed through his snout. *Well, I don't know that you should go about demanding things of a Guardian*, he said. *I may have kept secrets from you, but now that you know I am both Bear and human, you might as well treat me as such.*

"I will if it means you'll speak to me." She reached to his head again. "We will start again, shall we? As equal partners?"

Heppson allowed her to brush at his fur, nodding his snout.

"We need a plan for the future," she said. "We must move past what has happened and think of what lies ahead. I am out of ideas. Completely out. What do you suggest?"

Heppson thought for a moment, his mind going back to past troubles and plans, decisions that made up the zigzagging travels of his life. His mind brushed over memories of a blade swirling in the sky, of a life abandoned to evade forced murder. If he'd had more information then, if he had known his mother had a weakness, or that the Guardians even existed—what might he have changed? What might he have done?

First of all, he said, dropping to his hindquarters, looking her straight in the eye, *we need to share our information. We need to figure out what we know before we can possibly guess what we must do.*

"Yes," said the girl, "that makes sense."

In fact," said Heppson, "*I'm sure you've told Ant much more of your story than you've ever shared with me. For my part, I don't even know your name.*

"My name?" the girl said, dropping her hand to her side and fiddling with the bag of things she'd placed beside her. "I guess that's true. Well. I'm Heart."

Heart?

"Yes, Heart." The girl squinted at him. "And you?"

I am Bear, he said. *My human self is long gone by now.*

Heart opened her mouth, as though she might argue, but Heppson spoke first.

Did Summer or Autumn tell you of any name that they'd retained?

"No, but . . ."

It is because we are the Guardians. I am Bear. It is my name now.

Heart's eyebrows came down and she pressed her lips together. Finally, she spoke. "I suppose I can accept that for now. Though I don't know that it quite fulfills our equal partnership agreement."

Heppson snorted through his long bear snout, not surprised

she'd not given in completely. *Good,* he said. *Now, I think it best that you gather your things. We will walk as we talk, so that you might stay warm with the exertion. Though there is not much point in traveling quickly until we have some plan.*"

Bear stood from where he'd sat and began to lead their way out of the tiny alcove where they'd spent the night. Heart picked up her bag to follow him, one hand coming to rest itself on his shoulder when she reached his side.

It is time for you to tell me what brought you to this forest, said Heppson, trying not to think too much of the hand resting on his pelt. *So, tell me, Heart, what quest is this we follow?*

Once she began to tell him the story, the two of them spoke for most of the morning. Near midday, Heppson halted, his mind drawn back to a specific detail Heart had shared near the beginning.

Describe the witch again, he said.

"Young," said Heart. "Angry. Dark hair—closer to black than brown. She looked like . . ." Heart paused and looked to the sky, her hands to her hips, her eyes thin in concentration, as she looked backward in time. Her brow furrowed and suddenly she looked at Heppson again. "You know, she looked like you."

She looked like a bear? said Heppson, a bit of humor falling into his voice.

Heart shook her head. "Not like a bear. Like you. The real you. When I saw you last night. When you were a boy." Her face turned red, and she looked down. "I mean, when you were a man."

The hair along Heppson's back bristled. *But you said that she was young,* he said. *You said she was not an old witch. Not in face or temperament.*

"Yes," agreed Heart, looking up again, "she was young. Maybe a little older than me, but young all the same. But why should that make it less likely she reminded me of you? It's not as though you are old. Why would you look more like an old witch than a young one?"

In all their discussions that morning, Heppson had not spoken of his own path to the forest, which meant the troubles of his mother and his past were a mystery to Heart. He shook his shaggy head at her questions, not sure how to answer.

Every detail of Heart's story aligned with what he knew of his mother and her spells. This was exactly her type of trouble to cause; pain and anguish on the innocent, and a girl trapped in the form of a bird. But his mother's youth had passed long ago, and she had never bothered to convince others it had not. She hadn't needed youth to retain her power; her force of mind was more than enough.

Honestly I am not sure about the witch, he finally said to Heart, *or what I think of her. Perhaps from a different angle it might become clearer. Tell me instead about this wanderer of your sister's.*

If he was truthful with himself, Heppson had to admit he'd been glad the wanderer belonged to the Lark, instead of to Heart. Although he found it still rankled him a bit that Heart quested for this stranger, even if the man belonged to her sister. Regardless, the wanderer—whoever he was—played an important part in the puzzle, and was in fact the piece they now journeyed toward, however slow their pace might be.

"Well, he was kind," said Heart. "Even I could see that. Though I didn't wish to like him, not at first. In fact, his kindness was the reason I knew it would happen between them. So good, so hardworking, so honest—all those things you hear about in stories of perfect love. How could my sister not fall for him? All she'd ever met were neighbors near enough for trade or bumping into. And they were either too old, or too young, or too crazy to be bothered with. What could they hold to a strange and mysterious visitor, with all that charm and goodness rolling off his back?"

Heppson increased his pace slightly, his muscles tensing. This traveler of Lark's seemed quite the catch; miles ahead of any other options open to these common cottage lasses.

You never said what he looked like, said Heppson. *He must have been quite handsome to capture Lark's heart so quickly and completely.*

"Oh, he was handsome all right. Once he washed. Tall, well-built. Hands that could span a well-sized tree trunk. He had curls on his head. Blonde curls, almost golden in the sun. Why, when he laughed, you'd almost think you saw the sun. Of course, Lark would have loved him anyhow. Even if he'd been ugly and plain. But I'm sure she didn't mind that part. The handsomeness, I mean. Who would?"

But Heppson's mind had stopped at her mention of the wanderer's hair. Golden curls. And a witch. It could not possibly be a coincidence. Heppson had not stayed to kill Conrad, as his mother had intended. And what had his mother done? What could she do? Wouldn't it make sense that she had sent him away?

From the beginning Heppson felt the Queen could not kill the crown prince herself. But she wanted him gone, that much was more than obvious. And with Heppson in the desert, disobeying her orders in so permanent a way, her anger would have lashed out at those left behind. On Conrad. And perhaps even on Moiria.

Heppson's mind caught upon his sister's name. *The witch was young,* he said, and turning to Heart he flooded her mind with images of his own sister, unable to hold them back in his immediate desire to know. Unable to ask the question, when the memories came so much more easily.

Heart gasped, her eyes blinking rapidly under the barrage of information he'd sent her. Realizing what he'd done, he closed his mind again, shutting the images off as quickly as he'd started them. *I'm sorry. Did I hurt you? I did not think . . .*

"No, no, I'm fine. I just didn't know you could do that," she said. "It frightened me, it came so fast and unexpectedly, but no, it did not hurt me." She took a breath. "Anyhow, you're right. That is the witch. Whoever it is, you must have seen her as well. That is the girl who came and brought the curse to my sister. Of course, she felt differently when I saw her. Not so hidden, not so small."

Heppson dropped his snout to the ground, his shoulders caving forward. He was overwhelmed by what Heart confirmed. Moiria. Moiria was Heart's witch. What had he done, leaving her there to fall beneath their mother's power? What had she done? Had she come to serve their mother in every way? Had she taken the Queen's evil ways as her own?

Heppson realized he hadn't thought of his sister once since he'd left. That he hadn't thought of what might happen to her when he climbed over the garden wall and sought the desert as his grave. All this time, he should have regretted this as well: what he had done to his own sister when he left her at the castle. All this time, he hadn't known she lost life too, that fateful day. He had run, he had evaded his fate. But everyone else had been left behind to face what he had feared.

"What is it, Bear?" said Heart, coming closer to where Heppson bowed over their trail. "How do you know the witch? Is there a way we can defeat her? Tell me, what is the matter?"

I know the witch, said Heppson. This time his voice barely whispered into her mind. *After all, she is—or was—my sister."*

Heart

With Bear, she could forget her anger without any degree of effort. After all, Bear had saved her life when the strange soldier wolves had come to wring her throat. And he had been her companion, in her search for Ant, as well as in her continued travels to find Lark's wandering love. Besides, Bear was an animal in form. She could run her hands along his fur, and forget that he had lied to her. Even when he spoke inside her mind with human speech he still had paws and a snout, in addition to the short, bobbed tail. It was so easy to forget that he was a boy beneath that heavy pelt.

A boy who said he had a sister turned to witch.

Heart had not spoken to Heppson once he uttered these incomprehensible words. To think he did know of the witch, and knew her well. It made Heart tremble with both fear and exasperation. Bear had lied to her, and his lies had hidden even more truths than she'd imagined.

We will discuss this tonight, he'd said, his own voice tense and wary. *Around the fire. We will make plans.*

And she had nodded, not sure what else she might have said.

Bear, of course, retreated to the forest before the sun went down. He left to make the change from Bear to man beyond her sight. Unlike Summer, he did not make a production of his transformation; did not seek to overcome her with its magic.

Still, while she waited, Heart could not help but wonder, even with all the worry concerning the witch, about the transformation taking place. How did it happen? How did boy replace the Beast? She had barely looked at his human form the night before. She'd been so tired, so frustrated, and so frozen to the core. She'd seen just enough to notice the resemblance that changed everything. Just enough to make her curious to see him again this night.

He had stayed shaggy, as she remembered, even without the

animal's dark hide. He'd been unkempt and veiled in darkness, his features brown and black as the fur he normally wore. But when he stood beside the flames, insisting he had stayed to keep her safe, his form held power in it. He was acquainted with being obeyed and having control—that much she could tell. And Heart had felt protected in his presence, even without the claws and teeth her Bear normally bore.

Now she didn't know. He said this witch knew him as brother. Did he carry any of the evil the girl had on his own shoulders? Was the poison she held one that ran with blood? Should Heart be running from his side, rather than waiting for his return? She simply could not say. She simply could not decide. She only knew she had to see him for herself.

It had not been dark long when Bear stepped back within the glow of her fire, this time on two feet—his form restored to its human shape. She'd managed to start her own flames this evening, and all he had to do was crouch beside the fire's light to join her.

"You are not hungry?" she said, when he said nothing on his own. "You've never eaten with me before. Not that I have much to offer."

"No, I do not need your food." Bear turned and stretched his arm out to her, the hide hanging from his grip. "You should take the pelt again. I do not need it to survive. I will feel the cold, as a human would, but it will not harm me or bring me pain. You should use it to keep yourself warm."

Heart took the fur, her fingers brushing his as she did so. "Thank you," she said.

She pulled the covering over her shoulders, and immediately felt the frosty touch of winter make its retreat. The minutes passed, and Bear sat within arms' reach, his eyes intent on the fire's progress, his form unmoving. Both she and Bear remained silent, as he was apparently as unsure as she about how the conversation should progress. Despite the awkwardness, Heart could not keep herself from an inspection of her Bear—well aware that he must know she stared. His appearance was so different from Summer's; she with her glistening dress of scales, her gleaming shimmer of skin. Summer had been polished. She had wanted to be seen and admired. Bear looked exactly the opposite.

His clothes were worn, well-used, and obviously not washed. His hair hung long, uncombed and tangled to his neck. The beard she noticed before had no direction, no careful trimming. His skin looked grimy, covered with dirt. And yet, beneath this rough exterior, beneath the inattentive and uncaring manner he gave off, he looked fit and healthy. His arms were corded with strength. His hands looked capable of hearty grips. His shoulders set themselves as though to carry a substantial load.

"Who are you?" she asked, when the silence had gone on too long. "Who are you really? Not just Bear. *You.* It matters. Especially if she is your sister. It can't be let go. It can't be left behind."

Bear's head tipped into his hands. At first, he did not reply, and the fire crackled between them, confident in its right to remain the only speaker. Then, taking a breath, Bear slowly looked up, his face grown hard with a decision. He lifted himself, dug a branch from the dead growth about them, broke it against his knees, and threw its pieces into the fire before them both. Sparks flew upward in the air around them, darting to the sky.

"This is who I am," he said, his voice directed to the flames, "if you're so intent to know. I am Heppson. A name I have not heard for so long that it barely reminds me of myself when I speak it aloud. I am Heppson. The son of an enchantress—what you would call a witch."

"Your mother?" said Heart, her voice a whisper in its disbelief.

Heppson held up his hand, stopping her words. "My mother is a witch, and my father is a King. As such, I am the younger half brother of a golden-haired prince named Conrad, whom I believe you've met before." He looked meaningfully at Heart. "He is a few years older than myself; the heir to my father's throne. My mother did not wish him to live."

He said it simply, as though the words were not terrible in their meaning. Heart's mind raced to follow all he said.

"She couldn't kill Conrad herself—for some reason I never knew—and she demanded I do it in her stead. I could not slit his throat, and so I left. I disappeared into a nearby desert, traveling as far away as I could, knowing I must die. Before that happened, before I died, I became the Bear, in a complicated exchange meant to save my life. An exchange I have never worked out myself, and can certainly not explain to you."

"She asked you to kill your brother?" Heart said, her mind incredulous at the thought of such behavior to family, unable to advance to his other, even more inconceivable, claims.

"Conrad was not her son. I told you, he was my half brother—a son from my father's previous marriage. And my mother wished me to be King instead of him."

Heart stared at her Bear, at this Heppson standing in her sight. Could this dejected young man, who spent half his life as beast, truly be involved in such nefarious politics of the throne? Could he truly be a prince meant to rule and live above a common forest lass such as her? And what of his claims for his mother? What kind of woman would require her son to commit murder in that way?

Heart's life in the forest had been so removed from the nearby kingdom. She knew the castle and the village proper existed because her Granny told tales of it around the fire to put the girls to sleep at night. But she knew nothing useful of its rulers or their ways. Their forest was removed from the castle by a great expanse of farming land. Granny had always counted it a blessing that, as a result, they lived within their only little world. Because of this, she knew nothing of the life her Bear described. Her existence, her cottage; it had all been a distinct place where only her family existed. Only her family and the never-ending trees. Until the wanderer came. Until he changed everything.

"I don't understand," she finally said. "If your mother asked you to do such a thing, why didn't you tell your father? Wouldn't he have been the King? Why didn't he make her stop? Why would you need to run away? And how did your sister get involved? You said your sister was the one that changed my Lark, not your mother. Why would she do that? What would she have to gain from an act like that?"

"My mother," Bear said, "holds great power. I told you, she is a witch. A witch so strong the people wouldn't know to name her as such. Only those of us close enough to her influence would understand the term, and 'witch' is not a word we, any of us, have used for fun. She has done often the type of thing done to your sister since before I can even remember. And she has always forced Moiria to help her in some way or another. Before, I hoped Moiria was unwilling in her role; that she resisted the evil my mother offered. But perhaps things have changed since I left. Perhaps Moiria gave in to the pressure. It is not impossible. I know I would have killed my brother if I'd stayed. Her command is inexorable. That is why I left when I did."

"And after you disappeared, this something awful happened. Something to make Conrad the wanderer he was when Lark and I crossed his path. Something that drew your sister into it and brought her to change my sister. What was it? What changed?"

"I don't know," said Heppson. "I can only assume when Ant said I would be of use to you, that it had to do with my past. But I have been gone so long from the court. What I have to tell you is likely out of date and fairly useless. I would not have thought Moiria could do what you describe; it was not her way when I knew her. But the images from my memories and what you saw match. She is the one who cursed your sister."

"Yes," said Heart. "She is the one. And I felt of her darkness. It was very real. I am sorry to tell you so, but I did. Was there love between you?"

"Only a little. I must admit my brother and I were much closer than she and I ever were. She had been born before my mother became Queen, you see. She carried a past I knew nothing about.

And she always hung about the skirts of my mother, whether by force or by choice, I could not ever decide. It was not a safe place to stay and I could not join her there to ask."

"So, you and Conrad kept away from them?"

"We were boys together. I think my mother did not count on the strength in a childhood like that. She thought she could use it. She did not guess it would be used against her."

Heart sighed and gazed into the fire. "I hardly know what to think. It all seems so impossible. And yet, I've watched my dearest one be turned to bird. I've spoken to Fish, and Ant, and Bear. Why should this be so incomprehensible? That you are a prince. That the wanderer, Conrad, is your brother. Why should I be amazed?"

"I am sorry my family has brought you pain," said Heppson. "I often think I was wrong to run away from my mother. To not fight her. If I had stayed, you would not be here. I am not proud of the path my life has taken, or of the choices I have made."

Heart laughed, her tone dismissive. "If you had stayed, and if all you tell me is true, you would have likely killed your brother and turned to evil yourself. Let us not go back to the past anymore. We are done with it. The question is, what to do now?"

Heppson nodded, and bent down to his heels again. "We are following Conrad, I believe, under Ant's direction? It is the way I have led you until now."

"And Lark follows him as well. He is the pole her soul gravitates toward."

"Then we continue onward, and hope it becomes clear when we arrive."

Heart nodded her head and pulled Bear's pelt in more tightly. Beside her, Heppson picked at more sticks to feed the fire.

"A sorry companion I've made," he said. "I do apologize for that."

Heart let her chin fall onto her crossed arms. She eyed Heppson where he crouched, his hands twisting this way and that. He was so disheveled, so unhappy. His uncertainty was matched only by her own in its magnitude. He had nothing of the assurance of Fish or Ant, nothing of their confidence in the future coming to rights. And yet, she was glad it was he and not them that now accompanied her. She was glad, in all his humanity, that he joined her around this fire.

"You know, I am not glad my sister was changed to a bird," she said, her voice cutting across the frigid air to meet his ears. "To be honest, I was never glad your Conrad came and took her away from me. But I am glad you are here with me now. I am glad you are not some princely murderer instead, pressed beneath the heel of your mother."

And she watched as he allowed himself to smile, just a bit.

Moiria

Things had gone from worse to even more terrible. Of course, Moiria had thought she had it all in hand. She had thought the court subdued—no longer willing to question her methods. She had thought that the King was managed—his awakening dampened in the confusion surrounding Conrad. She had thought she would be safe and all her plans of a future unmolested would come to fruition. She had thought the sacrifices she'd made and the things she'd done had at least bought her safety and a new beginning.

But just as it had been when she fought her mother, all her confidence had come to naught. Now the King had Lark and the bird looked guaranteed to live forever, which made Conrad's will inaccessible to Moiria, and made all her meetings with him pointless in futility. The King had taken courage when he took the bird, and he carried more and more of the court with him daily. And now, advancing on her castle, she could feel the Lark's sister nearing the border of the wilderness. Yes, that enemy would soon arrive as well.

Moiria had no further plan of attack. No further way to defend. She had taken to pacing her mother's rooms, her fingers trailing the dusty tables of books, which held the dead Queen's wisdom. What would the witch have done, confronted with this task? This was the thought that plagued her, the secret she worked to ferret out. The Queen certainly would not have cowered and waited for her enemies to defeat her. She would have found a way to give them their desires, or at least trick them into believing that she had. Yes, she would have found a way to trap them at the last.

After all, even in that woman's death, a curse had been leveled and thrown at the two who dared to confront her. And if Moiria thought about it honestly enough, she knew the Queen had only given, in that curse, the desire that Moiria thirsted most for in her deepest heart. A banishment from a place she never had belonged. Of course, the curse hadn't taken Moiria away, and she had been left here to become her mother instead.

Which meant that even if they thought to conquer her, Moiria must at least take her last chance to succeed. She must not run. She must stay and fight. It was better than ceasing to exist. Moiria frowned, pushed two hands onto her mother's desk and frowned in concentration. Words from her memories seeped across her consciousness.

The trick, said her mother, from so very long ago, *is to make them forget it is a curse. The trick is to convince them they want what you give. It becomes simple that way. Simple, instead of complicated.*

"Simple," said Moiria, "instead of complicated."

And what was it they wanted? The King wanted Conrad, and even Heppson, if he'd had the chance. Conrad wanted his past, as well as his bird. And Lark wanted her love—the boy who took her heart and made it his. Meanwhile, the sister sought the bird as well, day after day, and month after month. All of them tied together in one happy bundle, drawn together despite time and wilderness and trouble. What did they want? They wanted each other.

Would it matter the way she gave them this gift?

Moiria's eyes hardened and she raised her head in realization. To find each other, they would go anywhere; they would do anything—no matter the cost. And shouldn't she help them in this task? Shouldn't she make their dreams a possibility?

Once you have them, said the Queen, *once you've given them their wish, that is when you pull the strings. You tighten the trap they've walked so willingly inside, and there is nothing they can do about it.*

Moiria turned from her mother's books, certain now what she must do. Without another thought or moment of indecision, she left the room. She followed the long, dank hallways of her childhood and moved downward in the castle until she'd reached the study where the King spent most of his days. She threw the door open and walked inside without any announcement or introduction.

The King looked startled, and his lone guard attempted to show courage. "Moiria," he said. "What are you doing here, in my personal rooms?"

"I have always refused to speak of Heppson," she said, the conversation begun without any preamble. "Ever since you awoke enough to ask where he had gone."

The King nodded, his eyes immediately hungry for whatever it was she might say next. He waved a hand at the frightened guard, and the soldier retreated to the wall, glad to be dismissed.

"I tell you now that I know where Heppson went, although it has also always been true that he went of his own volition and choice. I did nothing to make him go."

"Yes," said the King, his words impatient. "Fine. I will accept your words of defense, if only you are now prepared to tell me where he's gone. If you'll tell me where to find him."

Moiria twisted her head and looked to the King's left. Near the window the gilded cage she'd prepared for the Lark blew in a passing breeze. Within the cage, the Lark eyed her, its head tipped to the side, its beak partly open as though to sing.

"You must bring the bird, if I give you my information. And I will bring Conrad, as I'm sure you will request. We will seek Heppson together, all four of us. And when we arrive, we will make an exchange."

The King's eyes narrowed. "What kind of exchange?"

"As I said, you will bring the bird. I will bring Conrad. There will be no guards and no supplies. Only ourselves, traveling toward Heppson's last destination. These are the requirements you must fulfill in exchange for my leading you toward his location."

"And this is all I will be told before I am asked to agree? He could be dead for all I know."

"Yes," said Moiria, "he could. Though I'll tell you I don't know that he is dead. I have not felt him to be dead. It is a simple arrangement, and the only one I am willing to make. If you want both your sons, and not just the one, then you must be willing to take the risk."

The King rose and took his walking staff in hand. He leaned heavily against its strength to cross the room and moved to where the bird waited in its cage. Once he arrived, he dipped his head to look inside its depths and watch the Lark.

"The bird is important then, if you want me to bring it as well? I was right about that." He turned again to look at Moiria, his eyes somehow both wary and full of decision. "I cannot choose one son above the other, no matter how foolish that may be. It is agreed. I accept your arrangements. Now, tell me where to find my son."

Moiria took a breath, the first hurdle passed. "I never said I would tell you where we looked, only that I would lead you to his location. Bring the bird in the morning. The bird and your silly walking stick, for I know you will need that. Beyond that, bring nothing, or the deal is off."

The King turned again to the bird, before looking down in consternation. "It is what I have agreed," he murmured. "It is the only way."

"You are right, dear King," said Moiria. "Prepare yourself for our travels. Get your sleep."

And then she turned and left the room.

PART IV

Heart

Heart closed her eyes tight, not wanting the moment to fade.

This is what it feels like, she thought. *Rushing wind. Not the kind that makes your breath suck inward, but the kind that makes you want to stretch your arms into wings and soar upward, lifted away by its strength. And tips of new life. The wonder of growing that curls up in eggs, that unfurls in leaves, that bursts out in faint blossoms of pink.*

Spring, replied Bear inside her mind.

"Spring," agreed Heart aloud.

Now we just need to find her.

Heart grimaced at the practicality of his statement, opened her eyes, and moved forward. She picked her way carefully through the underbrush another foot or so. They had reached the forest's edge two days before, and were currently walking along its border, searching for they knew not what, all while waiting for Spring's appearance.

They had traveled for so long inside the massive forest Heart called home, and now, at its edge, they were both at a compete loss as to what they should do next. Luckily, they'd come to an unpopulated border; Heppson informing her that most of the farming land of the kingdom was still several days' travel away. He'd also told Heart of his limitations—how he could not venture beyond the outermost trees that made up the wilderness. Heart had not replied to this revelation, hardly knowing why it made her heart skip out of pattern to hear him speak such words.

I can't feel her the same way as I did Ant, Heart heard him say, her mind coming back to the moment at hand. *I think she's airborne.* He walked to the side of her, unable to come so close to the wilderness' border as she.

"This is insane," said Heart. "We've traveled northward as Ant said, and still no sign of Conrad. What can we do but wait for

Spring to give us more information? And yet, she does not come. It's not as though I wish to wait forever. It's not as though Lark isn't likely in grave danger as we speak."

The sound of amused laughter rang in Heart's mind, and she froze. "Bear?" she said.

It was not me, came the reply.

Then came a whisper, almost as if carried on the wind itself. *Spring must find you, you know. That is the way of it. Spring is necessarily a happy surprise. I do not come one day earlier than I wish.*

Heart spun in place, her eyes seeking what could not be found, her arms reaching outward to touch what could not be felt.

I will come to you, said the voice. *Make your camp and I will come.*

And all went silent again.

"She's found us," said Heart. "She's here."

To Heart, it seemed forever until sunset, minutes dripping from the day as imperceptibly as melting snow leaches into the ground. The movement of time felt mind-bogglingly sluggish, and Heart could barely stand to keep herself still, once they had made their camp and started a small fire. When Bear made to leave, to complete his transformation into Heppson, Heart reached out her hand.

"Please don't go. I've watched Summer change before, and I don't want you to be gone when Spring arrives. I can't stand to be here alone, wondering if anything at all will work out."

Bear hesitated, one paw still lifted toward his exit, his voice silent in her mind.

"After all the traveling. After all we've seen of each other, both good and bad, what could be so intimidating about me understanding this? You know everything there is to know about me. I've babbled long and hard along our journey. I assure you that I am not frightened of this part of who you are."

Bear lowered his head, obviously not certain she was right. But he did not move, which she took as some agreement.

Beyond him, minutes filtering away in a steady and established manner, Heart's eyes registered the momentary brightness, and then increased dimness, of full sunset. And before her—almost instantaneous to the end of day—Bear solidified and sunk inward, collapsing in size.

There was no flash as there had been with Fish, when Heart had seen her change. Instead, there was a slow shrinking and melting of pelt toward the ground. The massiveness of her Bear folding inward on itself, the broad and muscled form reducing downward to a more human size. Finally, the hairy fur rested over a moundish shape Heart assumed to be the form of a man.

So unassuming, without a show of any amazing ability. She watched as Heppson rose beneath the fur, his limbs unfolding to hold him upright. He straightened himself, and Bear's cloak rolled downward from his shoulders to the ground.

It had been weeks since she'd first seen him in human form. And he had changed during that time, though she doubted that he'd noticed or even meant it to be so. She had not spoken of it, not wanting to admit how terrible he'd actually looked at the start. Besides, she did not quite understand how the changes came to be, and she felt sure he wouldn't have known either. After all, there had been no one here to launder or repair his clothing. There had been no barber to address his hair and beard in all their wildness. And the winter season had meant it'd been too cold to even dip himself within a river to clean the dirt.

But Bear had changed, as night followed night after night, almost as though all those services *had* been available to him in this wilderness. His clothing became more serviceable and cared for. His hair was eventually trimmed, combed, and pulled back by a rather utilitarian string at the base of his neck. His countenance had lightened, and he'd lost the dark and abandoned shadows he'd carried with him when he first appeared to her as Heppson. Heart assumed that the magic of Bear made it so—that as Heppson's remembrance of himself as a human returned, so did his former self: the prince.

No, she did not remark on the changes, but she certainly noticed. How could she not?

Now Bear reached to his side, roughly pulled up the pelt, and wrapped it round itself, as one would roll a rug. "It is warm enough you do not need this anymore," he said.

Heart nodded in agreement, content with her fire's flames. "Thank you for staying. Thank you for trusting me. I know you didn't really want to, but it isn't frightening to watch, you know. It's not anything you need to spare me, ever again."

"I am not myself when it happens. Neither Bear nor Heppson. I'm not so completely now. That makes me uncomfortable." He looked away.

Heart smiled, attempting to brighten his mood and allay his worries. "Well, what does that matter to me? You are both my Bear and Heppson, are you not? It does not need to be one or the other, when it comes to my comfort."

She knew he noticed that, the way she made him her own as Bear, but he never said a word or mentioned how she spoke. It had been something she couldn't give up, when he revealed himself as human, no matter the awkwardness the extra word might have brought. When they'd first met, he as an animal, it had been easy to take ownership of her companion, almost as one would a pet. Then, when he became more than her Bear, when he became Heppson the Prince, everything should have changed. But she still called him her Bear, unwilling to let go of what rested beneath the term—no matter that he may once have worn a crown.

"She said she'd come," said Heart, her eyes still on Heppson's, though his slanted to the side. She wished she could speed his mind away from his discomfort, even if it required a change in topic. "How long do you think we must wait?"

But Bear did not have the chance to reply, as a small child tumbled in to join their camp at just that moment.

"Good evening!" said the girl, her gown swirling around her feet as a butterfly's wings in motion, her hands clapping themselves together. "You are here, exactly as I asked. And you have even built a fire."

Heart's mouth dropped open. She did not speak, not knowing what to make of the apparition before her. The little child reached its hands toward the flames, the fire's light glowing against her round, cherubic face. Chestnut ringlets framed her cheeks, their bounces exploding in almost every direction.

"I rarely start fires you know," said the child, her tone almost pouting, in a way. She sighed. "They are so much work for the form I choose. Still, I can't help but love them. Doesn't everyone feel better around a fire?" She looked expectantly at both Heart and Heppson.

Bear coughed as though to speak, but he seemed unsettled still.

"I have been waiting for the right moment to come to you," continued the girl. "Timing is everything, you know. And now that Heppson's sister has acted, everything is set to move forward. You must begin your journey immediately, if you are to make it in time."

"Spring?" said Heart, her mind still lumbering to make sense of the prancing child.

"Obviously," laughed the girl, her words dissolving into sparkling giggles. "I thought you knew that already?"

"It is she," said Bear, his spoken words unsteady in their effort to reach Heart. He was right to say the change from beast to man left him rattled.

"Well, she knows that *now*," replied Spring. "Pull yourself together, dear Bear, you mustn't let the sun's setting affect you so completely. Anyhow, we must get you both on your way as soon as possible."

"Well, we want to," said Heart, straightening herself, intent to take herself seriously in this conversation with what looked to be a child of five. "But we haven't found Conrad, and Bear . . ."

"Conrad has been moved," said the girl, her hand flitting to the side. "He no longer waits in the cottage as the Ant had led you to believe. Your efforts in that direction are ended, though at least it brought you here."

Bear made to speak again, but the girl raised her hand to pause his words.

"The Lark is with Conrad now also, as well as Bear's father and his sister. Quite convenient, don't you think? I knew if we waited long enough, that little witch would arrange it all quite helpfully. As for the old witch, she is dead. Dead as a post. So you see, all the important players are together. Except for the two of you."

"Dead?" said Bear. "But what? And how? And where has Moiria taken them?"

From where she sat, Heart gulped at all the girl had said, of Lark, of Conrad, of what the witch had done. She imagined her Bear's mind must have been spinning as well. This was his mother the girl spoke of when she spoke of Death. His mother, and his sister, and his step-brother. What was he to think?

But the child only looked at them and smiled from ear to ear, as though she knew the end to a good tale they both wished to hear. "Well, she's taken them to the desert—purportedly to look for you. I don't think she counts much on finding you, however. Only of losing them in its depths and then abandoning them to the waste."

"The desert? But . . ."

"Yes, very foolish for those common humans to enter there. Of this you are certainly aware. Moiria gave them no clue to where they traveled, only dragged them off with promises of finding you again. And she is the only one with water, or some method of escape."

Heart broke her way in to the conversation, barely understanding. "They have gone to a desert? You can't mean the East Desert? A bird like Lark would never survive in a place like that. Granny told us tales of it, but they were never the type to turn out well. It's even more massive than my forest, and it has not water or shade or plants within its bounds."

"Of course I mean the East Desert," said the child. "What other desert is there, anywhere nearby?"

"Then we have to go to them. We have to go immediately. They'll all die."

The child laughed. "I already told you that, when I first arrived."

Heart dropped her head into her hands. "But what can I do to make this right? How can I search a whole desert for a bird? Even if I were able to get there? Perhaps we traveled northward at Ant's direction, but the desert is several leagues east of this place!"

"And they are still even further to the north. Luckily, you have the gifts of the Guardians to assist you," said Spring smugly.

"Yes," said Heart looking up. "That is what they might be for. I can use them to save my Lark."

"To save the one you love," said the girl, all traces of laughter gone. Her eyes no longer twinkled as those of a game-playing child. Instead they held Heart tightly, the way Granny's eyes had often done, when Heart was young and her grandmother required some difficult action of her. They held her with authority, demanding a response.

"The one I love," Heart repeated, a realization building soundlessly at her core.

"And I must wait here?" said Bear to her side. "Useless as I've ever been? Trapped by this forest. Kept from a fight that is partially of my making?"

"Well, I do owe the girl a gift," said the child, her smile returning with an impish tilt. "Perhaps I could keep what I've hidden in my pockets for some other stranger, and give her another gift instead."

"Like what?" said Heart.

"I could help you with this little problem you have: the problem of your Bear and Heppson, the problem of this forest and its boundaries. They call you Heart, do they not?"

"Yes."

"Then why don't you trust your heart, dear? Tell me, do you want the conventional gift I've squirreled away, or would you prefer something a little different?" The child looked pointedly at Heppson, and Heart did as well.

His brow was furrowed, his hands clasped tightly at his sides. What Spring had said had obviously upset him. Talk of the forest. Talk of his family, and where they were now. She had never been able to see her Bear clearly in this boy turned man. No matter how she tried. He was a human, a prince—his past, with its many difficulties, was far beyond her knowledge. He would change each night, and she would catch herself sneaking glances, trying to understand who he might be. As Bear he was hers, but as Heppson—she could not say.

Of course, she could not deny the way her heart raced when he left as Bear each evening, nor the way it calmed when he returned each night to join her at the fire, no matter what his form. He had kept her safe along her journey. He had become a part of all she did. The pieces beneath the mortal exterior she saw now, were they not the same as the pieces beneath the exterior of Bear? Weren't the parts she cared for most both Bear and man?

Heart stepped to Heppson. She wished to reach and touch him. She wished to take his hand and know she did not face her witch alone. If he had been her Bear, she would have run her fingers through his fur. But he was not. He was a human instead. And so she signaled her intention with words.

"Tell me what you can do for us," she said to Spring, her eyes on Heppson. "Tell me what you can give."

Spring clapped her hands, the sound echoing around them. "Perfect!" she said. "It is the right choice, I am sure of it. After all, I am Spring. And if there is anything I can do, it is to make Winter leave. Correct? It is my privilege to banish Winter in that manner. So, that is my gift to you. I will make Winter leave this forest. He may no longer prowl its depths, not under my watch. Of course, he will need to return by the time his season begins anew, but until then, he must be gone from this place entirely. You, my dear, may do with him—and take him where you wish—during that period."

"I can leave the forest?" said Heppson, his jaw almost falling to the ground in disbelief.

"Did I not say you were banished?"

"You can do that?" he asked. "You can bend the Guardian rules in that way? No Bear has ever stepped beyond these boundaries."

"I can do anything I'd like, for another, when I believe it is in my power to do so," said Spring. "And this is what I want to do."

Heart laughed. The first real laugh she'd felt in weeks. "Well," she said, "if anything about a child is true, it is that she believes her way is the only right one."

"You are beginning to see," agreed Spring. "Now for the details, before I wave the two of you away and toward the desert. Heppson, you will continue to carry your pelt with you, and you will also persist in taking the form of Bear by day. He is a part of you, and Bear cannot be completely abandoned for this venture. Still, you will not have your powers of Guardian to assist you, only the strength of a normal bear and man. The Guardian powers may not go beyond this forest. It was always meant to be so, to keep them in check."

Heppson made to interrupt, but the child shook her head. "This I cannot change. No matter how you ask. As for your banishment, you may not return to this forest until your season breaks upon us—full of frost and all that irritating snow you tend to bring. At that time, regardless of what happens in between, Bear must return and take its place as Winter. Do you agree?"

"Yes," said Heppson, "as I must."

"And you, Heart? Do you agree as well? You may take Heppson with you to find the Lark. You may brave the desert together. But in the end, Bear must return and take his place as Guardian. Is this an acceptable gift I give to you?"

"Of course," said Heart. "It's more than I expected, to have Bear continue with me on my quest."

Spring smiled. "Then take his hand," she said. "After all, when he is flung from here, when he is catapulted away, you would wish to go with him."

Heart stepped even closer to Heppson and felt him take her hand in his. She squeezed back tightly, momentarily afraid of this pixie child before them. Meanwhile, Spring gathered her flowery skirts in hand. She lifted them up and held them at her hips, so Heart and Heppson could see her bare feet begin a sprightly dance. Gaining speed, she spun in circles beside the fire, her turns whipping faster and faster around. She dropped the skirts and pushed her hands to the sky, her head tipping sideways in a bend as she whirled.

"Spring," she sang outward. "Spring. Spring. Spring."

Then, suddenly, and without warning, she stopped. Her hands had reached their limits upward. Her skirt—wrapped about her legs by all her motion—began to reverse itself and slowly unwind.

"Spring has come," said the child, her voice clear and abrupt. She turned her head toward Heppson, brought her arms down and forward as though to push him from her sight. "And Winter must go."

Her eyes flicked to Heart's, so quickly Heart barely saw it before the forest fell away from her sight, blasted away by Winter's speedy banishment. "Protect your love," Spring whispered. "Protect him well."

Heppson

Once again, he traveled through the desert. But this time, he moved more quickly and with purpose. The sooner they found Moiria, and all the rest she had dragged with her, the better.

As he ran, Heppson tried not to think of the way his fur trapped the heat and held it tight against his skin. He tried not to think of his lumbering paws, slipping and sliding in the sand, taking them always a bit backward each time they attempted to move forward. He felt Heart's grasp upon his fur. He felt her will him on through the dryness and the heat. Both of them knew they must travel with speed before the desert defeated them. Before the witch won outright.

They'd begun their travels the night before. In the cool, they had gathered water from a useful spring located at the desert's edge, where the child Spring had left them when she'd whisked them away from the forest. Beneath the light of the moon they'd begun their all-important march through the desert sands. After experiencing all the pent-up energy of the child Guardian, Heart and Heppson had been at a loss for words with one another. They barely knew what to expect in the next few days; they only knew they should move where Spring had dictated. What was there to say at this point anyhow? All they could do was walk.

When morning came, and with it the change to Bear—Heart had gathered up the skins of water without hesitation and climbed aboard Bear's back to complete their flight. Once she'd settled, Bear began to run. As he did so, he tried to think beyond the moment. To what might come when they arrived wherever it was that Moiria waited.

How would they free Heart's sister or Conrad from her grasp? Could either of them succeed where they had both failed so miserably before? No simple conclusion presented itself, no formula to find success. He had no plan of defense, let alone of attack. He'd come all this way, yet he was as ill-equipped as before.

Heppson knew he ran too hard, for all this heat, but he could not bring himself to slow Bear's paces or conserve his strength. He feared what his sister might be doing, even now. He feared the thirst for blood he'd experienced before, when his mother dropped the curse upon his shoulders, the way he'd leaned toward his brother's death so irrevocably. He also feared the desert and the Death present within its bounds. He feared what it would do to Conrad and Heart's sister. He ignored his laboring frame, the quivering of his muscles, the rapid beating of his heart. What were Bear's troubles to what could be happening only miles ahead?

When he stumbled and fell from the exertion, it was almost dark again. He and Heart had needed to travel to the uppermost end of the desert, as Spring had only brought them to the bottom-most edge—the border closest to the wilderness. His sister would be at the far north, within walking distance of the castle and the villages surrounding it. Back where he had traveled before, when he had ran into the desert's embrace. But he was not to the end of their path. He had not covered enough ground. He had not had the strength.

Heart slipped from his back, ran her hand along his matted, sweating fur, and came to her knees beside him. She took the last of their water, opened his mouth and poured it down his throat. He could not stop her, could not make her take the water instead. He could not move at all, not anymore.

"We'll wait," Heart whispered near his ear. "We'll wait for night to come again." She looked to the sky, her hand resting on his shoulder, and he imagined she willed the sun to set and the sand to cool. Time ticked onward, both a burden and a gift with its advance. They must hurry, and yet they also must wait.

When the desert swallowed the sun, and the pelt detached as Bear retreated for the night, Heppson lay still beneath its weight. He was unable to lift himself from the desert floor, even with a smaller body. Without the rejuvenating power of a Guardian, his exhaustion overwhelmed him. Heart's hand remained at his shoulder. He felt her there. When he did not move, she pushed the fur from his back. She lifted at his frame, pulling and pushing until he'd flipped onto his back. She touched her hand to his chest and closed her eyes.

"You breathe, and your heart beats," she said.

"I speak as well," Heppson murmured. "But I cannot rise. You should go on without me. There is no other way."

Heart shook her head, her eyes brimming with a hysteria unfamiliar to Heppson.

"All this time," she said. "All this time I've been trailing my Lark. And you've helped me. You saved me from wolves and from Death. You've taken me to Ant and helped me chase Conrad. Now you want me to leave you? You want me to walk away and let you die? I hated Lark for it; I hated her for choosing another, for choosing Conrad. We were sisters. We were bound. That's what I thought. But I couldn't save her when the witch came. We were not bound in the way I thought, and it wasn't my place, not then."

Heart came to her knees. She stretched the pelt out beside Heppson and pulled and rolled him until he lay on it.

"But it is my place to save you. Do you see that? It is my place to make sure that you don't die."

Heppson pulled himself to his elbow, and she gently shoved him back again. "I can do this," she said. "I grew up in the forest, after all. No father. Only Lark and Granny to do the work. I am used to making do and pressing onward. I've carried dead game; I've brought wood for fuel. I will bring you as well." She stood and yanked at the pelt, dragging Heppson along behind her.

"Heart," said Heppson, from where he lay on her makeshift bed.

"We will find them together," she said, not bothering to look down. "You have carried me, and now I will carry you. I will not leave you behind."

He did not try to stop her again. He wished he could end her efforts and give her relief, but he could not. The day had worn him to breaking, and he must let her do her part.

Before he knew it, seconds had turned to minutes, and minutes into hours. The moon had risen high in the sky, and still Heart dragged him behind her. Heppson wished that he might come to his feet, but was left instead to think. About her words, about the meaning hidden behind them. About his sister and what had happened to his mother when he left.

It would all come to a head soon enough. All his past missteps had managed to bring him back to the fight he should have finished in the beginning. And yet, he couldn't wish his wrong turns away anymore. Not his run from the castle, not the agreement with Trickster. His decisions may not have been perfect, but they had brought him here. To this place. With Heart. His weaknesses were what they were. He could not change them. But he could act where he stood. Or lay, as it happened to be.

The dragging came to a stop, and Heppson looked up to Heart. They were both exhausted, in many ways forlorn. They'd been thrown upon this desert, but they'd traveled here together. He turned his head to see where it was she looked now, what held her gaze so completely. He found it did not surprise him to see him sister standing there.

"This is unexpected," said Moiria to Heart. "Even for you."

Heart dropped beside Heppson, pulled his head into her lap. Her chest heaved from the exertion of the past day and night. Her hands shook and trembled in fatigue.

"You will not best me this time," Heart said to Moiria.

And Heppson heard his sister laugh.

Moiria

She'd known the girl would arrive before morning broke. She'd felt her presence and the constant headway she made in her sister's direction throughout the night. But she had not felt Heppson until the very end. His appearance had been a completely unexpected reality—a surprise Moiria could not even begin to internalize. He should have been dead.

Of course, she'd told the King they came to seek Heppson. And then she'd dragged him into this dreary and dead place, full of heat and dust that clogged the lungs. At that point, even the King had not been fooled into believing it might happen, but it was too late. He'd been trapped, driven onward both by the power in their agreement and a desperate need to be certain of his second son's fate, whatever the cost.

Moiria had only been waiting for the girl to arrive, so she might abandon the lot of them to the sand's embrace, taking Conrad back with her once the bird had died. How the bird's Heart had found Heppson and dragged him to their rendezvous seemed impossible to comprehend.

Still, unwilling to be undone, Moiria straightened herself. She was determined to play to the crowd she'd gathered, no matter what confusion boiled inside her belly. There would be no turning back today. Besides, her absolute confidence would matter, once the King realized who the desert had managed to cough up into their presence.

"I see you've decided to join us," she said, her voice cool and deliberately calm.

"You have my sister," said the girl named Heart. "I had to come."

"I have much more than that," said Moiria, beginning her shaping of the future. "I have your sister and her love. I have you and . . ."

"Not this time," said Heart, cutting her off. Her words were filled with weariness, as though the girl did not have the energy to wait her turn in the debate Moiria had begun.

In fact, Moiria could hear the physical exhaustion from the girl's battle with the desert. She could hear it in her rough voice and in the breaking of her words as she forced them from her lips. This girl hadn't had the magic or water that Moiria did as she traveled into the desert's depths. Her journey had covered more distance. She was not nearly as well situated as Moiria, as a result. And yet, even as she failed to sound capable of attack, her demeanor was resolute.

"Excuse me?" said Moiria, taken aback by the interruption, and wondering in the back of her mind when the King would wake from his parched stupor and clue in to all that happened.

"I said you can't stop me this time. When we last met, I couldn't move at all because you wished it. Your power willed me to inaction, to ineptitude. I didn't understand how it worked. I couldn't face you then. I couldn't free my sister. But now I know what I want, and I know why that matters. And because of that, I know what I can do. You will not take my love from me again."

Moiria could not help but step toward the girl, drawn to the battle line that Heart had drawn. It was intoxicating: this girl's flimsy challenge. She reached down and pulled both of Heart's elbows upward in a firm grip, a fever roiling in her blood, begging to be set loose.

The girl rose, and Heppson's head fell from her lap to the ground. Moiria did not look toward her brother, prostrate on the desert floor. When he'd last been in sight, she'd not been the witch yet. What could possibly be between them now? Instead she eyed the girl.

"What do you mean by this?" said the King, his voice rasping from behind her.

With Heart's foolish declarations, and the tremor inside Moiria's gut calling for an attack, Moiria had almost forgotten the King. Until then, he'd hung back beside a disoriented and dazed

Conrad—as though he might protect his befuddled son from the debilitating Death the desert offered.

Earlier, when she'd signaled for him to stop, the King had placed the birdcage on the ground and wrapped his arms about Conrad. It had been a terrible walk for the old man, and his strength was past its prime. This did not keep him from his son. Perhaps he'd assumed the figures she spoke with were a mirage of some sort, his mind not capable of further understanding. But now with Heppson's head dropping to the ground before him, the truth had become clear.

"Is that my son?" she heard him say. "Is that Heppson? Did you truly bring me to his side? Who is that girl you're pulling at?" His voice began to rise in anger and increased anguish.

"You will wait your turn," said Moiria, without glancing his direction, hoping against hope that her power would hold. She flicked one hand toward him, freezing him in his place, just as she had done to the girl so many weeks before. Luckily, he was too weak to fight against what she had done. Luckily he stayed, his voice caught deep within his chest, unable to protest all she would now do.

Meanwhile, in her grip, Heart wavered from side to side, barely staying on her feet. The girl had done too much to make her way through this desert. She had helped the heat complete her own undoing. The desert had prepared her for her own demise. All it would take was a few choice words, and Moiria would be completely done with her and all her blasted interference. She had nothing to fear from this broken shell of a girl.

"You've discovered what you want, have you?" said Moiria to the bird's sister, shaking her slightly, with tightened hands. "Well, tell me what it is, and I will give it to you. What do you think of that? I will give you exactly what you wish. I am willing to make a trade." Her eyes flashed with all she might do, knowing it would be more than the Heart could ever imagine, or possibly fight against.

"But I don't need you to give it to me," said Heart, her eyes, in those simple words, triumphant. "I already have it."

Moiria's world spun. Her fingers tightened on Heart's arms, suddenly frightened it was the only way she could hold her any longer.

"You turned my sister to a bird," said the girl. "But she found him anyway, don't you see? And if he took her from that cage, and broke the band, all would be right between them. He only needs prodding, and they will have each other. And Heppson, he is alive. Here to join his brother and his father, just as they wished he would. And I have him, to guide me onward and keep me safe. The same as I have done for him. You cannot hold us any longer, with your many spells and tricks. You cannot make us think we need your help to make things right."

"But how? How would you know?" hissed Moiria. "Why won't you take what I can offer?"

"Spring told me," said Heart. "She said if you believe something enough, you make it so all on your own. Well, I believe you are too weak to take the things most dear to me. I believe I have the gifts I truly need to win this fight. You cannot stop me. Not this time. I will not cower before you, as I would a common bully. I have the strength to do my own will here today."

And with those last hard words, the girl shook herself from Moiria's hold, yanking her forearms from her grasp. Moiria let her go, her mind tumbling with a sudden loss of direction. What had she meant to say? What had she meant to do? All of her plans flew from her mind, a bird she could not catch. Heppson here, unexpected and alive. The girl, refusing to do as she wished, refusing to be cowed. What now? How could she keep the rest of them caged and docile? What would her mother do to make things right?

She watched, as though from the moon above, while Heart dropped to her knees and pulled at Heppson again. She tugged him upward beside her, her arms wrapping around his dusty frame. And he looked at her, intent on what she'd said, on her stand against Moiria and all her demands. Moiria watched his eyes take in this girl who had done what no one in his life before had dared to do: speak back to a witch. Moiria had never been so brazen with her mother. Perhaps if she'd had such courage, it would all have spun another way. Perhaps, even in the beginning, she had been wrong in her shadowy method of attack. Perhaps she should have just said 'no.'

But now, as Heppson gazed at Heart, Moiria felt a renewal of the anger in her blood. It had been dampened for a moment, but it still begged to be let loose. She would have helped her brother, if he'd let her, and then none of them would have been in this mess. She would have helped him fight his mother and refuse the Queen's demands of murder. But he had never asked—he had disappeared instead. And all that had happened since then, all that had come, was because of what he'd done, and how she'd acted as a result. Because he'd left her to face it all alone, as no brother ever should his sister.

"He is what you want?" said Moiria, the words spitting out between her teeth, fueled by a rage that brought to mind her mother's knife. "Am I right in thinking he is what you already have? You came to save your sister, so sure that your devotion was what she needed. And now you will save him instead. You will forget the one you are bound to by blood, the one you were meant to protect from the beginning?"

Heart did not even glance toward her, but her words were certain. "Conrad will save her."

"I see," said Moiria. "Conrad. And what if, despite your cheers of victory, your Heppson doesn't make it?" said Moiria. "His heart already fails from the heat—this heat which I have dragged the two of you inside. He will get worse, you know, and he may slip between your fingers to the world beyond our own. There is more than one way for me to take what you desire. What will you do then? Will you wish you had let me give you what I offered? That you had kept me on your side?"

Heart's mouth straightened to a line, her spine lengthened in defense. "You do not frighten me," she said. "And neither do your threats of Death."

As she said this, the King spoke again from where Moiria had bid him wait behind her.

"She is right," he said, his voice shaking with the realization. "The girl is right."

Whirling in surprise, Moiria turned to see him. The King was not frozen in place, as she had demanded. His staff had fallen to the ground, and he dragged one leg behind him as he moved toward the gilded cage where he had dropped it. It seemed the world around her had turned to a puppet show where she no longer pulled the strings. Moiria's mouth fell open wide, a bit of fear beginning to press inside her ribcage.

"We have been fools to let it continue this way—to believe you might control the future," he said. He turned his gaze to his son. "You must open it, Conrad." He lifted the cage and, reaching, handed it to the waiting prince. "She spoke of an exchange, and of the bird wrapped tight inside it. I am sure you must claim your past, and all its memories, beginning with this fowl."

Where he stood before his father, Conrad's eyes were fuzzy. His gaze lacked any intent or comprehension, a fact that played to her own chances for success. Moiria knew it was not only the heat and the exertion of long walking that Conrad battled. It was also her mother's failed curse, which wrapped itself solidly about his mind, dampening any parts of who he used to be.

"You must act now," said the King, his voice raising in alarm. "Do not wait to claim what should be yours. Do not let her hold you back."

With this one last chance before her, Moiria blocked out thoughts of Heppson and Lark's sister. She would deal with them again, after she finished with the bird, after she kept Conrad from his full recovery. She could injure Heart this way as well, making her more vulnerable to later attack.

Moiria stepped toward the King and Conrad, her arm

beginning to raise. It was true, she could not do it all as she had planned before, but it was still possible, with the help of the desert's heat, and with a few of her mother's words to stun Conrad into inaction. The bird could not last much longer, if she was denied the freedom her love could offer her. And if the bird would die, she would be one step closer to her goals, no matter what Heart declared.

Moiria's fingers spread by degrees, her mouth stringing the words together that would bring the crown prince down in overwhelming pain. The King, his eyes catching her movements in his vision, turned and looked toward her. He would know the look of a spell. He would recognize what she meant to deliver. He had seen it enough, in that life of his before. But it was too late, he could not stop her. The charm had erupted from her hands.

And the King stepped into the curse's path.

Moiria gasped as the darkness crashed into his already weakened chest, throwing him backward into the sand. It had been a powerful collection of spells she'd built, as she knew how difficult killing Conrad had been for her mother. She had planned merely to stun the prince, to reduce him to an incoherent mass until the Lark had died. Now her hatred and weakness bit into the King instead, convulsing his body with the strong reverberation of her words.

Behind him, watching the old man fall to the desert floor, his son's eyes sprang open wide. Moiria could almost see the memories replaying. Memories of when he had done the same as his father did now, when he had stepped between the Queen's curses and Moiria. When he had saved her, and given all his past in the attempt. A key had turned, releasing what had been hidden, and Conrad's past had become his own again. Moiria watched the light spill through his eyes, the knowledge and self that he was returning. For with the memory of this sacrificial act within his past came all the other memories. His identity. His brother. And, of course, his father.

A father who now lay upon the ground, hands clutched to his

heart in crushing defeat. Moiria saw that what would have only injured his son brought a finality of life to the King that could not be denied. Death. She had not meant for it to be so, but it had happened all the same. Once again, Death at her hands. Conrad yelled with realization and fell across the King's dying frame. One of the prince's hands still held the cage, while the other grasped his father's clothes as though to hold him tightly in place.

"Father!" he said. "Father!"

"You remember," came the whispered reply.

And Moiria could not help but watch them in that moment, her murder-stained hands falling to her sides. Stunned into inaction, she watched the dreadful scene play out upon the desert floor. Why should she, the one who brought this pain and its resulting spiral into Death, show any interest in the last moments they shared?

And yet, long before, Conrad had been her stepbrother. And watching him watch his father die, she remembered once again what he did for her that day she fought the Queen. Was it possible there were two Moiria's standing inside her? The one who now existed? And the one who once had been? She felt them both, their breaths heaving inward and back again, fighting for dominance inside her frame.

"Open the cage," said the King, his voice a rasping grating noise, barely distinct in intonation. "Do it now, while I might watch."

"Of course," said Conrad, weeping and overcome by all he now remembered. "Whatever you wish."

The crown prince turned to the gold contraption at his side. He pulled at the latch until it opened and gathered the bird inside into his hands.

"What do you find?" said his father. "What has she put there?"

Moiria listened for his answer as well, her hands limp and lifeless now that she had all but killed the King. Hadn't part of her always hoped the Lark's release would happen this way? Isn't it why she had given the bird to its sister that day far in her past? Didn't a portion of her want to see?

"It wears a collar of some sort," said the Prince, his words punctuated by labored breath and swallowed sobs.

"Remove it," said the King. "There will be no more bindings in this kingdom. Not even for a bird."

And Conrad took the ring off.

The desert swirled. It tipped and collided with the sky. Rushing, rushing, all around. Before her, Moiria watched as the bird shucked its feathers from its wings. Wind rushed in waves about the Lark, spinning granules of flying sand outward as she grew to her full height. Her tattered gown hung from her hunched shoulders. Her tangled hair wrapped down to her waist. She stood as a human again.

"Lark," said Conrad. "Lark." His hands reached out to the love he had known.

Moiria watched the maiden tip upon her feet. She imagined the girl must be feeling all she'd lost, in those many months she's spent as bird. What must that change mean? What must it feel to come back now? So many days passed by, so much of life misunderstood. But now, she'd returned to herself.

"Go," said the King, the words barely a sigh. He pushed his son toward the girl, a rattle from his chest escaping outward. "Go and be glad."

And with the King's last breath, Conrad stood, reaching to catch the Lark as she fell.

And there it was, the bird returned. Was it all that Moiria had imagined? That and more? She turned in place, taking in the unfathomable scene around her. Her brothers freed from the Queen, joined to those they loved. And what of her? What did she have? All she had lost, all she had done? What was it for? For a kingdom? A kingdom she never wanted? She'd been a fool. She'd been a fool caught in a trap.

Moiria raised her hands to the fading stars above and screamed a frenzied scream. The day was almost here, the night almost gone. She should have conquered by now, and been on her way home. She should have had everything she wished. But what was it she actually wanted? And what had happened over all these weeks and months to bring her here? Everything inside her had schemed and fought for his moment, but now she could not for the life of her think why.

"Moiria!" croaked Heppson, his words barely reaching her ears.

She turned to him. He had raised himself to his feet, his legs barely managing to keep him upright. Heart knelt beside him, one hand tightened at his ankle.

"Moiria, this must end. All of it must stop."

"You should have been the first to go." The words escaped her without thought, her anger grasping her will and making it its own. The pain and fury flamed from where she'd cut her arm so long before, from where she'd begun this long and misdirected path. The aching beneath it drove her to wreak havoc, in any way she could. "You knew what she was, when you left us to face her alone."

Lifting sand with a rushed and desperate incantation, her arms held widely to her sides, Moiria heaved the spinning mass at her brother. He stumbled backward into the ground, one knee bending to keep him upright before the storm of wind and dirt.

"I will not submit to you, Moiria," he said though gritted teeth, one arm raised before his eyes, "no matter how much sand you pile upon my body. I should never have submitted to our mother. I will not make that mistake again. I have learned to accept the role I play. And if it means I must guard these others from your wrath and helplessness, so be it. Even as an ordinary man, I will stand here and do it. Even if you kill me."

"It would only take one word," said Moiria, her teeth gritted as she spoke. "You must know that. One word to end your life. I feel you shaking in Death's grip even now. The desert has brought you to the brink of death for me. It has made it all too easy. I need only heap this sand upon your head for you to go. And then I will heap it upon the others. Your father is already gone. Conrad can barely hold his shaking Lark up from the ground. And that Heart of yours will break to pieces once you're gone."

"Yes, I know," said Heppson. "It is no surprise what you could do. I have felt this desert's hold before, and I know how close I stand to Death. But tell me, Moiria, would it make you happy to see me die at your feet? To see them die at your feet? Is that who you want to be? Would you let our mother make you that?"

With his words striking out toward her, Moiria felt every moment of her life halt and swirl around her frame. Beneath her feet, the ground shifted itself a million times over on tiny shavings of sand that would not keep their place.

"You can kill all of us, if it's what you really desire," said Heppson. "It would not be difficult at all. And we certainly have no strength to go about attacking you. You can take everything from us that you desire. So, tell me, Moiria, tell me now—what is it that you want? Is it this? I am a Guardian. I am meant to guide people to where they seek. I am meant to see the way they cannot see. And I beg you to see. I beg you to see that this cannot be your path."

What do I want? thought Moiria, her mind empty and rattling with his questions. *What do I want? What have I ever truly wanted?*

And she realized she had never managed to know exactly what she sought. That had been the problem all along, the source of all her failed attempts and beginnings. She had not dared to really desire the Queen's death. She had not wanted to completely take the throne for her own. She had not wished the bird to die with any immediacy. She had not torn her prodigal brother to pieces when he showed up alive. Of two minds, always, she had been.

Now she looked around. At Heppson. At Heart. At Conrad. At Lark. Even at the dead King. Happy, in his death, to know his sons returned. They were weak, they were broken, and they were there for the taking. Was that what she wanted above all else?

Perhaps not. Perhaps not really. But the fire inside her told her it didn't matter. Not anymore. And the fire was all she could hear.

"You cannot give me what I want," she finally whispered. "And so why should I not take all this instead?"

Heart

The night Heart's faint and mewling cries first broke the still of darkness, her mother died. The arms that took her in their tender, trembling grasp were small and slight. Her sister's hair, a falling shade of darkness, lent protection to Heart's barely pulsing frame and fuzzy, fire-hued brow.

Lark, a sister turned to guardian in an instant, worriedly smiled at the babe. Amidst the wails and darkened candles of the room, she stretched her love out wide, determined not to let this tiny life blink out before her eyes.

With fumbling hands, she tightened a blanket around Heart's body and tucked the fabric's warmth around the fresh and chalky infant skin. Pulling her newborn sister deep within the curve of her strong arms, Lark dredged what joy she could from the bottom of her freshly shattered soul to whisper hope. In doing so, she determinedly kept Death back from his second prize that night.

And somehow, in that moment, both were safe. Sisters, joined by love, protected by the care they'd given each other that day and every day that followed. Heart's sister Lark had a way of healing in her, and Heart had always known it. After all, she'd healed Heart in those first few hours of her life. And then she'd healed Conrad when he stepped into the shelter of their family cottage from the wilderness that was his past. It was her gift, the one she carried always in her grasp.

Heart did not notice Lark moving toward Moiria at first. She only saw Heppson, one knee in the sand, pushed to the limits of the man he was. She'd kept the witch from binding her tight and prescribing her future, stood strong where she'd failed before, but she couldn't halt Heppson from facing his sister—even if it did mean that he offered his life. By now she knew the circular nature of magic. She'd watched the seasons turn from one to the other, each of them retaining their strength only by giving it away. And just as she'd finally dragged her Bear through the sand at the end, she must let him play his part in this particular battle, no matter the cost. This was not her place.

She did not think of Lark's role in this final confrontation, as it had been so long that she'd only been a bird. But after the removal of the golden ring, her sister had returned, and with her came a human heart and soul, broken and exhausted, but complete in all its pieces. Hers was a heart used to offering love and healing, no matter what loss she had carried on her side.

When it happened, when her sister's arms wrapped tight about the witch, tight about Heppson's sister, Moiria, Heart knew the end result before she even saw it. Those arms were closed, not in an attack or even in defense, but in an embrace Heart had felt herself so many, many times before.

"Shhhh," said Lark, her mouth soft against Moiria's ear, calming in its aching understanding. "We are here with you as well. You are not alone."

And, as Moiria crumpled in half and shook with the pains of a battle she never should have fought, Heart could only watch, her own body unable to do more. Moiria released her anger and her curses, and she fell backward in time to the girl Heppson had shown Heart in her mind those many weeks before. The image of the sister he remembered, before she changed into a witch. This then, was Moiria as she had been. She let her heart be taken into Lark's protection.

And even from this distance, Heart felt her do it.

Heppson

In the end, it did not matter that Moiria came to her senses. Heppson knew it was too late for him. After all, he had felt the advance of Death before, and that being's arrival was unmistakable this time as well. Of course, this time there was no Trickster to carry him off and toward safety. But it was right that it came to this. He should have ended the evil before, by standing against his mother. Things had been brought to where they always should have been, and what could be more appropriate than that?

He wondered for a moment, about the Bearskin. About what the forest would do when it needed its Bear back. But then he remembered how his end had not actually come at the hand of violence, how Moiria had been stopped before the last blow fell. And he remembered how the other Bears had eventually slept, and new Bears been called to take their place, in a natural order of things. The forest would move on, pulled along pathways both powerful and long established. There was nothing to be feared, in that regard.

Heppson looked beyond his sister, where she rocked in Lark's arms. Death stood waiting, his dark frame lit from behind by the first tendrils of a rising sun. Heppson could not see Death's face or features, but he knew the silhouette meant an end to the life that had once been his. He knew it with certainty.

As though a rope stretched between them, he felt Heart stiffen where she waited. She must see Death standing there as well, though he would not have thought she would be capable of such a thing. Heppson gulped another struggling breath, and worked to keep upright within her sight. It would be painful to leave her here. If he'd had his Guardian powers, he might have resisted Death's pull for her. But he gave them up when he joined her in this desert, when he helped her seek her sister and finish her fight. Coming here had been Winter's final gift.

Death advanced. His steps were silent and invisible to the others around them, but they were deliberate in their purpose.

"No," said Heart, and she came to Heppson's side, her arms pushing him upright a little longer. "It can't happen this way. Not after all we've done. We only need some water. We only need to leave this desert in your past."

"I am too weak for us to get away from here. The sun will rise soon, and I cannot last another day inside a heavy pelt, beneath its rays." His hand reached out to touch her face. She had reached to him this way a thousand times as Bear, but he had never dared to do it on his own, let alone with his human hand. Now he took the last chance offered him to hold her cheek in his palm. "Death must come. We both see him. You cannot save me now."

Heart froze, her eyes trapped by what he'd said. "Save the one I love," she said. She reached to her side, hurriedly pulling at the bag still tied there, despite all that happened in the night. "My gifts from the Guardians."

Death's shadow fell between them, and Heppson looked up to meet his fate. There was no horse, but the shadow was familiar all the same.

"The strings of your life are ragged and twisted," said Death. His voice felt like a memory, a delayed imprint of knowledge once known and understood. "But I am not Death for nothing. I will make your ending quick despite the difficulties."

"Wait," said Heart. She pressed into Heppson's line of sight, between him and the specter. "I have a gift. An exchange to make for his life."

Both Death and Heppson wondered at her act. Should she not be afraid of Death and what he did? But Heppson watched as she pushed a cloth-wrapped box toward the dark form, the gift he knew she'd received from Fish almost a year ago now. As she lifted up her offering, Ant's gift fell from her hands, tumbling and unwrapping itself as it fell forgotten on the desert floor beneath their feet. Heppson opened his mouth to tell her, but the tugging of Death upon his soul drew him away from what could not concern him.

"It is meant to save the one I love," said Heart to Death, not blinking beneath the specter's gaze. "The Guardian told me that, though I didn't understand at all what she meant. I thought it would save Lark, but it is for Heppson, for my Bear. It is for you."

Death leaned toward Heart, and with his close proximity to both her and him, Heppson finally saw his face. It was a human face, not so surprising to a man who lived his days as Bear, and it was stubbled with a half-grown beard of black. His eyes were gray and overhung by thick unyielding brows.

"Death halts for none," he said. "Death does not exchange souls for silly gifts."

Heart did not flinch, and Heppson wondered at her strength. "Open the box," she said, her words firm and clear. "Open it and see. You may have it, whatever it is, and whatever you decide. Even if you won't make the trade. But at least look, at least give it a chance."

"Demanding, aren't we?" said Death, his words a somewhat amused drawl.

"Please. Open it," was all she said.

Her eyes flickered back to Heppson's, her hands wrapping about his arm. As she watched him and he watched her, Heppson heard the click of the box's latch. Together they shifted their gaze to Death and the opened box. Death pulled from its hidden insides a slinky darkness. On its surface, faint specks of glitter reflected the shimmer of sand around them over and over again.

"What is it?" said Heart.

"I can't believe it." And Death, surprises of surprises, grinned. Of all the strange and wondrous things. He lifted the mass of dark and light higher into the air so the two might see it more clearly. "Quite the exchange you propose, my girl. One you can't even understand. A soul for a soul, as it were."

Heart turned to Heppson in confusion, but he knew no more

than she did about that fabric of dark and moonbeams held by Death.

Death looked toward the two of them, his eyebrows raised in deep amusement. "I have a brother," he said. "A brother who troubles the world and evades my censure no matter what unreasonable actions he chooses to take. He has done so by hiding his soul, so neither I nor my other siblings might hold him fast and give him punishment for his ills. We have sought this hidden soul, each of us in our travels, and now you bring it to me, without any reasonable thought of what you offer."

Trickster, thought Heppson, his memories gliding back to the creature who made him take Bear's place. *He'd hidden his soul away, and now it has been found.*

"Then you want it," said Heart, not caring about any details beyond the trade. "You'll make the exchange?"

Death wrapped the soul over and over, folding it gently back into the box. "You give me the chance to offer my brother retribution. What better trade could you ever have offered, no matter how you tried? Yes, I will make the exchange you suggest. I find it fitting, especially considering an earlier exchange made by this boy—in the absence of Trickster's soul."

Heart's brow furrowed, but Heppson watched as she let the worry pass. "Heppson will live," she said.

"He will live," said Death. "Though what you'll do about that Bearskin at his feet, I cannot say. Even Death cannot change the boundaries of that agreement for you."

"No," said Heart, her eyes taking on a shade of sorrow. "No one can do that."

Moiria

A witch takes things from people. That's what Moiria had been taught. Her mother took and took, unable to quench her thirst, driven by some force Moiria never understood. She swallowed the wills of others. She thought only of how the future would serve her own goals and desires. There was nothing to her but the want for what another had.

Moiria had seen Death come for her brother, though she doubted the others knew she had. She had seen Heart's offering and watched as that being allowed Heppson to live. It was the gift that troubled her though. The forgotten gift, which fell to the ground when Heart handed Death the box.

Drawn to the gift, she shook Lark off. She was determined to see it more clearly. And so, she pointed Lark back to Conrad, back to where she belonged, and took her own path to where the package had fallen. Moiria's steps were halting on the sand in her approach toward the object. Somehow, she knew what she would find, knew it would require firm action on her part. She must have resolve. She must have strength. After all, she felt the aching pulse the package emitted. Felt it reflected in her own flesh.

Taking the package in her hands, she unwrapped the knife she'd known would lay inside. Its familiar etchings and patterns winked with dried blood, reminding her of all she'd done in the past year. Begging her to do more. Her mother's blade. Back again. Brought by Heart to tempt her once more. This was the blade she'd been sent to retrieve in the cottage. The blade she'd cut her arm with and taken to the witch as lying evidence. The blade that held her mother's last heart's blood as well.

And now, holding the knife, she found she could remember further. The dry desert air cut through the knife's force, guiding her memory's paths in a fumbled remembrance of half-understood and childlike recollections. She recalled the blade when it entered her mother's life. The change its appearance had wrought in the woman who had been her mother. The strange and green-tinged man who had offered it in exchange for warm, cooked food. Trouble: that had been his nature. She could see that now.

Before the blade's arrival, Moiria had spun in her mother's arms, a simple village child. Happy and content in the forest life. And the blade had changed everything, gripped in her mother's hand. It had brought pain. It had brought sorrow. Why had her mother let it into her life? Why had Moiria let it come to her? This she could not see exactly, she only knew the knife lay at its center.

Moiria grimaced at the knife, its pain and terror and influence washing over her again. She could hear it speak its darkness to her, willing her to stand and take more blood, regardless of whatever else her heart might wish. But she could also feel the ghost of Lark's arms about her, holding her together, reminding her of who she was. And because of this, she understood that she could not give into the pulsing any longer; she would not let it choose her path.

Knowing no other way, she took a water skin from where it hung at her waist, and, trembling, poured the precious drops of water over the knife. She only hoped it would make a difference. Moiria rubbed and rubbed at the blade, pressing at the bloody ridges until it finally came clean, clean from her blood, clean from her mother's blood.

As she did so, the pulsing in her arm lessened in intensity, snaking backward to the site where the blade first bit her, until eventually it rolled in upon itself and ceased. She had wiped the knife's ache and influence away with a finality that could not be erased. She had made it end. Her actions would no longer be dictated by the evil of the knife, or how it had tied her to the monstrous Queen her mother had become. Moiria was free again. She would no longer do the bidding of her pounding blood.

Could her mother have escaped as well, given such a chance? Was that woman just as trapped by the blade's murderous dictates? Was that why the knife had driven both her mother and herself to hide it away, deep in the forest's cottage, where it could not be made clean? It was impossible to say. She was only glad the girl had brought the blade here, and that her sister had given her the strength to stand against it, in the end. It would make trouble no longer.

"Can you send us back to the castle quickly?" Heart said from behind her, her voice breaking into Moiria's moment of reverie and unshackling. The girl had dragged Heppson with her, his labored breathing painful to any who listened. "Have you power enough for that? Even with Death's agreement, he cannot live inside this desert one more day. Death would only have to return."

Moiria nodded and pocketed the knife, knowing it must be hidden away from any who would fall beneath its power. She would do this thing; she would get rid of the blade. It would be a beginning to her change, a recompense for all the evil she had done. And perhaps it would help her understand her mother. But for now, the transportation spells Heart had requested tumbled in her mind, ready for her use.

"I will do it," she said, turning to her brother and the girl beside him, thinking all was done.

As she turned, the sun broke free from the ground, tumbling the long night behind them into the newest day. Sunrise had been bulging upward, and now it broke loose. Moiria's eyes went bright with light, and she pulled her hand before her face to block the pain.

By the time her eyes had focused again, her brother Heppson was gone.

And in his place there was the Bear.

Moiria

Heart had pressed at Moiria to complete the transportation, one hand knotted in the fur of the weak and weary Bear kneeling beside her, the other held upward to delay the questions and exclamations of Lark and Conrad. "You must move us now," she'd said. "I must hide him in the castle without anybody knowing he is there. He cannot return to his forest yet, but we cannot stay here inside the desert."

Moiria's eyes had only widened, unable to comprehend.

"He is a Guardian," Heart had said, pulling on her hand to make her listen. "It is the way he survived the desert, when he should have died before. He was made into a Guardian of the forest. The forest that is located south your kingdom. His power is meant to help all. But because of the power, he must live as Bear when the sun rises. He must wear this rugged pelt as skin when day arrives."

The girl had gone on, pouring out the details to Moiria, begging her to awake and send them back to the castle. Details of Heppson, trapped inside a pelt, tied to a forest. Lark and Conrad had slipped nearer and nearer as well, no longer frightened of the beast that was their brother, their own ears gulping down the words Heart spun around them.

Moiria's brother would never return to his kingdom as the prince he was before. He would never make Heart a princess. His future had been torn away after his escape to the desert. Together he and Heart had managed to vanquish Moiria as witch. They had even vanquished Death. But they could not vanquish Bear, this one they called Guardian.

Eventually, Heart had turned from Moiria, her narrative ended, her hand still wrapped in Heppson's pelt. Moiria had seen her eyes center on the Bear, where he crouched with troubled breath. She couldn't quite believe it, though she could tell there was truth in what the girl had said. Conrad had also reached out to touch the fearsome Bear, feeling the reality of their brother's new existence as well.

"Please move us now," Heart had said, her eyes lifting up to the circle of concern wrapped around her. "The heat is too much for him as Bear. We cannot stay here."

And Moiria had finally pushed aside her confusion and incomprehension to complete the spell she'd needed, the spell that took them away from the desert's heat and to a certain portion of the castle's lower chambers. There they carefully hid the Bear in a large and cool root cellar no longer used by the castle's kitchen staff. A place where no one would come unawares and find the massive creature Heppson had become. Where no one could take fright and pull a weapon of attack.

Moiria watched Heart squeeze her Lark's hand at that point, once her Bear was somewhat safe and she had a moment to think of the sister she had followed for so long. She let herself be embraced and held by the sister she loved. Then, no longer afraid of being parted forever, Heart pressed Prince Conrad to take her sister and find her the rest and care she needed after her long captivity as a bird.

When the pair had disappeared, hands gripping tightly to each other, Moiria did not leave the cellar's chambers with them. What was for her in the castle above? She would leave it to Conrad to sort out the mess of Alastair. It was his kingdom, and she would not take part in its government ever again.

Instead, she stayed and watched Heart nurse and cool the Bear as best she could. Instead, she stayed and waited for the night to bring her brother back again, a man inside a Bear.

When night did fall and the hide fell loose, she worked with Heart to lay Heppson out along the bed. Heppson really was there, inside the Bear! She and Heart dropped the pelt in the corner until her brother must wear it again when morning broke.

Heppson's breath continued to rise and fall in shallow patterns, and he barely drank the water Heart continued to pour into his mouth. But he would live. Death had left him behind for this life, though Moiria now understood he would have to return to his forest's boundaries.

"I suppose once he is well," said Heart to Moiria, when Heppson had finally dropped off into a somewhat restful sleep, "I will have you send us to the forest's furthest boundaries. He cannot enter the forest just now, but we can live along its borders until winter comes. He certainly cannot be kept here. There is no way to keep that kind of secret for that length of time."

Moiria nodded. "Of course I will send you, but what kind of life does that mean for you? You are a forest lass, it is true. But will you wander always as companion to this Bear?"

Heart only sighed. "I don't know," she said. "I don't know. But I cannot let him go alone." And her own eyes closed in deep exhaustion, her mind unable to offer more.

Moiria watched the two before her and trembled at her thoughts. So much had happened since her mother demanded Conrad's death. And so much would eventually be made right. Regardless, this Bear of a brother was beyond any simple solution. What could be done?

But a witch takes things from people, she remembered. And so does a sister, a sister can take things as well. Especially burdens.

In the beginning, is that not what she'd planned to do? Wasn't all she did meant to help Heppson and Conrad? To be a tool to bring them peace and happiness? She had fallen from her course. She had done evil. She had hurt people in her kingdom, and manipulated those left in her family. But it could stop now. And she could choose a new direction. Lark had shown her this.

Her blood no longer beat for vengeance and for pain, not now the blade was clean. She had the power to make things right, beyond just hiding the knife, beyond leaving Conrad to his kingdom.

And so, as Heppson shallowly breathed in and out, his body struggling to repair itself and gather strength, and as Heart watched Moiria's movements with wide and sudden awareness of what she planned to do, Moiria took the Bearskin. She hefted it in her hands, felt the pressure of its weight and what it might mean for the days ahead. Finally, in firm decision she lifted it over her shoulders.

Leaning down toward her brother and calling together the spells she would require, she gathered a strong net about herself, readying herself to travel far, far away from this place. This had never been her home—she knew that now. Her mother had dragged her to this place, driven by a blade that wanted destruction and pain. But that was ended now, and she could go. She could find another path to follow.

She would leave them here. Heppson and Heart. Conrad and Lark. Even the King to be buried by his people. She would leave them to lead their lives. She would leave them using the magic she'd learned from her mother and the strength of her sister heart. Men and women. Kings and Queens. Nothing beyond that. Not a bear or bird between them.

And Moiria?
She would wear the Bearskin.
She would be Bear.

"Good-bye," Moiria whispered to her brother. And with those words, she took herself away. Far away, and to a new beginning.

About the Author

Jamie Robyn Wood is a full-time wife and mother and a part-time writer. Over the years she has handed out money at banks, taught ballet, and managed to make dinner for her family semi-regularly. Jamie never imagined the wind could blow so hard and so cold until she moved to the Midwest. Now she prefers to hunker inside the house with a story to write. *Bearskin* is her first novel. Jamie, her husband, their five children, and their "pet" squirrels currently reside in Coralville, Iowa.